DENTIST MAN

BY THE SAME AUTHOR:

Max Lakeman and the Beautiful Stranger

The Man in the Window

DENTIST MAN

JON COHEN

VICTOR GOLLANCZ

LONDON

My thanks to three terrific dentists –
Dennis Hoffman, Robert Chideckel, and
Lester Levin. Thanks also to Joseph
Gangemi, and Mary Hasbrouck, as
always.

First published in Great Britain 1993
by Victor Gollancz
A Cassell imprint
Villiers House, 41/47 Strand, London WC2N 5JE

© Jon Cohen 1993

All rights reserved. No part of this publication may be
reproduced or transmitted in any form or by any means,
electronic or mechanical including photocopying,
recording or any information storage or retrieval system,
without prior permission in writing from the publishers.

The right of Jon Cohen to be identified as author
of this work has been asserted by him in accordance with
the Copyright, Designs and Patents Act, 1988.

The names, characters, places and incidents either are the
product of the author's imagination or are used fictitiously,
and any resemblance to actual persons, living or dead, or
locales is entirely coincidental.

A catalogue record for this book is
available from the British Library.

ISBN 0 575 05566 9

Typeset by CentraCet, Cambridge
Printed in Great Britain by
St Edmundsbury Press Ltd, Bury St Edmunds, Suffolk

For Peggy and Bevo

Chapter 1

War, famine, pestilence, throat cancer, depletion of the rain forests, Daddy in a nursing home, the ozone layer, the national debt, teen pregnancy, Alzheimer's, homelessness, oil spills, urban decay, moral decay, tooth decay . . .

Actually, that last one, tooth decay, Henry Miles, DDS, could do something about. Sure, patching a hole in a mandibular molar wasn't exactly the same as patching a hole in the ozone layer. But it was something, wasn't it? My little contribution, thought Henry. Making the world a safer place for teeth.

Henry opened his eyes to the new day. He stared at the bedroom ceiling, painted white as a polished incisor, and wondered if everyone woke up in the same way: in panic and despair. The List, as he had come to call it, War / famine / Daddy / etc., was the first thing his brain dished up each morning. Henry had learned that the best way to counter his instant panic was to open his eyes immediately and stare at his ceiling. Its whiteness comforted his dentist's soul. White is hope, Henry thought. Health and hope. White, white. Hope, hope, he chanted against The List. War and famine go away / Henry fixes tooth decay.

'Henry, my God.' June, his wife, was up on one elbow glaring at him. 'You scare me half to death looking like that. What a thing to wake up to.'

Henry continued to stare wide-eyed at the ceiling, doing battle with The List.

'Like a corpse,' she said. 'That's how you look.'

White, white, thought Henry.

'Blink or something,' said June, poking him.

He blinked several times, rapidly. SOS – SOS. June, come to my rescue.

'Speak, Henry.'

'Woof,' he said.

'You are such a strange man,' said June. 'I share my bed with a barking corpse.'

Henry turned and smiled at her. The List had begun to mist away. He'd beaten it. Dentist Man wins again. 'Do you love your dentist?' he said.

'Not when he's strange,' June pouted. 'Not when he goes into his trance. You've been doing that a lot, Henry.'

'I start my day thinking.'

'Stange is how you start your day.'

'June,' said Henry, his smile suddenly gone. 'Tell me, what's the first thing you think about when you wake up?'

'Gee, Henry, I don't know,' she said, falling back on her pillow. But she did know. She felt the heat rise to her face, and elsewhere, and scrunched away from Henry so he wouldn't see. Every day for the last month she'd awakened dreamily to thoughts of Jeffrey Lyons's T-shirts. He was the eighteen-year-old next door, twenty years her junior, and he bulged magnificently in his T-shirt. For a month she'd had visions of herself in Jeffrey's backyard, running through a multicolored sea of his T-shirts drying on endless clotheslines in the summer sun. This morning June had gotten herself particularly worked up: in the middle of one of her imagined clotheslines, something new hung amidst the T-shirts – a pair of dazzling red boxer shorts.

'Surely something comes to you,' said Henry.

'Oh, you know, just sleepy thoughts. Nothing in particular.'

'Like . . .?'

'Like, well, breakfast, the kids, listening to the house.' T-shirts and red boxer shorts.

Henry looked at her, envious. Now why can't I do that? he wondered. She lies there thinking of waffles and Raisin Bran, and I have to worry about world famine. 'June,' he said, moving closer to her. 'Do you ever wake up filled with dread?'

She stared at him. 'What sort of dread, Henry?'

'Are there different kinds? You know, overwhelmingly paralyzing absolute dread.'

She stared at him some more. 'Henry,' she finally said. 'That doesn't sound very healthy.' She drew him to her and began to stroke his head. 'That's why you've been staring at the ceiling, isn't it? That's why you barked like a dog.'

'Yes,' he said. 'I believe it is.'

'Would Dentist Man like his Juney June to do something special for him?' she cooed in his ear. 'Something to make that mean old dread go away?'

Henry nuzzled her. He loved to hear her use his secret name. 'Yes, he would,' he whispered.

She touched a finger to the tip of his nose and winked at him. 'Wait right here.' She pranced across the room to the bathroom.

Henry leaned back against his pillow and watched her bottom disappear into the bathroom. It was still a fine bottom, a bottom he should spend more time thinking about than he actually did. Tomorrow, first thing, he would try to think about her bottom instead of The List.

June reappeared in a jiffy, holding something in her hands. Henry saw what it was and shivered in anticipation. She moved slowly, provocatively, across the bedroom and sat on the edge of the bed. Almost involuntarily, Henry's lips parted.

June leaned over him, her breasts straining against her thin nightgown. She held her fingers in front of his eyes and pulled the green strand taut. 'Peppermint,' she whispered. 'Waxed.'

Henry could hardly bear it.

'Are you ready, Dentist Man?'

'Floss me,' he said.

And she did. For a brief time in that morning bedroom they were as happy as a married couple can be. No dread, no dreams of T-shirts. June flossed Henry until he could stand it no more.

'Morning, Dad.'
'Morning, Dad.'

Henry, still in his pajamas, his gums throbbing ever so slightly, stood in the kitchen doorway and studied his twin sons. Frederick and Edward, thirteen years old.

'Morning, boys,' he said, giving each a big smile. There you go, Ed, one smile for you, and Fred, another smile for you. Or was it Fred he smiled at first, Fred eating his Cheerios and ignoring Henry now? Or, goddamn it, was Fred the one eating Cocoa Crispies, and Ed eating the Cheerios? Which? He'd never been able to tell, not from the first day they came home from the hospital. Utterly and bafflingly identical, all the way down to the tips of their little weenies. He should have nicked one of their ears early on, like you do on a cow, or had the doctor tattoo them right there in the delivery room. Big letters on the forehead. ED. FRED.

'Ed, slide over so your father can sit down,' said June, who had come downstairs before Henry.

So Ed *was* eating Cheerios. What was June's system? Had to be that intuitive maternal thing that links mothers unerringly to their children. It wasn't fair.

'So Fred,' said Henry, turning to the one eating Cocoa Crispies and reading the sports section of the paper, 'how about those Phils?'

Fred looked up. 'How about 'em?'

Henry's stomach bubbled uncomfortably. Fred challenging him already. Nothing rough yet, but definitely a foreshadowing of the teen years soon to plague this house. A double plague! Ed and Fred coming at him relentlessly, hopped out of their skulls on testosterone.

'Well,' said Henry in soothing tones, 'you know, RBIs, at bats, homeruns. That sort of thing.'

'Dad, you don't like baseball. You don't like any sports.'

'That's not true,' he said. 'I like horseshoes.'

'Dad,' Ed now joined in. 'Horseshoes isn't a sport, it's a pastime.'

'Hey, call it what you want. You still can't beat me. Either of you. How about a game right now, before my coffee, even. Ed? Fred?'

The twins looked at each other and rolled their eyes. 'Sure, Dad,' they said simultaneously. 'Right.'

'Now Henry, don't be a bear. Here's your coffee.' June sloshed a big mug down in front of him. 'You want sausages or bacon this morning?'

Ed and Fred instantly clutched their chests, pretending heart attacks, then resumed eating their cereal as if nothing had happened.

Every morning the same thing – the twins never let him chew his fat in peace. Henry was a cholesterol addict, worse these days than being an alcoholic.

'Got any *bran* muffins, Mom?' said Ed.

'I'll take some Raisin *Bran*, Mom, if there's any left,' said Fred.

'You boys leave your father alone,' said June. 'He can't help being what he is.'

Henry twisted around to her. 'And just what is it I am, dear? A tub of Crisco?'

The boys snickered.

'Well, you could try a little harder to eat right, Henry.'

'Have you ever seen even one granule of sugar pass between my lips?'

'Never. But you're a dentist, after all.'

'And if I was a cardiac surgeon you'd never see me eat a sausage. Now give me three – no, four links please – and everybody leave me the hell alone.'

They were right, of course. Absolutely goddamn right. Cholesterol was right up there at the top of The List. Next to oil spills. Cholesterol spills, greasy globs washing up against the major arteries. June slid the plate of sausages in front of him like a sentence of death. The twins smirked, daring him to put one in his mouth. Henry pushed at one with his fork. Fat seemed to ooze out of it like sweat. Come on, the sausage goaded, are you man enough to eat me? Henry looked up. June and the twins were watching. So was the sausage. Henry lifted the thing to his lips, steeled himself to bite off its little head.

'Do it,' the twins began to chant in a whisper. 'Do it, do it, do it.'

Henry pushed the sausage against his lips, but he couldn't seem to get them open. Come on, the sausage whispered from the fork, do it, do it.

Henry dropped the fork like a hot match and it clattered down on to his plate. The sausage bounced across the table and on to the floor, where it lay, as ugly and out of place as a turd on the shining linoleum.

'Eeeewh, Dad,' said Ed.

'Look what Dad did on the floor,' said Fred, pointing.

Even June would not, as she usually did, come to his defense. See how she squints at my mess on her linoleum. First he'd barked like a dog, and now this second act of canine misbehavior. He half expected her to roll up the newspaper and whack him on the nose.

Ed jumped out of his chair, snatched up the sausage, and began to wiggle it at Fred. 'Gonna get you,' he said. 'Gonna make you eat it!'

'Mom!' Fred held his sports section in front of him and danced away from Ed. 'Make him stop.'

The twins laughed and screeched and chased one another around, banging against chairs and kitchen appliances. June made grabs at them as they bounced by. 'Ed, put that sausage down. Fred, stop hitting him!'

Henry slumped in his chair and glumly watched the commotion. Tomorrow, he told himself, tomorrow I eat bacon. Ed, Fred and June whirled out of the kitchen and were gone. He stared a moment at the sausages, shoulder to shoulder on his plate, then pushed them away. How quickly the day had escaped his control. Did my father have such a hell of a time controlling his days? How had Stu managed? Henry got up and looked out of the window above the sink. Could it be that in the kitchens of the houses he could see, and on and on in the houses he imagined, families were seated amicably at the table, munching toast and sipping orange juice? Had his own family ever done such a thing? Only in his dreams. Hey, Ed, please pass the toast. Fred? More orange juice, son? June, is that a new bathrobe you're wearing? Quilted, yes, I see, so it is. It looks so lovely and warm. And dear, if you could just pass the Mighty Bran, I think I'll have myself another bowl – but let me say first, God bless us each and every one.

From upstairs, a piercing scream. Ed successfully cramming the sausage into Fred's mouth? Or Fred into Ed's? Who knew, who knew? Another scream, followed by laughter. Henry lowered his eyes from the ceiling. He picked up a half-eaten slice of toast from someone's plate and began to chew. Chewing was such a comfort to him. All his parts working in perfect harmony. How beautiful it must look from within – the marble mountains of teeth tearing and kneading the toast, the muscular pink tongue manipulating the mass from the teeth to the pharynx, the six salivary glands hosing it all down like a car wash, the orgasmic act of swallowing. God. It was a wonder he didn't weigh three hundred pounds. But he knew that food was not really his friend, no indeedy. Remember, he'd tell his patients, every time you bite into a glazed donut, you might as well be gargling with battery acid. You had to scare them a little bit, especially the younger ones. He used a lighter touch with his older patients; the ladies especially seemed to enjoy it. Patting their ample arms, he might cheer them on with, 'Rinse and spit / Rinse and spit / Help those pearly whites stay fit!'

June appeared in the doorway, looking stormy. 'Well, you sure were a big help.'

'You seemed to have things under control. And really,' he said, not meeting her eyes, 'all in all, you manage them better.' Hell, he thought, at least you can tell them apart.

'I chase them better, you mean.' She turned and called over her shoulder. 'The school bus will be here in five minutes, you two. No monkey business, hurry up!'

'There, that sort of thing,' said Henry. 'That's what you do better.'

'Chasing and yelling, Henry. How nice that I do it better than you. It makes me feel so feminine.'

Uh oh, thought Henry. 'Childrearing has nothing to do with femininity.'

'Precisely,' she said, icicles dripping off the word. She brushed past him with a handful of breakfast dishes and dumped them in the sink. A sudden cough and a deep growl from a motorcycle starting up next door. June went up on her tiptoes in front of the window. She gripped the sink. Vroom, vroom, she growled back under her breath. Jeffrey Lyons, I see you. Oh Jesus, you're wearing a T-shirt, just for me. He always wore a T-shirt, but never mind that, never mind that one bit. He gunned his engine, his back muscles rippling. June steadied herself.

'Honey?'

Henry's voice barely reached her. She was far away, heading down the highway of her imagination astride Jeffrey's motorcycle. She clung to him, cheek to his thick back, the pulsing energy of eight hundred pounds of hot steel moving up and out of her. She whimpered.

'June?' She having a seizure or something? Look at her trembling. Henry touched her shoulder, and she immediately turned and took his face into her hands and pulled him to her.

'Kiss me,' she breathed.

'Mmmph,' said Henry, as she practically chewed the lips off his face.

'Eeewh,' said the twins in unison from the kitchen doorway.

Henry jumped away from June.

'You guys done or what?' said Fred.

'Yeah, we're only thirteen, you know,' said Ed. 'We shouldn't have to see that stuff.'

'Yeah, like ever,' said Fred.

June held their lunch bags out in front of her. 'Moms and dads kiss,' she said. 'Get used to it.'

'It's unnatural,' said Ed, snatching his bag.

'Yeah, twisted,' said Fred.

Well, at least surprising as hell, Henry had to admit, giving the boys an unrequited wave as they ran for their school bus. He stepped into the living room to watch the metal mouth of the bus open for his children. To whom had he entrusted them today? The drivers seemed to change weekly: midgets, ex-cons, octogenarians, substance abusers – or so they appeared to Henry. Fred and Ed climbed the black stairs and headed for the rear of the bus. The driver looked straight ahead through the big windshield. Was that the same guy as yesterday? Henry couldn't quite see. The doors began their jerky close. The driver turned to Henry, revealing himself in the final half second before the doors closed completely. A Death's Head! Henry pressed his nose and both hands to the picture window as the bus took off. The eyeless sockets, the gappy grin – Death driving his two boys to school.

'Henry, I just Windexed that window yesterday,' came June's voice from behind him.

Henry, pale and sweaty-lipped, whirled around.

'Dear?' she said, approaching him carefully. 'You look like you saw a ghost.'

'I did! That's exactly what I saw, a ghost. Or some sort of skeleton, some sort of dead-looking thing driving the bus.'

'Oh, for goodness sakes, Henry. What a thing to say. That's Millie Robinson's husband, you know, Lyle, he's got that disease. Poor guy. Retired from Boeing in the spring, thought he'd do a little part-time driving for the school, to keep busy, and then he got that disease, the one where you feel fine but you waste away? What's the name of that?'

Henry could just hear the bus grinding its gears in the distance. 'How much more does he have to waste? I mean, I think he's there.' He strained to hear more bus sounds. 'What if he passes out at the wheel or something? Our boys happen to be on that bus, you may recall.'

'He's fine. They wouldn't let him drive if he wasn't fine.'

'You kidding? They let anybody drive those buses. Two weeks ago I saw a lady with an eyepatch, for Chrissake.'

'Oh, Henry.'

'Hey, look. I'm a health professional. I worry about people's diseases.'

'You're a dentist. Worry about teeth.'

'And that's another thing. Ol' Lyle didn't have the healthiest looking set of choppers.'

'So they shouldn't let him drive a bus?'

'Fine, fine.' Henry moved past her and started up the stairs. 'When they make the call, you be the one who takes it.'

'What call?'

Henry shouted from the bedroom. 'The call that tells you Lyle Robinson has driven a school bus full of children into Crum Creek, and two of them were yours!'

Mother of God, how he loved his new Ford Taurus station wagon. Henry sat in it a minute before starting the ignition. He reached up and stroked the padded rectangle in the center of the steering wheel. Within that rectangle resided the feature he most loved about his Taurus: the airbag. There was no place on earth Henry felt safer than in his driveway, surrounded by his new car and protected by his airbag. Nothing could touch him. He'd walk away from anything, like Mario Andretti rising from the wreckage and waving jauntily to the screaming crowd. He was dying for the bag to go off, to see what it would look and feel like. They tell you on impact it's there in your face and gone again in less than a second. Pop! Like a champagne cork, a celebration, you survive while the other guy, airbagless, gets scraped off his windshield. Henry did feel a twinge of guilt whenever June rode with him, bagless on the passenger's side. On the long drive up to the mountains three weeks ago, when his foot went numb and he was visibly nodding off, he still wouldn't let her take the wheel.

'But Henry, you're going to kill us all,' she'd said.

No, not all, he'd thought, secretly stroking the edge of the padded rectangle with his thumb. 'I'll pull over for another cup of coffee. I just need to stretch a little.'

'I don't know why you're so stubborn. You never used to like driving so much.'

'Oh, it's just the new car thing. You know. I'm sure it'll wear off in another month or so,' he lied.

Henry started the car. Well really, it's Detroit's fault for putting in only one airbag, making you choose between you and your loved ones. He backed out of the driveway wondering, Am I really such a monster, always thinking about saving my own neck? He sighed. The curse of advanced technology. Life was so much easier with the old Honda Accord, when a car crash was guaranteed to kill us all.

He managed to drive three blocks before the first patient of the day materialized before him. He rarely made it to work without someone approaching him for free dental advice. This morning it was Lotty Daniels standing on the corner of Park and Cedar, her heavy flesh packed into a running suit that strained to contain her. He should pretend not to see her, be looking the other way. But no, dammit, she was already waving and stepping into the street on the passenger's side, and he had to slow down. Then again, if he sped up he'd hit her, and he'd get to see his airbag in action.

Henry pulled to a stop, drumming his fingers on the steering wheel as he waited for her to come around to his window. But she didn't come around, she was opening the passenger door, squeezing herself into his brand new Ford Taurus! The car listed to her side and Henry felt himself begin to slide toward her.

'Oh Dr Miles, thank you so much,' Lotty began. 'I just don't know what I'd have done if you hadn't stopped.'

Made an office appointment, perhaps? Henry tried to lean away from her, fighting her gravitational pull. 'Well, Lotty,' he said. 'Tooth problems?' He tried to sound kindly.

'The worst. The absolute worst,' her fingers prying into her mouth to reveal yellow teeth, and gums that somehow looked as pinkly overweight as the rest of her. 'All night long,' her words garbling around her fat fingers, 'the pain right here, this tooth 'ight 'ere, like a red hot knitting needle jabbing into it, like little sparks of white shooting lightning. Oh doctor, it's just awful, the pain.'

Henry listened dreamily. He'd often thought of starting a dental poetry magazine, filling it with his patients' descriptive renderings of their toothsome woes. *Tusk*, he'd call it.

>   Red hot knitting needles
>   Jabbing
>   Sparks of white –
>   Oh doctor, doctor.

Or yesterday, poor suffering Mr Lyman gave him a few good lines:

>   Take them all
>   They rot
>   They smell.
>   These are not
>   The teeth of my youth –
>   Take them all.

Next dental convention, he'd try the idea out on his colleagues.

'Do you see anything, Dr Miles?' insisted Lotty, pulling his attention back to her. 'It's got to be this 'ooth 'ight 'ack 'ere.'

What does she want me to do, snap off the rearview mirror and go in for a closer look? 'Really, Lotty, it's hard to tell.'

'Please look, doctor.' Her eyes started to moisten.

'I'm looking, I'm looking.'

Lotty suddenly grabbed his hand and stuffed one of his fingers into her mouth. He squinted in anticipation of her chomping down. Would he still be able to work a drill with three fingers and a thumb? He was relieved when she just poked his forefinger up against a molar.

Lotty was right up on him now, crunching him against his steering wheel, her pink face weaving inches in front of his own. She generated a lot of heat on this May morning. Henry tried to reach his other hand behind him to roll down the window. A red minivan honked. He was blocking the intersection. The minivan cut around him. From the corner of his eye, Henry could just see the woman in the minivan stare, then shake her head as she drove by. Oh Christ, she thinks . . . with Lotty squirming around and practically on top of me, she thinks we're getting it on! Did she recognize me?

'Do you see anything?' Lotty said. Then she cried out: 'Uuuhn, 'ight 'ere,' her wet words spraying on to the back of his hand.

'There?' he poked.

'Uuhn.'

'Or there?'

'Uuhn-UUUHN!'

He was tempted to give her one more jab to indelibly associate, deep within her subconscious, the interior of his car with surging pain. He did not want the word to get around that his Taurus wagon was a mobile dentist office.

'Lotty.'

'Yes, doctor.' Her eyes grew wide and she pressed her lips tightly together, bracing herself for the news.

What a moment. Dentistry always hurts twice: hearing the diagnosis, and then the actual intervention. What I could do to your day, Lotty. You're lucky I'm not a cruel man. Just a harried one. He glanced at his watch and looked up at her with a frown. 'Your gum's a little puffy, that's all. You're fine.'

'I can't be fine.' She pulled away from him, eyes narrowing.

'But you are fine.'

'But the pain. It's kind of going now, but last night . . .'

'You flossed too hard.'

'I don't floss.'

'Then you brushed too hard.' He pointed to his watch.

'Really.'

'I Water-Pic, Dr Miles. Like you advised.'

So now she turns surly because her tooth doesn't have to be extracted? 'Listen, Lotty. Actually, your gum didn't look too good,' (see how her face brightens) 'so I did a kind of a new thing in there.'

'You did?'

'Yes, I did. I performed a periodontic acupressure.'

'It does feel better,' she said, rubbing her jaw.

'I bet,' said Henry. 'And now, really, I'm late for the office.'

She backed herself out of the car and Henry felt the springs lift in relief. 'Oh thank you, thank you. You're a wonderful man, Dr Miles. Really, everyone says you're the best.'

Henry wished Fred and Ed had been in the backseat to hear that. *Look what Dad did on the floor.* 'Call the office if you need to, Lotty. So long now.' With a wave he was off again, Henry Miles, Dentist Man. The Best.

Henry loved to be loved. He drove along the familiar streets, feeling cozy and mildly high on himself. I matter. I make a difference. I am not tumbling endlessly into the void. I have my health. I have my teeth. I have my relative youth. My Taurus wagon, my wife June, the twins. I put my father in a nursing home, but it's a *good* nursing home. I am a skilled practitioner. I am a healer. I am good in bed.

Am I? Henry turned on to MacDade Boulevard. He felt his mood slip as he glimpsed the void. Why did he bounce around like this? Why couldn't be he Dentist Man all day, and all night too? This morning was pretty good with June, but really, things had been a little dull lately. I'm forty-two and she's thirty-eight: we're supposed to crackle with sexuality? Did we ever crackle? For that matter, did any couple he knew crackle? It's all a lie, a TV and advertising lie. Or maybe not. Maybe in bedrooms across the country people were crackling like crazy, and expertly, too. He was the only one who couldn't make his wife squeak with pleasure. The best he'd ever gotten out of June was a kind of a hiccuppy sigh. Why were women's orgasms so difficult to detect and decipher? Did she had them constantly? Or at all? I mean, she could be having orgasms at the breakfast table and he'd never know. And they never did anything weird. Oh, maybe the floss, but that was just good cleaning fun. She never raked his back and growled. Did he want her to?

He pulled into his parking space right in front of the office. He smiled. The sight each morning of his very own office gave him a sort of . . . well, yes, orgasm. Not down there, but all over, a rushy satisfied release.

The office, not his home, was Henry's castle. He got out of the station wagon and surveyed his kingdom, which consisted of an asphalt parking lot with spaces for six cars (not including his own, with its DR MILES stenciled in bold letters), a ten by ten foot square of immaculately tended green grass bordered by a knee-high yew hedge, and the office itself, single story, white stucco, on top of which crouched a large rectangular sign that read HENRY MILES, DDS – GENERAL DENTISTRY. It stayed lit twenty-four hours a day. Pushy, maybe, but it pulled them in.

Next door to his office, looming with evil intent, was a Dreami Donuts. They shared a driveway. Two cars sneaked past his office as he watched and pulled into the Dreami Donuts lot. Sure, drive by now, I'll get you soon enough. Chow down on that sugary slop, go right ahead. He walked over to pick several discarded donut wrappers out of his hedge. Every damn morning, same thing. The place breeds rot. Breeds business too, Henry. Rot is your business. Marty Marks, manager of Dreami Donuts, waved to Henry from his glass-enclosed sugar palace. Henry waved back to him with his handful of crumpled wrappers.

Marty stuck his head out the door, a guy at least Henry's age who looked like an imbecilic teenager in his Dreami Donuts paper cap. 'Sorry about that, Dr Miles. Little bit of trash blow over? Dogs must've got in the dumpster or something.'

Dogs on pogo sticks, you fool? 'Been happening kind of regularly, Marty,' Henry called back across the lot.

'What do you say to a box of Tiny Tasties, doc? For you and your crew. Forty-eight in a box. Tempted? How about it?'

'I don't do donuts, Marty.'

'These aren't really donuts. They're the centers.'

'No.'

'Not even for the gals?'

'No. Listen, Marty, the wrappers. I mean, if you could confine your trash to your own property.'

Marty's eyes went flat. 'Those wrappers serve an important sanitary function, Dr Miles. They give the customer peace of mind.'

'It may be peace of mind on your side of the lot, but when it blows over to my side it's a piece of trash. OK?'

Marty's face flushed, and he started to pull his head back inside the door. Before Henry turned away, Marty popped into view again. 'Say, doc.' His hand started to move toward his mouth in a gesture all too familiar to Henry. 'My crown, this one up here,' he said hooking a finger inside his cheek and giving it a tug, as if Henry could possibly see from where he stood. 'It's coming loose, you know the one you fixed last time?'

Do women in parking lots lift their dresses if they happen to run into their gynecologists? And proctologists, God knows what sights are forced upon them by patients in supermarket aisles. These bodies devour us. 'Sure, Marty,' said Henry wearily. 'Give Rita a call. I'll tell her to fit you in if we have a cancellation.' He made a dash for the office before Marty had a chance to show his gratitude with another offer of a box of Sticky Sickies, or whatever the hell he called them.

Rita Hoops, his aging and bewigged receptionist, attempted to stand when Henry walked in.

'I'm not a general, for Pete's sake, Rita. Please don't rise when I come in.' He said this every morning, to no avail.

It took her a while to get out of her chair, so Henry was forced to wait in front of her desk, smiling politely, until she completed the maneuver. He usually spent the time admiring the thin spots on her precarious wig. Did she have it on backwards today? Weren't those her bangs hanging down around the back of her neck? He was waiting for the day when she wore it inside out. Surely she could afford a new wig on what he paid her. Perhaps her attachment was sentimental – had it been a favorite of the late Mr Hoops, say in the 1950s? When she wore the wig properly, with the bangs in front, she had a kind of Mamie Eisenhower look. Maybe that's why she stands when I come in – she really does think I'm the General. Ahh, there. She's up.

'Morning, Dr Miles,' she said in her strange and delicious tones. What a voice. As if the aging process had somehow bypassed her vocal cords: youth's last stand, sensuality imprisoned by decrepitude. Thick and throaty like Lauren Bacall, candy for the ears. Henry had seen patients come in, the young guys, all hot to meet the receptionist who'd scheduled their appointment. Thinking about her voice, thinking maybe she's going to be one of those phone-sex goddesses come to life. And then pow, there she is, Rita with her motheaten wig on backwards, older than their grannies.

'Yes, good morning, Rita. What do we have first in today's lineup?'

'He's already in the chair. Charlie Carnes.' Rita began her slow descent back into her chair. She would not rise from it again until her twelve-thirty lunch break. She was all business.

'Oh, right.' Novocaine Carnes.

'Operative. You have four ops this morning, two prophylaxes. This afternoon, crowns and bridges. A moderate day, I should think, doctor,' she said, her voice making it all sound so tempting. Rita was the brains of the outfit, the organizational nerve center. All day long Henry listened to her seductive telephone voice arrange and rearrange the patient schedule, order supplies, untangle the Byzantine workings of the insurance companies.

A rustling behind him and a whiff of something lovely.

Henry turned, a smile instantly lifting the corners of his mouth. If Rita was the brains, the body was all Jennifer's. Jennifer Olmstead, his twenty-year-old dental assistant, her cupcake ass and gumdrop nipples within nibbling distance eight hours a day, five days a week. Such a collection of parts, how he craved her. He smiled, showed his perfect whites and healthy pink to her, *his* best parts, and prayed, as he did each morning, for God to strike her mute.

'Hi, doc,' she said in her lifeless monotone. 'Patient's here. I put him in room two.'

Henry nodded sadly. 'Fine. Good. Tell him I'll be right there.'

'OK, doc,' she said, shrugging as she turned away.

Because if you never spoke, he thought, checking first to make sure Rita wasn't watching him, then riveting his eyes on Jennifer's departing rear end, if you never spoke, you would never reveal to the world and to your employer your excruciating dullness. She wasn't stupid; she did her work, robotically but well. Her body screamed excitement, but her mind yawned. How he struggled to make conversation. He had to. He couldn't just look at her all day.

Say, Jennifer, he'd ask, bending over somebody's mouth, *see the plane crash coverage last night? Crashing into a mall. What a way to go, huh?*

Yeah, I guess, she'd say, suctioning spit. *I don't know. Roseanne was on. I kind of watched that instead.*

Say, Jennifer, the Bosnia crisis. What a can of worms, huh?

Yeah well, you know, it's weird, I guess. People killing each other and everything.

Say, Jennifer, what do you do for fun?

I like TV, I guess. Some of the shows. I do some cooking, you know, with the microwave. My boyfriend likes his pizza waved. So we do TV mostly, I'd say. TV and microwave.

What a unique form of torture you are, gumdrop Jenny, you exquisitely proportioned android. Those poor guys who come in lusting for Rita, who change their appointments two or three times just to hear her voice, and then stroll into the office with their loins tight, only to discover the voice belongs to a crone with a, a *rodent* on her head. Down they droop – until they look up and see you crooking a finger at them, beckoning them into an examination room. Boing – they're in business again! How they try to win you with their hot looks and hopeful bantering, ignoring me, chatting you up even as I stuff their mouths with cotton wads and suction tubes and probing instruments. They are so distracted I don't have to bother with the local anesthesia. Hell, I could chip out an impacted wisdom tooth with a rusty ice pick and they wouldn't know it. You stand there, Jennifer, and suction their drool, which you cause them to excrete in excessive quantities, you suck them absently, tune them out completely. Like news of plane crashes and foreign wars, they are one more dull thing to ignore. What a daze they're in when they leave the office, all thick and confused by you and Rita. Only I don't disappoint them, though they don't know it until that night when they stand brushing before their bathroom mirrors and see how well I have attended to their real needs.

Henry stepped into his office to change. He never used this tiny room in the back except to hang up his coat or sweater and change into his white dental top. He'd crammed an oversized oak desk in here like he was some corporate big cheese, but there was no reason to sit at it since Rita handled most of the paperwork. Well, a man was entitled to a status symbol or two, something to impress the wife and kids. When they were toddlers, the twins had been so impressed they'd gotten hold of one of his newly sharpened scalers and scraped zigzags in the finish. And June, she'd been back here exactly once, to help him choose the wallpaper.

Before his first patient, he cut across the hall to the bathroom for a quick piss, a function he performed whether he really needed to or not. He didn't like the unprofessionalism of an insistent bladder while he was working on patients. They expect you to be there totally for them, not worrying about when you can hightail it down the hall to the toilet. Henry watched his thin stream start, hesitate, start up again. Not as much power behind it as there used to be. And the trickling off instead of a clean finish: that was happening more often these days. So let's see, I'm forty-two. I'm edging up on the prostate years. Lovely. He gave himself the once over in the medicine cabinet mirror: hair OK, nothing wedged between the teeth. Why'd he have a medicine cabinet put in here, anyway? He never used it, couldn't remember ever even opening it. He opened it now. Oh my. Look at that. Panty liners, thirty-six to a box. Jennifer's panty liners. His heart skipped a beat. It's open. She opened it. She's *used* them. What are you, Henry, twelve? Put the box back, put it

A staccato knock on the bathroom door, and the box flew out of Henry's hand, airborne panty liners fluttering everywhere.

'Doc?' came Jennifer's voice. 'Dr Miles, your wife's on the phone. You want her to call back, or what?'

The last panty liner landed on the floor. 'Yes, yes! Put her on hold. I'm coming,' Henry shouted through the door.

'You OK in there, doc?'

'Fine. Absolutely great. Put her on hold. Be right out.' Henry got down on his hands and knees and snatched panty liners from behind the toilet, off the pipes beneath the sink, out of the corner where they had gathered in drifts. Christ, more like five hundred to a box. Did he get them all? He rose and banged his forehead on the corner of the sink. Tears blurred his vision as he tried to repack the box neatly. He returned it to the second shelf (or had it been on the third shelf?), then dabbed his rising welt with cool water from the faucet. Steadying himself, he stepped out into the hallway.

Jennifer stood by the front desk talking to Rita. Rita looked up at him, pointed to the phone with its blinking hold light and frowned. She didn't like him tying up her phone with outside calls.

Jennifer squinted at his forehead. 'What happened to you?'

He touched his finger to his wound. A zing of pain. 'Slipped in some water. Pipes leaking or something, you two be careful in there.'

He picked up the phone. 'June. You're not working at the mall today?'

'Henry. I thought you died in there.' June's voice jumped at him through the phone. 'Today's Tuesday. You know I don't work Tuesdays.'

'Right.' Then, 'Died in where?' he said guardedly.

'Jennifer said you were in the bathroom.' Henry glanced at Jennifer. 'Actually,' said June, 'what she said was, "He's using the toilet." That's a vulgar little girl, Henry.'

June did not like Jennifer. Her beauty, her youth, her youth, her beauty. Rita did not like June. June called the office and tied up the phone. June, however, liked Rita. Rita was not beautiful, not youthful. Rita liked Jennifer. Because Jennifer did her job well? And Jennifer, bless her heart, was indifferent to both June and Rita, as she was to all things.

'So, June,' said Henry, 'what's up?'

'Well,' she said, her voice going gooey, 'I just wanted to say—' She stopped abruptly. 'Is Jennifer standing there?'

Jennifer was standing there, a panty liner length or two away. Henry's forehead throbbed. 'No,' he lied. 'Say what you were going to say.'

'This morning, Henry.'

'Yes.' From where he stood, Henry could see Charlie Carnes fidgeting in his chair in room 2.

'You remember?'

Remember what?

'Do you?' she nudged.

'Of course I do.'

'It was nice for me, was it nice for you?'

'Yes, it was . . .' His voice dropped to a whisper. 'Nice.'

She breathed into the phone. 'Fantasize today. And whatever your fantasy is, we'll do it tonight, OK?'

Rita and Jennifer stared at him. Charlie Carnes coughed in the next room. Henry turned his back to them. 'Uh, yes, June,' he said, trying to sound businesslike and neutral, 'well, that's an interesting option, and I'll look into it.'

'Promise?' June cooed.

Henry winced and stretched the phone cord taut trying to get away from the desk. 'That's a possible affirmative.'

'Only a possible? And just how firm are you, Henry?'

'Right. I'll pick up a dozen eggs and a loaf of bread,' he said loudly, glancing over his shoulder at Jennifer and Rita.

'Henry?'

'Yes, and chicken breasts too,' he said. 'Goodbye, dear, see you at supper.' He hung up quickly and turned back to the desk.

'June doesn't drive?' asked Jennifer.

'She drives. Car's out of whack.' No, car's fine, wife's out of whack. Henry started for room 2. 'What do you say, Jennifer, shall we begin the day?' He could see Charlie Carnes tighten, the body language of fear. Henry smiled. At last, the day seemed to be in his control.

Chapter 2

June gripped the phone until it started to bleep at her, then, without taking her eyes from the bedroom window, lowered it to its cradle. Henry, she thought, you did not hear me cry out for you.

Outside, in the driveway below June's window, Jeffrey Lyons stood up from his partially dismantled motorcycle and stretched in the sun. He pulled off his T-shirt and tossed it on to the grass.

June reached for the phone in a panic and began to dial Henry's office number again. When Rita answered, June quickly hung up. She hurried into the bathroom to splash water on her face. She could hear the metallic sounds of tools at work and a muscular grunt as Jeffrey lifted something heavy. She moved back to the bedroom to watch.

Think, June. If you go near that boy, the earth will open up and swallow you, lightning will strike you, vice squad cars with flashing lights will surround you. Henry will load up the twins, the house, your new leather sofa and whisk them all away. Think, June, list those negatives. The negatives will save your marriage. Rejection – that boy will laugh in your face if you make the tiniest overture. Despair – if he rejects you. Loss of creature comforts – if he doesn't reject you and Henry does. Humiliation – if he does or doesn't reject you and everyone in town finds out. Which they definitely will. You listening, Juney June? They definitely will. Diseases – turn on the news, everybody's a carrier now. No more free dental care, no more dentist – that's Henry we're talking about, your husband and mate for life. June sighed and let the shade fall against the window.

Sometimes, when she mated with Henry, it did seem to go on for a lifetime. He was so relentless, sometimes, as he hovered above her and – she winced to think of it – drilled away at her.

That's not fair, June, he can't help it if he's . . . a bit methodical and he certainly can't help being a dentist. So what's the issue here, his dentistry or his sexual technique? Is there a difference between the two? Oops, there you go again.

June fell back on the bed and stared at the white ceiling, the ceiling Henry had begun his day staring at as he battled his morning panic attack. Images flashed before her, Jeffrey Lyons in his second skin of a T-shirt. Henry in his polyester dental top. Jeffrey brandishing a metric socket wrench. Henry holding a drill. Jeffrey lifting a tire off his motorcycle. The spare tire around Henry's slack waist. Jeffrey's rippling arms. June went blank for a moment: she couldn't really remember Henry's arms, or ever once having looked at them. She moved on to other parts. Jeffrey's thing. Hmmm. She smiled at the tingling pressure the thought caused. Henry's thing. What *did* she think of it? It was OK, she guessed, the little she saw of it. He was so furtive about it, even after all these years. Scampering naked out of the bathroom if he'd forgotten his bathrobe. Or reaching to click the light off before they had sex. The pink bat that hung hidden in the cave of his pants, venturing out only in the safety of darkness. Men needed a way to devalue their parts, take away some of the charm and mystique. Male menstruation, that'd do it. A few babies passing between their legs, doctors and the whole world looking on.

Would Jeffrey Lyons be the same way, hiding so she could never get a good look? Well, you'll never know, June. It's the stuff of fantasy, T-shirts fluttering in imagined breezes. She closed her eyes and drifted through a clothesline heavy with his freshly washed T-shirts, the soft cloth fluttering against her skin, cottony kisses.

The doorbell rang. She got up, gazed at the bed a moment as if something other than a daydream had occurred there, then hurried downstairs to the front door. She opened the door and stood blind and squinting, dazzled by the sudden morning sun shining directly in her face.

'Mrs Miles?'

At first, only the voice, as if spoken by the shimmering light that filled her doorway. As her eyes adjusted, a form appeared, yes, a human form. And then Jeffrey Lyons materialized before her, outlined in the bright gold of the May morning sun.

'You OK, Mrs Miles?' Jeffrey stepped forward.

June stepped back. 'Jeffrey?'

'Did I wake you? I can come back later.' He tugged at the hem of his T-shirt.

June's blood pulsed in her ears. She held on to the doorknob for support. He'd read her mind. Her lascivious thoughts had danced out of her brain, the musical notes of her siren song dancing through the air, out her bedroom window and down down down to Jeffrey Lyons's unprotected ears. Or had it been hormonal? The invisible traces of her sexual chemicals exuding from her pores, penetrating the walls of her house, flying toward Jeffrey, a thousand microscopic arrows of desire piercing him. Then we're both victims, Jeffrey, blameless victims of our animal urges, bodies in heat, let's make friction, how about it, kid? Or at least let me launder that T-shirt of yours, toss it in with my panties and bra, splish splash, tumble and churn, you'd enjoy that, wouldn't you? June thought the doorknob would snap off if she gripped it any harder.

She managed to say, 'No, no Jeffrey, you didn't wake me. Please come in.' Run away, Jeffrey, save us both.

'Sure, Mrs Miles.'

June winced. *Mrs Miles.* There was an awkward moment as Jeffrey waited for her to step back from the doorway. She started to move, then hesitated, so that he bumped into her, one of his elbows nudging her left breast.

He went red. 'Sorry, Mrs Miles. I guess I tripped.'

'My fault, Jeffrey,' she said, leading him into the living room. She turned to face him. 'So?' she said, meaning, Your move, kid, you planning to make a go for my right breast now, or what?

'So,' repeated Jeffrey, looking blank. Then he brightened and smiled. 'Oh, yeah. So. So I was wondering, Mrs Miles. Dr Miles has a set of standard wrenches I borrowed once before. I was wondering . . .'

'Tools,' she sighed. 'You want to borrow some tools.'

'Tools, yeah, wrenches. You know, if that's OK and everything.'

Jeffrey, I am woman and you are man and here we are standing on the creamiest, softest carpet imaginable, a carpet I'd gladly rest my backside on if you'd care to climb aboard, now are you sure you're really asking me about standard wrenches?

'You say Henry has a set of these wrenches?' she said. 'Because he's not particularly handy, if you know what I mean. He's not what I'd call big in the tool department.' She looked straight into his eyes.

'Oh yeah, he's got them,' said Jeffrey. 'I remember he said you gave them to him for Christmas last year. Great set, too.'

'Christmas, is that right?' she said. 'Maybe so. Maybe I did. He's always asking for tools, I don't know why. They're toys to him really. I've never seen him fix a thing with all his tools.'

Jeffrey shifted. 'Well, you know, some guys are better at that stuff, is all.'

'You're very good, aren't you?'

He tugged at his T-shirt. 'Dr Miles is good at what he does, too,' he said. 'I mean, with his own kind of tools, his dentist stuff. I hardly feel a thing when he works on me.'

Ditto, thought June. Hardly a thing. Why is this boy coming to my husband's defense? I'm spooking him. He's figured out I'm coming on to him. Ease up. Give him the goddamn wrenches and let him go.

'Shall we venture to the basement, Jeffrey? That's where he keeps everything.'

A conversational beat or two passed before he said, 'Sure, Mrs Miles.'

June looked over her shoulder at him as she led him into the next room. 'Afraid of basements?'

'Uh, not really,' he said. Again, that beat or two.

Her hand on the basement door, 'Of me?'

He coughed. 'Look, uh, Mrs Miles, if this isn't a good time I can . . .'

June, my God, do something. Alarms going off everywhere, you're blowing it, girl. She grimaced and slapped her hands to her forehead. 'Mmm, ow, my head again.'

'Mrs Miles?'

'Migraine, Jeffrey. Been coming on all morning. Ooh, just,' she gave him her best pained look, then moved past him, 'just let me sit down a minute.'

Jeffrey took her arm and helped her to the leather sofa. She could smell his T-shirt, sweaty, but clean, too. 'You gonna be all right?' he said.

'Sure, sure,' she said, her eyes closed, but her nostrils dilated, taking him in in deep sniffs. 'I get so weird when they first start. They just kind of possess me.' She opened one eye. He looked concerned but relieved. Mrs Miles had been possessed. 'I just need to lie here, I get them once a month or so, I'll be fine.'

'Really, you sure now?'

'Get your wrenches, Jeffrey. His workbench is downstairs on the left. Get whatever you need. I'll rest here.'

'I can come back some other time.'

'Don't be silly. Get what you need, then let yourself out. Just need to rest. Mmm, yeah, I'm feeling better. Go on now.'

Jeffrey hurried downstairs, rooted around a minute, then noiselessly reappeared, the wrench set under his large arm. 'Mrs Miles, I'm going now,' he whispered. 'I'll tell my mom to look in on you later.'

Eyes closed, June dismissed him with a flutter of her fingers and he was gone. When she heard the front door click shut, waves of heat and cold passed over her. She squirmed and trembled on the sofa; she really did have a headache now, a pounding one. *Tell my mom*, he'd said. Oh shit, June, that was close. Shit, shit, shit. When you were twenty and losing your virginity, Jeffrey Lyons was a fetus! Compared to you, he still is! What if you had touched him? He'd have told his *mom*. And she'd tell all the other moms. And Oprah and Phil would have to do a show on you. 'Mrs Miles, your sickness was neighborhood boys, wasn't it?' they'd whisper into their microphones in confidential tones. 'Couldn't keep your hands off them, could you?' while an entire TV nation of moms widens their eyes in horror.

June curled on the sofa. But Phil, oh Oprah, I don't think it's lust, not really. It's passion. Now she opened her eyes and sat up. Outside, a motorcycle engine sputtered a minute and died away. She looked around the living room, the familiar landscape of objects somehow remote, museum pieces of a life. Her own, yes? Inside, beneath her breasts untouched by Jeffrey Lyons, something in her heart sputtered a minute and died away. June sighed and looked around. She was safe here. Across the room on top of the cherry wood console of the vast TV, a framed photograph of the twins and another of her Henry, his beautiful teeth smiling. Henry, you'll protect me, won't you? In your arms I know I'll always be safe from passion.

'Charlie, Charlie, Charlie, what am I going to do with you?' sighed Henry.

Charlie Carnes's jaws were clamped tighter than a bear trap. His fingernails clawed deep into the padded vinyl arm of the examination chair. His breath came in tight little gasps; his face was white and filmy with sweat.

'Charlie,' said Henry. 'The Valium I prescribed. Did you take one before coming in?'

'Two,' said Charlie through his teeth.

'I didn't prescribe two, I prescribed one,' said Henry sternly. 'I'm the one with the Dr before his name, not you.'

'My hands were shaking so bad,' said Charlie, 'two came out, and before I knew it they were in my mouth.'

Henry looked at him. 'Well, Charlie, if your mouth opened so easily for all those pills, how about letting me get in there for a second.'

'What for?'

So I can extract your bicuspids with a pair of red hot pincers while I drool and cackle like a madman. So I can drill your teeth down to pulpy stumps, so I can jab your gums with needles as thick and long as pencils. 'Well, Charlie, so I can have a little bit of a look-see.'

'Will it be as bad as last time?' whimpered Charlie.

'Last time I didn't do anything.'

'Which means it will be worse.'

'Charlie. We found a cavity, you know that. Which is why you had to come back. Right?'

Silence, except for the rapid pounding of Charlie's heart, which Henry thought he could actually hear. Christ, Charlie having a heart attack in the chair, that's all I need. Am I paid up on my malpractice? Gotta remember to check with Rita. Charlie dead in my chair: boy, that'd be great for business, wouldn't it? Henry felt a sudden urge to slap him. That's what I'd have to do in battle, slap some courage into him, right? Buck up, boy. It's only pain. Pain is life.

'Pain is life, Charlie.'

Charlie's eyes widened. He went a whiter shade of white.

'Which is a good thing. No pain is a bad thing, I'm telling you, Charlie.'

Charlie sucked air like a fish.

Henry patted him and went on. 'No pain, dentally speaking, is the worst thing that can happen to you. Now listen to me. I don't mean to go religious on you, but don't you think it's interesting that God, in all His wisdom, chose to provide the tooth with the most sensitive nerve structure in the entire human body? The name we give to that supreme state of sensitivity is: pain. And since the only way we know we're alive is through our senses, then pain, as I see it, is the ultimate expression and embodiment of life. Pain is life. Life's a good thing, so pain's a good thing. Do you read me, Charlie?'

'Oh my God. Oh my God,' whispered Charlie between fish gasps.

'I always feel a little like I'm interfering with God's work when I deaden pain. But, as I say, don't want to keep going religious on you, except I guess to point out that God made man and man made anesthetics, so it all works itself out.' So nice and tidy. Henry beamed down at Charlie, who didn't seem to appreciate the beauty of Henry's intricately constructed logic.

'Don't tell me any more,' said Charlie. 'Even what you say hurts. Everything in this office hurts.'

Hey, thought Henry, is that my fucking fault? If you brushed your scuzzy teeth once in a while, you wouldn't be sitting here. If you didn't keep sneaking over to Dreami Donuts – don't think I haven't seen you in there – you wouldn't be requiring my hurtful skills. What a lousy job this is. Ungrateful, time-consuming, cavity-ridden slob. Look at you sweating on my newly upholstered chair. Help me but don't hurt me. What am I, a faith healer? It's all about paying your dues, Charlie boy, taking the sour with the sweet. The meter's ticking, I got a job to do, so open wide, buddy, Dentist Man is coming in.

'Jennifer,' Henry called. 'Gonna need suction in here in a minute.' Henry wheeled his stool closer and positioned Charlie's head. 'We really need to get this show on the road, Charlie.'

Charlie suddenly reached up and grabbed Henry's hand. 'Hold my hand for just a second,' he said weakly.

Jennifer appeared and without changing her expression (not that Jennifer ever really had what could be identified as an expression) smoothly wheeled her stool to the other side of Charlie's chair. 'Hey, Mr Carnes, how about holding my hand? Dr Miles really needs both of his to work, OK?'

'OK,' he answered gratefully.

Bless you, Jennifer, you efficient no-nonsense thing. Whatever it takes, you'll do it. Keep that patient traffic flowing. Henry winked at her and she shrugged in reply.

He readied himself just above and behind Charlie's right shoulder. 'Open,' he said with unequivocal dental authority. To Jennifer, he said, 'This Xylocaine have Epi in it?' He held the syringe up.

'No Epi.'

Charlie's mouth was slowly coming open. His eyes were screwed shut.

'You know the routine, Charlie. Numb you, clean you out and patch you up. Really, there won't be much to it.' Henry held the X-ray from Charlie's last visit up to the exam light and squinted at it. *The man's got an overbite he could use for a bottle opener.* 'Yes, right there on your number seventeen molar. Little bit of leakage around an old filling. Nothing to it.'

'For you,' said Charlie.

'Ha, ha,' Henry forced out a laugh. 'Nope, not for me, you got me there.' *Then again, I wasn't the one shellacking my teeth with jelly donuts, now was I?*

'A little pinch to numb you.'

Charlie's eyes opened and his mouth snapped shut.

'Don't look at the needle, Charlie. You know how you get.'

'I can't help it.'

Henry hid the syringe behind his back.

'I have to see,' urged Charlie.

'No.'

'Please.'

'No.'

'I have to know what's coming.'

'Same needle that's been coming for the fifteen years you've sat in that chair, Charlie.'

'Just one quick look.'

'Oh for God's sake, here.' Henry flashed the syringe before Charlie's eyes, then hid it again. 'See?'

'It's bigger! You're using a bigger needle this time!' Charlie lurched forward in his chair.

Jennifer gripped his arm and Henry forced his shoulders back against the chair. 'It's the same damn needle, Charlie, the tiniest one they make, it's so thin it's practically invisible.'

'It won't feel invisible.'

'Open,' demanded Henry.

'Mr Carnes,' said Jennifer. 'Do you think it would help if I held both of your hands?'

Henry watched him consider his options. To a fifty-three-year-old homely and forlorn man, an offer to hold the two hands of a luscious dental assistant was tantamount to an offer of unimaginable pleasures. Would this chance ever come his way again? Had it, in fact, ever before come his way? Was hand sex enough to induce him to take the needle?

Charlie took Jennifer's hands and opened as wide as a garage door. 'Do me,' he said.

Henry raised an eyebrow. Charlie Carnes, you conniving rat bastard. So that's your game. Get us feeling sorry for you so you can cop a feel, if you can call kneading Jennifer's knuckles a feel. That's what *he's* calling it, look at his fingers go. Henry was about to tell him to ease up when he caught sight of something odd altering Jennifer's normally blank look. An expression! A smiling expression. He was stunned.

'Jennifer?'

She smiled up at him. 'Yes, Dr Miles?'

'Everything . . . OK?'

'Sure, why not?'

'It's just that . . .' He jerked his head to point down to where Charlie sat, mouth open, eyes closed.

She leaned over Charlie and said to Henry in a whisper, 'It's OK.'

'No.'

'In fact, I sort of like it.'

Henry held up his hand. Tell me no more, Jennifer, whoever you are. Your pleasures are your own, it's not something I wish to delve into, it makes my head ache just to consider the possibilities.

Charlie opened one eye. 'What are you two whispering about?'

'Nothing. Turn your head this way, please.' Mouth agape, his body turned one way toward Jennifer and his head twisted the other, Charlie looked like the Elephant Man.

'Here comes the pinch,' said Henry, moving in with the needle, 'yes, there, good . . . good . . . uh huh, yes, you're doing great, doing great, there, almost, and . . . that's it. Done.'

Charlie jerked once when the needle went in, then almost immediately began to melt into the chair as if Henry had injected him with some sort of bone-evaporating chemical. Henry regarded him nervously. 'You with me, Charlie?'

Charlie smiled sloppily and half opened an eye. 'You betcha,' he said, letting his big mouth fall open. He rubbed his thumbs on the backs of Jennifer's hands as he spoke.

Hmmm, thought Henry. Have I discovered the perfect patient cocktail? Two Valium, a dash of Xylocaine and a touch of Jennifer. Jennifer, she seemed to be the key ingredient. Henry revved the drill near Charlie's ear. He didn't move an inch. Look at him smiling with his mouth wide open, the goof. I'll have Jennifer hold all their hands, every patient who comes in here. No, for the ladies I'll have to hire some young stud. I'll make a new sign for out front: DR HENRY'S HEALING HANDS DENTISTRY.

'Here I come, Charlie,' he said.

'Come ahead,' said Charlie, opening still wider.

Henry touched the whining drill to the surface of Charlie's molar. Charlie's eyes fluttered briefly and that was it. Amazing – no peeling him off the ceiling this time. Henry pressed on, squinting against the spray of water and pulverized enamel misting out of Charlie's mouth. Still he drilled, deeper, until the spinning drill bit broke into the tiny hidden cavern of decay. A barely perceptible pop, a sensation felt, not heard. Henry was a miner working in reverse: his job was to chop through priceless enamel until he reached a pay dirt of rot. The burning organic stink of drill-heated tooth rose to Henry's nose. I'm sorry, he whispered silently to the tooth, so sorry I'm forced to kill part of you so that the rest of you might live. Charlie destroys you and I destroy you further, on and on. If only he had not treated you so sweetly you'd have remained intact for all his years and even after, into the bony centuries, to smile up out of the grave at those who might some day unearth you. Tooth, forgive us.

Henry sighed. 'Well, time to put you back together, Charlie.'

'So soon?' said Charlie, his eyes opening dreamily.

And Jennifer, look at her still smiling, holding on to his hairy paws. 'Gee, I hate to separate you two,' he said, trying to make it into a ha-ha joke, 'but Jennifer, think you could start up the amalgam mixer?'

'Sure, no problem.'

He saw Jennifer and Charlie lock eyes for an instant. Don't think about it, Henry, don't even think about it or your head will explode. 'And I'll need the carver, it's not on the tray.'

'It's being sterilized.' She flipped on the mixer and left the room.

Charlie's head twisted to watch her go. Henry took him by the chin and turned him back, said, 'Gotta slide a matrix band in there. Open, please.' The poor molar looked like a strip-mined hill.

Jennifer returned, slid on to her stool and handed him an amalgam carrier, then the carver. 'Give me another double spill, this is a pretty big hole,' he said.

Charlie tried to speak, but Henry cut him off. 'Don't move, not yet.' Patients got real chatty when you finished drilling them. They were on an endorphin rush, a survival high. Henry always hurried to finish so he could turn them over to Rita for billing before the high began to wear off.

He carved and scraped the new silver filling. 'Clamp your teeth together gently so I can check your bite.' Ooh, that bottle-opener overbite – Charlie, where were you when they were handing out the braces? 'Looks good, real good. Keep off that side for the rest of the day, OK?' Henry undid Charlie's paper bib and hit the foot control to bring him upright. 'There you go, all done, you were a trooper today, a real trooper.'

He hooked an arm under Charlie's arm and helped him out of the chair. 'OK, Charlie, remember: no chewing on that left side and please stop and talk to Rita on your way out. Nice seeing you and take care now, all right?' He patted Charlie on the back and let Jennifer guide him to Rita's desk. My God, he's got hold of her hand again. Don't look – but he had to. Jennifer flirting, has the world gone mad?

Henry stepped back into room 2 to wash his hands and splash

water on his face. He'd worked up a little sweat doing Charlie. He noticed he was sweating at the end of each hour with a patient. Nothing heavy, but even so. What did it mean, all this sweat? Used to feel good when he was young, out on the ball field, or horsing around on a summer day. But now, at forty-two, it was another body fluid to worry about – like his fatty blood. Or a little while ago, fretting about taking a piss. He didn't used to fret – he just did it, for Pete's sake. But this sweat thing. Was it his heart, was it The List? Or was his body simply changing, excessive sweat one of the humiliations of the approach of old age? Did old Stu, his father, sweat like this? Thinking about Stu in the nursing home made him sweat. Christ, thinking about sweat made him sweat! He splashed more water on his face which made his wound from the panty liner incident throb, which reminded him he'd been in the bathroom to piss and that it was more dribbling than pissing, his body fluids going to hell, blood sweat piss, round and round, until aaaaahh, get me out of here, I better see that next patient before I drown in my own juices. Deep breath, you're fine, you are Dentist Man, he who controls the drill. Into room 1 you go, atta boy, on to the next patient. Yes, it's the patient who sweats, not the dentist, I feel great, yes yes yes.

Chapter 3

'June?'

'Mmm?' June answered the phone foggily. She'd fallen asleep on the sofa where she'd faked her migraine. She held the phone receiver in one hand and slowly opened an eye to look at the watch on her other wrist. Eleven a.m. She'd been asleep for over an hour.

'June?' came the voice again. 'This is Margo Zimmerman.' Hesitation. 'Am I interrupting? You sound . . .'

June slowly sat up. 'Sorry, Margo. I'm a little out of it. I guess I overdid it with my new aerobics tape, had to lie down a minute, catch my breath. You have the new "Susie"? God, she puts you through the leg lifts at a pace you would not believe.' Why was she rambling on with this dull lie? To erase Jeffrey Lyons, of course. To plant in her brain the possibility that she really had been doing something reasonable like aerobics and not getting her exercise running after eighteen-year-olds.

'June?'

Why did Margo keep repeating her name? It was beginning to feel odd. 'I'm here, Margo.'

A deep inhale, then, 'I really should be telling you this face-to-face, June.'

Punishment time. You make a move toward an eighteen-year-old and the messengers of doom promptly seek you out. Could this be the call Henry predicted this morning, the one that tells me that Lyle Robinson has driven the school bus into Crum Creek? Or is it Henry, he never made it to work, they've been prying him from the wreckage of his Ford Taurus as I napped. June tried to speak but the words gummed in her throat. She coughed and tried to clear it.

Margo went on. 'But I don't have the guts. I just don't want to see your face, I just couldn't take it. The look you'd get.'

Not the look, Margo, but this thing in my throat. June coughed and cleared. Or is it *around* my throat, your impending words of doom like squeezing hands; for God's sake, tell me, Margo, before I pass out, you sadistic bitch. Oh, you must love this, begged them to let you be the bearer of the message. Cough cough. You've always savored a bit of bad news, eh Margo, but then, cough, who doesn't? I'd have gladly called you. Gladly.

'You all right, June?'

At last, June croaked out a pair of words. 'Tell me.'

'Henry.'

Injured, dying, dead. The three choices danced and dangled before her. For some reason the rules of the game were very clear to her. If she selected one of the three, uttered the word, Henry would be spared that fate. The gods were severe, but somewhat accommodating. The hands tightened around her throat, but still she managed to get the word out. 'Dead.'

Silence, as Margo gathered herself, and then she said, 'You may wish he was.'

So terribly injured I wish him dead? Oh Henry, and you counted so on your airbag. Speak to me, Margo, because I no longer can. She grunted into the phone for Margo to continue.

Margo needed no urging. 'OK, here goes. I'm so glad I'm not there to see your face. But. This morning on the way to work, I pulled on to Cedar Lane, you know, to cut over to MacDade. Sometimes Henry goes that way too, and this morning, on the corner of Cedar and Park, I ran into him.'

Margo ran into my Henry, crashed into his Taurus. June saw that clearly and then the rest of it became a blur of flashing red lights and men in uniforms, police, ambulance crew, fire rescue team, uniforms all over Henry, using the Jaws of Life to pry him loose from the jammed metal mess of the dashboard and steering column, Henry's bloody face engulfed in an uninflated airbag.

'You won't believe what I saw,' said Margo.

Oh, I do believe, I do. What wife has not imagined the scene a thousand times, her beloved injured and helpless, of course I believe. This calamity has been at my door since the day I married him, is at all our doors, and your phone call has simply opened the door and let it in. 'Uhnn,' she said.

'Brace yourself, June.'

She was so braced she felt the phone receiver bend in her grip, could hear the arm of the sofa creak, the upholstery begin to pull away where she pressed her knee against it.

'I saw – oh June, your face – on the corner of Cedar and Park, as I drove by his car, I saw Henry and Lotty Daniels in a sexual situation in the front seat of Henry's car.'

June barked out a laugh, it just leapt out of her. Suddenly the choking hands of doom released her and relief erupted from her. Her rigidly braced body slumped back on to the sofa and she laughed again. Henry was unscathed. The Lotty part lagged unprocessed in her overheated brain. Henry lived!

'June?'

Now she could speak. 'Margo – you didn't really run into him, did you?'

A confused silence. 'I did. I absolutely saw Henry,' she said.

'You *saw* him, but you didn't run into him. With your car.'

'Like an accident?'

'Yes.'

'You thought . . .?'

'Yes.'

'June, you are so morbid. I kind of wondered why you said, "dead".' Margo didn't say anything for a moment. Then she said, 'Still, you must be pretty upset and everything.' June could hear the hope in her voice.

'About?'

'About!' Margo's voice jumped through the receiver. 'About the fact that in broad daylight on the public roads your husband was having relations with Lotty Daniels! With Lotty "Size Eighteen" Daniels,' she added for emphasis.

June's brain, having digested Henry's uninjured status, now turned itself to the matter of Lotty. Margo had already gotten it wrong once, she thought, making me think Henry had been smashed in a car, maybe not with words exactly but her tone certainly suggested something awful had happened to him – so that if she messed me up on that, maybe she's got it wrong again, Margo being not terribly bright or always accurate in the gossip department. Better move into this slow, thought June. Better get this right and straighten Margo out, too, since as soon as she finishes with me she'll be dialing up this town A to Z, if she hasn't already. Could be she's just calling me because she's reached the Ms, and I'm simply the next on the list to hear about Henry Miles humping Lotty Daniels on the corner of Cedar and Park.

'So,' she said cautiously. 'You think you saw Lotty talking to Henry this morning.'

'Talking? June, if Lotty was talking to Henry he must be deaf, because she was right on top of him in that car.'

'She was *in* the car.' Now that was strange. If Margo really had it right, that is.

'In the car. I saw the car jiggling, June. Which was why I slowed down and looked. I thought maybe Henry was having a seizure or something, the car moving like that.'

'Jiggling.'

'Jiggling in a rhythmic fashion,' said Margo, getting into it now.

She could almost hear Margo smacking her lips in delight. June tried to envision the scene in the car. But try as she might, she could not even imagine Lotty being able to squeeze her size 18 butt into the Taurus. And sex with Henry in the front seat? Physically impossible. 'Tell me more, Margo. Details.'

'You don't want my next detail, June. Honestly, you don't.'

Then why did you call, you wicked little shit, if not to torture me with your evil details? Margo, I envy you, how lovely you must feel delivering this news to me. So much nicer to give than to receive, isn't it? And you believe it protects you, don't you? One bit of bad news that won't be coming your way now. For

Margo to be safe, June must be sacrificed. Law of the jungle, fair is fair. 'Let's have it, Margo,' she said wearily.

'Well,' said Margo, suppressing a snort.

'Must be pretty good, hunh?' said June.

'You're taking this so well, June. You are such a strong woman.'

'I'm a walking miracle. Now get on with it,' she said. 'Do it.'

'I will. Remember, though, you made me tell you.'

June was silent.

'OK. OK, I was going by in my car, and Henry's back was to me – he was in the driver's seat turned toward Lotty in the passenger's seat – so I couldn't see him real clear except that he was moving around a lot. A whole lot. And Lotty, her I could see. She was kind of leaning forward, scrunching over him, her head bobbing all around and up and down.'

June stopped breathing. Even as Margo's next words came to her over the phone she had begun to envisage the scene in the car.

'This is going to kill you,' Margo said, her words coming in a rush. 'Just before I drove all the way by, Lotty's face came up and into view one last time and I saw her open her mouth wide and reach for Henry. She put something in there, as God is my witness it's true, June. Lotty's mouth open so wide you'd have thought she was having him for dinner!'

June slammed down the phone, hoping the sound exploded Margo's eardrums. Lotty and Henry on the corner of Cedar and Park. Henry cheating? Cheating on her in broad daylight? In a car with other cars driving by him? Henry letting someone see his precious penis, a privilege rarely bestowed on me, his wife of fourteen years? Who always had to fumble for it in the dark. But Lotty Daniels, he sticks it right under her nose for her to examine at her leisure. Lotty Daniels? This is craziness. Has Henry secretly craved overstuffed women all these years? And the more I dieted and did my aerobics, the more I repulsed him. I've never been big enough for you, is that it, Henry?

June rose from the sofa and moved deliberately back and forth across the living-room carpet. She began to see the symmetry of the morning's events and the divergent paths she and Henry ultimately chose. Both of us were offered the possibility of fantasy sex, me with Jeffrey Lyons, and you, believe it or not, with Lotty Daniels. Both of us brought our dream partners into our family spaces, Jeffrey into our home, Lotty into our car, intending to violate all the rules of marital and familial decency. June tried to understand the situation rationally, objectively, so that any actions she might take in response could only be viewed, perhaps even in a court of law, as reasonable and fair. So that when I shoot Henry to pieces in his goddamn Taurus, the judge will be understanding and even lenient. She paced like a lawyer before a jury, an all middle-aged female jury nodding sympathetically to her words.

So, she thought, both of us are adulterers, both of us brought our dream partners into areas hitherto sacred to the family, both of us, ladies of the jury, walked knowingly to the sexual brink, yet – June froze, her eyes narrowing, imagining the activities in the front seat of the Taurus – yet I pulled back, while Henry unzipped his fly and thrust himself into infidelity. I did not commit the act and he did. I did not, oh Henry, and now the tears began to blur her vision, I did not touch some stranger and you did. She saw Henry and Lotty swim through her tears toward one another, as if they were alone on a *From Here to Eternity* secluded beach instead of inside a station wagon on the corner of Cedar and Park.

She hugged herself and dropped to her knees on the carpet. What have you done, Henry? It's so unlike you, I never thought you really cared about sex. But then, maybe it is like you, really, maybe it's the dentist in you that's driven you to this: the compulsion to put things into people's mouths. Yes. Her tears suddenly stopped as she moved from courtroom thoughts to the realm of the psychiatric. Dental. Sexual. God, they're pratically the same word.

Her mouth was very dry and she moved slowly into the kitchen for some water. She filled a glass and raised it to her lips.

She lowered it again without drinking. She stared down at the linoleum. This morning at breakfast. The sausage. We watched him try to eat it but he couldn't. His face went all funny, he began to tremble, and the sausage practically jumped off his fork. Henry couldn't put the sausage into his mouth. Mouths, sausages, Lotty: yes, his subconscious was already working on him, judging him guilty, guilty, guilty, in the court of Freudian law.

Outside, a motorcycle kicked to life. June wandered over to the window above the kitchen sink and slowly went up on her toes to have a look.

It was to be a day of unlucky phone calls. Henry received his just before noon. He'd made it through the usual mix of morning patients: the fearful, the odorous, the suspicious and the ungrateful. The patient who did not exhibit at least one of those qualities during a visit was rare; most patients revealed all of them and more.

Yes, he was feeling almost good, almost in control of the day, as he hoisted his last patient of the morning from the chair and unclipped her paper bib. He was thinking lunch at Rio's Diner over in Morton would be just the thing, they cook their French fries in lard, none of this born-again vegetable shortening stuff like at McDonald's. God, your teeth crunching through that crispy brown, the squish of warm greasy potato. You can bathe your teeth in grease and never get a cavity. So how much of a health risk could it be? Besides, he hadn't had his sausages this morning, he was due for a dose of cholesterol. He was due a lot more than just a few French fries, the aggravation he'd suffered so far today. He washed his hands and, as he'd done several times already this morning, touched a finger to the bump on his forehead. Pelted with panty liners, struggling with unruly patients – dentistry is a front-line job, people don't appreciate that. OK, maybe I brought the panty liners on myself, but even so, there's a constant potential for danger when I walk into this office. And if I want French fries, dammit, I'll have French fries.

And a large Diet Pepsi, plenty of ice. He smiled guiltily, because he was forever warning his patients not to chew on ice, while he chomped and gnawed his way through freezers full. Something about crushing a solid object with his teeth: a validation of absolute dental health. Like in prehistoric times when our teeth were tough enough to pulverize bone. Yes, he was almost feeling bone-crushing good when the phone call came.

'Dr Miles,' Rita called to him over the intercom. It wasn't like he really needed intercoms installed in the exam rooms: Rita was only fifteen feet away in the reception area. But he enjoyed hearing his name paged, like doctors in city hospitals. Impressed the patients, too, he thought.

He punched a button. 'Yes, Rita?' He could see Rita out at her desk and she could see him. It felt a little like children talking through two Dixie cups and a string.

'You have a call on line one. Personal call,' she said disapprovingly. 'Insisted they speak to you.'

'Fine, Rita. Put it through.' Better be quick. There's an order of French fries with my name on it waiting for me. He picked up the extension phone. A click, a pause, and another click. 'Hello? Dr Miles here.' Grilled ham and cheese would be pretty good, too.

'Henry Miles?' came a loud female voice.

'Yes, this is Dr Miles.' Please – when you call me at my office it's *Doctor* Miles.

'Mr Miles, this is Betty Speers, day nursing supervisor at Fox Glen.'

Daddy! Henry slumped against the wall. Fox Glen Nursing Home. Henry flashed to a year ago, filling out the admission forms for his father's placement. The sinister little box in the corner with the words, 'Whom to call in the event of an emergency – Home, Office.' He should never have given them a phone number. Give them a number and they use it.

'Mr Miles?'

But I'm *Doctor* Miles. Maybe they've got the wrong Miles. No, she said Henry Miles, didn't she? 'Yes,' he replied weakly.

'Mr Miles – oh, I see on the form it's Doctor, isn't it? That's right, you're a dentist.'

That's right, no doubts now, are there? In the event of an emergency, call me. When did I last see you, Daddy? Two weeks ago? A week? Henry felt dizzy. He wasn't even sure what day today was. Tuesday? Wednesday? Time was speeding up and slowing down. But he seemed fine when I saw him last . . . didn't he? Eighty-three, and still chowing down on the food, getting around all right with his walker. Mostly making sense when he talked – hell, more sense than June and the twins ever make. Daddy . . . gone? Henry's next thought made his knees buckle. Daddy gone; me next.

Betty Speers went on. 'Actually,' she said, 'it's good you're a dentist, because what we have here is a dental situation, you might say. I need you to come in, Dr Miles. To see about your father. We really need you to come in right now, if possible.'

Daddy not gone. Henry squinted, trying to make sense of it. Daddy not gone. Me not next. Dental situation. Come in now. No French fries. 'You want me to come in because of my father's dental situation?'

'Yes. Exactly.'

'Miss Speers.'

'Mrs.'

'Mrs Speers. I'm sorry, I'm not quite following you. There can't be anything wrong with my father's teeth because he has no teeth. He wears dentures.'

'No, Dr Miles. He does not.'

'Has he lost them? Broken them? Why do I need to rush in?' Yes, French fries! Maybe I'll get a baco-cheeseburger, too.

'Not lost or broken them. Worse.'

'Worse?' Henry echoed in a weak whisper.

'Worse.' Mrs Speers paused ominously. 'Your father refuses to put his dentures in.'

'Impossible,' Henry immediately countered. The room tilted for an instant, then righted itself.

'Absolutely refuses, Dr Miles. The boys, the orderlies, have been having quite a time with him. They're with him now.'

'Are you sure it's my father? Stu, Stuart Miles? Don't they wear ID bracelets or something? Did anyone check?'

'It's my job to know all the residents here at Fox Glen,' Mrs Speers said icily.

Henry held his hand up in front of him. He could see his fingers trembling. 'Yes of course, Mrs Speers. I'm sorry. But you see, my father is such a tidy man. A careful man. Him not putting his dentures in is like, I don't know, like having him walk outside without his pants on.'

'I wouldn't be surprised if that's what he tries next.'

'What!'

'Once they start going downhill they're capable of just about anything.'

Downhill? A week and a half ago Daddy was bantering snappily with the nurses and eating like a horse and now he's about to start running around naked with his gums flapping?

'If this continues we may be forced to restrain him. Or even sedate him.'

'Because he won't put his teeth in? You tie old people up and drug them for that, Mrs Speers? Christ, what do you do when they talk back to you: take them outside and shoot them?'

'Don't you raise your voice at me, Dr Miles! That's precisely why I've called you. He's doing a good deal more than talking back. Two orderlies, two very big orderlies, are in his room right now trying to calm him down. Your father has already drawn blood on one of the boys.'

'What did he do, gum him?'

'Hit him with his lunch tray. Now you'll have to come in or we simply must proceed to the next level of intervention.'

'Well, you just keep your needles and ropes away from him, you got that? You tell him I'll be there in fifteen minutes. Good enough, Mrs Speers?'

'I hope so, Dr Miles.'

Henry hung up. His stomach bubbled nastily. Great. 'Rita!'

Just great. Daddy in the clutches of Nurse Ratchet and two of her goons. Henry rushed out to Rita's desk. 'Cancel my afternoon appointments. All of them. My father's gone off the deep end and I have to run over to Fox Glen to straighten things out.'

When Rita tilted her head up to him, her wig slipped backwards, revealing an extra three inches of wrinkly forehead. 'Well, you give my best to him,' she said. 'He's a dear old man.'

Henry hurried down the hall to his office, struggling to take off his dental top as he went. 'Not so dear today, from what I hear,' he shouted out to her. He threw his top on to his big oak desk and pulled on his shirt and his seersucker coat. He eyed the bathroom door on his way back up the hall. It was closed. He could hear someone in there. Jennifer, of course. Counting her panty liners. She could probably smell his fingerprints all over them. He moved faster. 'So Rita, cancel the appointments, because I don't know what's waiting for me out at Fox Glen. Then finish up here and you and Jennifer take the afternoon off.' He looked down at her, trying hard not to watch the progress of her wig. It was moving perceptibly, crawling down the back of her neck like a stealthy weasel. If it falls on to the floor while I'm standing here, should I acknowledge it? What would Miss Manners advise?

'Dr Miles?'

'Yes, Rita?' Please let me leave, Rita. Before your hair hits the floor, before Jennifer comes out of that bathroom, before my naked, toothless and bloodthirsty father escapes from the nursing home. Henry's eyes flickered for an instant and he saw a wild parade running across the rolling green lawn of Fox Glen. A chase scene, with himself in the lead, pursued. They pursued him, one after the other, Daddy flashing his spitty gums, Jennifer angrily waving a fistful of panty liners, Rita clutching her wig, Charlie Carnes, Lotty Daniels, Marty Marks tossing Tiny Tasties at him, the twins taunting, June with a plate of glistening sausages, and Lyle Robinson as the Grim Reaper, taking up the rear, gunning the engine of his yellow school bus and roaring over the green grass. If this has been the morning, he thought, bringing Rita into focus once more, do I stand even the slimmest of chances of making it through the afternoon?

'Well, doctor,' said Rita, 'have you thought of hobbies?'

'Hobbies?' he said. Yes, that sounds like just the thing. Maybe take up ham radio, or perhaps build model airplanes during my carefree morning schedule. Rita, have you gone mad?

'For your father. A hobby might help to settle him. Focus his mind.'

Henry envisioned the current scene at Fox Glen. His father, wild-eyed, gnashing at the two bewildered orderlies with the disembodied dentures he held in his hands. What sort of hobby might focus the mind of a man like that?

'Well, Rita, I thank you for the suggestion, but somehow I think my father has moved beyond hobbies. The way Nurse Speers described him, he really didn't sound like he was in a hobby sort of mood.'

'I just have to say, when I'm out of sorts and I tend to my African violets, or rearrange my Hummels, I am soothed considerably.'

Henry eyed his watch. 'Again, thanks, Rita, and I'll keep what you say in mind. And if you come up with anything more, please let me know.' He could hear Jennifer starting to open the bathroom door down the hall. 'Rita, I gotta run now.'

Which he literally did, straight out of the office and into the parking lot. If Jennifer had been holding her violated panty liners box and readying herself to confront him, he'd never know. He started up his Taurus and, as he often did, patted his steering wheel with its hidden airbag for luck. Given the tenor of the day so far, the gesture seemed too little too late. He pulled out of the parking lot and on to the stretch of driveway he shared with Dreami Donuts. As he started to drive by, he glanced over and saw Marty Marks clutch his jaw and hurry toward the glass door. Henry tried to hit the accelerator, to leave Marty in the dust, but once again events conspired against him. For the first time in over twenty-six years of driving, his foot actually missed the accelerator and hit the brake. The Taurus jerked to a stop and Henry's head snapped forward with just enough force to bump the steering wheel. It was a very mild tap, but evilly placed: he hit dead center on the raised welt he'd suffered earlier in the bathroom. Zing, double zing.

'Ow, goddamn it,' he cried, blinking back tears.

Tap tap tap, went Marty's knuckles on his car window.

Are these tears of pain, or tears of frustration, or tears for Daddy? Or maybe just anticipatory tears – he opened his eyes and gazed through his window at Marty. Tap tap tap. Henry's eyes teared up again and he looked away a moment to compose himself before rolling down his window and allowing Marty's voice to taint the sanctity of the interior of his Taurus. Not that its sanctity had not already been heavily tainted this morning by Lotty Daniels.

'Dr Miles,' said Marty plaintively. 'You're leaving for the day. I just talked to Rita on the phone and she said you're leaving for the entire rest of the day.'

'Yes, Marty. I am.'

'But my crown is beginning to throb. You said you'd squeeze me in today.'

'It had been my intention, yes, Marty.' Henry touched a finger to his forehead where his own wound was throbbing.

'But now you're leaving,' said Marty. 'For the day,' he repeated in disbelief.

Did Rita tell you it was just for the day, Marty? I believe she meant to say for ever. That's right. For ever and ever. I won't be coming back and your poor tooth will throb and swell and maybe even explode. Think of it, Marty, one by one your teeth exploding, like kernels of popcorn on high heat, pop, pop. 'Well, Marty,' said Henry shrugging.

'You can't go,' said Marty. He started to reach for the door handle.

Henry locked it in the nick of time. 'Now, Marty.'

'But this is an emergency.'

'I'm on my way to another emergency.'

'A house call? Dentists don't make house calls. You're making it up. You just don't want to see me.' He rubbed his jaw mournfully. 'And I bet that's against some dental Hippocratic oath. I bet by law you're required to see me if it's an emergency.'

'Don't get hysterical, Marty. Take some Tylenol. I'll be in tomorrow and see you first thing.'

'Now!' He jiggled and tugged on the door handle.

So what's he going to do, pull me out of the car and hold a gun to my head, force me to repair his crown here in the parking lot? 'Marty, control yourself, it's only pain. It's not death, it's pain, and from a dental standpoint, pain is often a measurement of health. So revel in your pain because it's an indication of your vitality. Lucky you, Marty. Lucky you!'

'You bastard,' Marty hissed, wincing as his tongue moved against his crown. 'You sadistic prick. You hate me. That's why you're doing this. You hate me, you've always hated me, you always will hate me.'

Wow. Present, past and future hate. That's a whole lot of hate. He's right, I do hate him. 'I don't hate you, Marty.' Henry peeked down at his watch. Tick tick tick. He could almost hear the time bombs ticking: his fangless father ready to strike out at the orderlies again, Marty deciding whether to drag him out of the car and kill him and all the other bombs he wasn't even aware of yet, ticking. He thought of June and wondered how her morning was going. Blissfully, no doubt. No time bombs ticking for her. And she wondered why he came home from work as tense as a cat, why he began each new day anxiously mulling over The List.

'You hate me, yes you do, and I'll tell you why.' Marty jerked his thumb over his shoulder, pointing at the pink and maroon Dreami Donuts behind him. 'Because I work there.'

'People got to work. I don't begrudge people having to work.'

'Yeah, but I work *there*.'

Marty, you're not as dumb as I thought. Yes, I hate you because you are the commandant of a death camp for teeth. But it's not just that. I hate you because you are a middle-aged man who wears a paper cap embossed with the Dreami Donuts logo.

And it's not even the fact of the hat, but that you wear it at a jaunty angle. Jaunty means it's not just a job to you, but a vocation. You enjoy your work, peddling sugar with a nod and a wink, catering to the sweet addictions of the nutritionally impaired. You are, to use a current term, an enabler. And you dare come to me with your emergencies, your crown of thorns. 'Marty, you're making me late. I have somewhere I have to be.' Henry eased his toe toward the accelerator. He wasn't going to miss this time.

'So I sell donuts. Is that such a sin?'

The biggest there is, thought Henry. 'You'll have to decide for yourself, Marty,' he said.

'Sure. I know what you really think,' said Marty, a rising desperation in his voice. 'And I understand that. And appreciate it. You got reason to hate me. OK.'

Henry touched his toe to the accelerator and the Taurus began to inch forward. Marty inched along with it, his face still bent to the car window.

'OK,' he continued. 'But even hating me, you and I, we're both professionals. I have customers I hate coming into my store all the time. Does that mean I don't serve them?'

Henry pressed a little harder on the accelerator in reply.

'Of course I serve them.' Marty hop-trotted alongside the car, probably wasn't even aware he was moving. 'I mean, the grief I take from customers sometimes, you wouldn't believe. But hey, hate 'em or love 'em, I'm a professional, and a professional does his job.'

Henry was moving now, ten, fifteen miles per hour. He'd reached the end of the driveway and had begun to turn on to MacDade Boulevard. Marty, are you nuts enough to stay with me?

Marty was nuts enough, or in pain enough. He ran beside the car at full speed now, his skinny legs pumping. His Dreami Donuts hat bounced off his head and fluttered into the street. Cars honked at him. 'So you got to do your job too, you sonofabitch dentist! Hating me doesn't count. I'm what you do!'

Henry floored it and at last left Marty behind. If you're what I do, thought Henry, watching Marty's arms flailing in his rearview mirror, then I must be really screwed. He raced down MacDade Boulevard, moodily scanning the blur of roadside scenery so known to him it was almost invisible. Scenery, was that the right word? Doesn't something have to be scenic to be part of the scenery? Look at this crap. He usually liked the cheesy stores on this part of the strip, the urgent pushing variety of it all. Hoagie shops and hardware stores and shoe outlets and meat markets. It tickled him, the ways humans sought to occupy themselves and be useful to others. Marty calling himself a professional. The owners of these places, did they all consider themselves professionals? Hi, how are you, I'm Frank Jones, professional hoagie maker. These absurdly inflated egos. Sure, I'm a little inflated myself, but I'm a dentist, not some guy who flips burgers, or an asshole who runs a donut franchise. Fucking Marty Marks.

He screeched to a stop at a red light he'd noticed at the last second, his bumper millimeters from the delivery van in front of him. His heart thumped, sweat beads crawled down his back like insects. He slumped forward and rested his head on the padded center of his steering wheel. Don't die here, he thought. Don't die on MacDade Boulevard, surrounded by hoagie shops and shoe stores.

A car honked, then another. He looked up at the green light. I'm not dying. I'm holding up traffic.

He lurched forward into the intersection. So what if I sweat, he thought. Sweat doesn't necessarily mean death. It's like pain. Just means your body's functioning. Pain's a part of life, an *indication* of life, really. So is sweat. Don't get so worked up. Calm yourself.

Off MacDade now, on to Riverview. Ahh yes, better. Residential, no stores. Off Riverview, on to Hillborn. He slowed down. There's the junior high school. Teenagers everywhere. Must be lunchtime. His stomach gurgled. God, look at them all. Hanging out on the steps, on cars, in trees, against the chain-link fence.

They moved too rapidly, in and out of groups, dividing and coming together like the cells of a dangerously active disease.

He drove slowly by. How much time had passed since he'd gotten the call about Daddy? And here he was dawdling in the school yard. He was about to pick up speed when he spotted one of the twins hunkering beside the fence with a group of kids. Henry's skin prickled. He pulled the car over to the opposite side of the street and pressed his face against the side window. The kids looked right out of an anti-drug TV commercial. They all wore army fatigue jackets. They hunkered. They furtively passed secret unseeable things back and forth. Easy, Henry. Which twin was it? Which of his twins was he going to have to enroll in a drug rehab program when he got through tending to Daddy at the nursing home? Oh Fred. Oh Ed? The generations are caving in around me. I don't want to go to weekly family therapy at a rehab center. I don't want to go make my father put his dentures back in.

Tap tap tap.

Henry froze. Had Marty Marks caught up with him?

Tap tap tap.

He slowly turned to the passenger side window. His son! His other son, not the son in the drug commercial across the street. His good son. Now, the question was, Fred or Ed? Henry slid over and unlocked the passenger door. The son slid in.

'Dad, what are you doing here? Is Mom OK?'

'Of course she's OK.'

Ed let out a big breath. 'Phew. I was sure you were coming to get us and take us to the hospital to see her or something. Parents never come to school this early unless the other parent is dead or something. That's what happened to Buddy Iozzi last week, his mom came and got him at lunch 'cause his father like stroked out at work or something.'

Henry looked at Ed – hell, I've got to call him something – Henry looked at him and thought, My God, a little me. I've spawned a little Henry, have passed my nervous genes on to the next generation. Fear and anxiety will live on forever in the

Miles family tree. Ed has his own version of The List, of course he does. I wonder what's on it: parents dying, acne, braces, geometry, homework, voice cracking in front of a girl, nuclear holocaust, wrong haircut. Shit, that's a List I'd give my eye teeth to have again. 'No, no. Mom's fine. Don't worry about Mom,' he said.

Ed nodded. 'How about you, then? Everything OK with you?' He eyed Henry.

'Me? A hundred per cent. Two hundred per cent,' he said too loudly.

'Good, Dad. That's great.'

Henry flicked his eyes towards the school-yard fence. His other son still being sneaky with those army fatigue boys. Look at that one's hair, shaved to the scalp in places, with a kind of lanky pony tail hanging off the side. Jesus, that's creepy. Used to be you had two choices: short hair or long hair. Not this demented mix. 'That your brother over there? That Fred over by the fence?'

'That's Ed, Dad. I'm Fred.'

Henry's face went hot. 'Yeah, I meant Ed. Did I say Fred?'

The boy shook his head and smiled. 'Jeez, Dad, just joking. I'm Ed.'

Henry couldn't look at him. He forced out a laugh. 'Ha ha. Had you going there, didn't I, Ed? Or should I say, Fred?' Stop, stop while you're ahead, you fool. He's looking at you like you're crazy. 'Anyway, so that's your brother over there.'

Ed's face hardened. 'Yeah, so?'

He thinks I'm spying on his brother. I am spying on his brother, but I don't want him to think it. 'I guess those are some of his lunchtime pals.'

'Dad, I gotta get back. I got class in five minutes.' He made a move for the door.

'Oh, hold on a minute, will you, please. You're treating me like I don't belong here.'

'Well, Dad, I mean, you don't belong here. It's lunchtime. Parents don't come here.'

'I was on my way to see about Grandpa Stu. The high school's on the way. I saw Fred, thought I'd say hello.'

'So how come you didn't go say hello? How come you were sitting here watching him?'

Watching as in spying on him, you mean. 'He looked busy.'

'He's not busy. He's just with some guys.'

'What sort of guys? Are they friends of yours, too?'

'Some of them.'

'Nice guys, are they? The one with the hair, he's nice, too?'

'They all have hair, Dad.'

'He really has the hair. You know what I'm saying.'

Ed was silent.

'Well, anyway. I bet they're all nice guys.' Henry hesitated, then tried to say casually, 'Sure are busy looking, though.'

'If you say so. I gotta go, Dad.'

'Busy doing what, I wonder?' Henry placed a hand on Ed's knee, gently restraining him.

'I don't know. Probably making deals. A lot of dealing goes on at lunch.'

Henry felt something rise in his chest and flutter to his brain – his scalp tingled as that something went up and out of him in waves. Why didn't Ed just lie to me? It's the times. We devastate each other with openness. Fred is dealing and being dealt to on the playground. Crack? Marijuana? Speed? I won't have to wonder long. This new openness – Ed can't wait to tell me. I don't want to hear. I want it to be breakfast again, before Daddy flipping out at the nursing home, before I find out my beloved son deals—

'Baseball cards.'

'I'm sorry?' said Henry.

'They deal baseball cards back and forth. I'm not that into it, but Fred kind of is. Jackie Brickson, the guy with the hair, really is. You should see his collection. It's pretty cool, I guess. He has a Ted Williams he won't let anyone touch.'

Thank you, thank you, thank you. Henry beamed at Ed. He felt an overwhelming urge to hug him, to bring him close to his chest in a deep and grateful embrace. He didn't dare try. Instead, he patted the boy's knee, then quickly pulled away and closed his hand into a fist as if to keep safe that brief and precious moment of contact.

'Baseball cards,' he said. 'Yes, I thought so. I pulled off a few good deals myself when I was his age. Still have those cards somewhere, I think.' Deals. The word practically danced off his tongue now.

'So why were you on your way to see Grandpa Stu?' said Ed. 'Is he OK?'

Henry wanted to hold on to the good feelings – he didn't want to have to think about Grandpa Stu and the calamity he knew was waiting for him at Fox Glen. Just sit here and shoot the breeze with his boy. Hell, maybe he'd even pull Ed out of school for the afternoon, drive around the rest of the day talking.

'Dad?'

'Yes, Ed?'

'How come you go off all the time?'

'Sorry?'

'You're always drifting away. It's kind of creepy.'

'I do? It is?'

'See? You don't even know it. I ask about Grandpa Stu and you kind of look out the window and disappear.'

'Oh no, Ed. I don't disappear. I just have . . . well, you get older and you have all sorts of things on your mind, stuff that clutters up your thoughts. I mean, man to man and everything, I've had one hell of a morning. But I don't disappear. Your dad does not disappear on you.' He pressed closer to Ed as he spoke and Ed shifted back against his door.

'OK, Dad. Easy. I was just, you know, pointing it out. It's not like that big a deal or anything.'

Henry looked at the boy with what he hoped would be interpreted as absolutely focused concentration. I'm right here, son. Not disappeared, not tumbling endlessly into the mental void. 'So, in direct answer to your question, which is a good one, and a legitimate one: I am going to see your grandfather because he is having some sort of problem of a dental nature and I have been asked to intervene.' There. Now do you think I'm all here?

If Ed took any comfort from his father's answer, he didn't show it. He looked at Henry a moment, then said, 'Do I make you nervous or something, Dad?'

Shit. 'No, of course not!' I overdid it. I could feel myself overdoing it even as I overdid it, but I couldn't stop myself because the kid makes me so damn nervous I don't know what to say. I go one way he nails me, I go another he nails me worse. You want me focused or unfocused? Give me the dialogue and I'll do it.

'It's the twin thing,' said Ed. 'That's what throws you off, isn't it?'

'I never think of you as twins. Only as individuals.'

Ed looked out the window at the school yard beginning to empty of kids. Fred and his little group dispersed and drifted back into the school building. 'OK, Dad.' He reached out and patted Henry's knee, then opened the door and got out. He came around to Henry's open window. 'One more thing,' he said.

'Yes?' said Henry, softly massaging the spot on his knee.

'I really am Fred.'

Henry winced.

'Just kidding.' The boy smiled and turned toward the school, waving goodbye over his shoulder.

Henry called out, 'Hey Fred.' When the boy stopped and pivoted, Henry winked at him and merrily yelled, 'Gotcha!' then pressed on the accelerator and got out of there as fast as he could.

Ah, he's a good boy whoever the hell he is, thought Henry. Both of them are good boys. Every boy in that high school is probably a good boy. He drove along enjoying this rare, life-affirming moment. Good boys in a good school in a good little town. Good people in this town, too. He thought about that one a minute. Except Marty Marks. He's no good. He's a prick. A sugar-coated prick. Probably fucks the holes in his donuts. Now, now, Henry, that's not a life-affirming thought. He drove along, turned left when he should have turned right, stopped at yellow lights when ordinarily he would have roared on through, slowed his advance on Fox Glen, dawdled. Another thing that's no good is what's waiting for me there, he thought. What waited for him there was something beyond teeth. He did not feel equipped to deal with matters that were beyond teeth. Why can't the nursing home just handle it? He remembered the way Mrs Speers said they'd handle it, the needles and restraints, and hurriedly turned right where he was supposed to turn right and shot through the rest of the yellow lights until he reached Fox Glen.

He pulled into the parking lot panting, as if he'd run instead of driven the remaining distance. Jesus, what a creepy place. In fact, Fox Glen was not at all creepy. It looked rather comforting and efficient, landscaped so as not to offend or endanger, its main building and smaller outbuildings freshly painted and attended to. OK, so it looks good, but it's still creepy. Henry stepped out of the safe confines of his Ford Taurus and frowned at the scene which surrounded him. Wheelchair ramps everywhere. Railings. Inside, he knew from previous visits, all the signs were printed in big bold letters. The whole place focused too much on the body, the body in decline. It was supposed to, of course, but still.

He listened intently, trying to pick up the yells and sounds of crashing furniture that would indicate that his father's battle with the two orderlies was still underway. Silence. Not good. The orderlies must have won. He pictured his father wrapped mummy-like in restraints, porcupined with syringes, out cold, his snoring mouth open to reveal dentures jammed into place. More silence.

From behind him came a cough. 'Ahem.'

Henry jumped, whirled around and saw nothing at first until he looked down into the upturned face of a little white-haired creature occupying a wheelchair. Henry decided it was an old man, although he wouldn't put money on it. Then he considered again and decided it was an old woman in a man's shirt and pants. So old the sex had drained out of him. Or her. Why was something so old allowed to roll around unattended in the parking lot, sneaking up on visitors?

'Ronnie,' the white haired man-woman piped up at him in a scratchy voice.

'No sir,' Henry said. Then he muttered, 'No ma'am.'

A hand reached up out of the wheelchair toward Henry. 'No sir? No ma'am? I don't get ya. I'm Ronnie. Ronald D. James. Shake my hand, will ya?' he piped. 'Old as I am, it's liable to drop right off, I hold it up here much longer.'

Henry took Ronnie's hand, then released it quickly in case there really was a danger of it suddenly dropping off. 'Dr Henry Miles,' he said. 'Dentist.' Ronnie's skin was cool and slippery, as if it had been coated lightly with silicone.

'Henry the dentist, how ya doing?'

'Pretty good, Ronnie. Pretty good.' How'd you get so tiny, Ronnie? Did you start out that way, or did size go out of you over the years, like your sex did? How small and how sexless will we all be if the scientists keep us living until we're a hundred and fifty? Ronnie's feet didn't quite reach the foot rests on his wheelchair. He didn't look strong enough to give those big wheels a full rotation. Had a strong voice, though. Maybe when you're as old as Ronnie, you direct your energies into the running of a single body part. Guess Ronnie chose his vocal cords.

'You checking into this hotel?' said Ronnie.

Do I look like I'm checking in? Ronnie, the question is, are you checking out? Henry scanned the grounds for an orderly. Were they all in his father's room beating up on the old man, leaving no one to watch Ronnie? How many escapees did this place have a day? 'Actually, Ronnie, I'm here to visit my dad. Stuart Miles in room 414D. You know him?'

'Older-looking fellow with white hair?' asked Ronnie in his strong elfin soprano.

Henry nodded. 'Yes, that's right. That's him.'

Ronnie chuckled. 'That's all of them, son. I'm just pulling your leg.'

Henry nodded again and tried to smile. His neck was getting

a little cramped from looking down at Ronnie. What a specimen. Is this really what will happen to Dentist Man, too? I'm not going to live forever, am I? How long have I got until I turn into a Ronnie, thirty years? What's the matter with his lower eyelids, how come they droop like a hound dog's? How'd his earlobes get so long? What are those grey lumpy things growing on the side of his neck? Old age is a party I don't want to get invited to. I hate coming here. Every time I come here, it scares me – and I haven't even gone inside yet to see Daddy. Henry let out a long sigh.

'Whatsa matter, Henry? You sound kind of pooped. That why you came to this rest home? Heh, heh,' he chuckled again.

This guy obviously hasn't looked in a mirror in the last decade or he wouldn't be laughing. I shouldn't begrudge the old fool. He's doing OK, I guess. Still, I wish he didn't have so many of those grey lumpy things on his neck. 'Tell you the truth, Ronnie, I am kind of pooped. It's been a heck of a day for me.'

'Count yourself among the lucky then, Henry. I can't do much any more, so I never have the luxury of getting pooped. I'm always kind of the same – asleep or awake, I'm pretty much always revving at the same r.p.m.s, if you know what I mean.'

'Say, Ronnie,' Henry said, looking around the place again but seeing no one, 'pretty loose with the rules here, are they? Let you do what you want, for the most part?'

'Watcha figuring on doing?' Ronnie said conspiratorially, inching his wheelchair closer. He looked ready for anything.

'No, no. What I mean is, I was just wondering if they always let you wander around the grounds alone like this.'

Ronnie did one of his high-pitched elf chuckles. Teeth still surprisingly good, observed Henry. Could use a little work on that bridge, though. 'Oh sure,' said Ronnie, 'they always let *me* wander around alone.' He jerked a thumb at the main building. 'But I don't imagine they let *them* wander around alone.'

Out of it. Sure sounded with it, but I guess he's one of those old guys who comes and goes. Hope this doesn't get too pathetic. I never know how to talk to the senile. He tended to speak louder and use a sort of baby talk, like with a puppy. 'That right, Ronnie? You're not one of them, are you, buddy?'

'Hell no!' And with that, he hopped up out of the wheelchair and gave Henry a playful slug on the arm. He had to reach high to do it, since he was very short. 'I'm not one of the inmates, Henry,' he laughed. 'I'm here visiting my mother.'

Henry realized his mouth was open. He shut it, then opened it again to say, 'Your mother?'

'One hundred and two. I'm only eighty-one. I got a few years before I wind up here.'

'What about that wheelchair?'

'Stole it on the way out. I get a kick out of riding around in them.' He pulled it close to Henry. 'Here. Sit down. Give it a whirl. Fun!' He tugged Henry down into the chair.

'But . . .'

Ronnie dangled a set of car keys in front of Henry's face. 'Well, Henry, great to meet you, but I got to go.' He shot a quick look over Henry's head. 'Gotta go.' He skipped across the parking lot to a blue Buick sedan and started it up.

'Hey!' shouted a voice in the distance.

Still sitting, Henry turned around in the chair and watched a group of nurses and orderlies, a blur of agitated white, erupt out of the glass door of the main building. 'Hey! Hey, Mr James. Ronald, get out of that car!' they screamed.

But Ronnie, his little white head barely visible above the steering wheel, already had the Buick in motion.

'Mister,' they yelled to Henry. 'He's one of our patients. Stop him, he's stealing that car.'

Before Henry could untangle himself from the rolling wheelchair, Ronnie zoomed out of the parking lot and tore down the long tree-lined driveway. Ronnie was out of there.

Several of the nurses and orderlies ran up to Henry and stopped. A few drifted farther into the parking lot and watched Ronnie's stolen car vanish from view. When Henry looked up from the wheelchair, they were all glaring at him. He read the name tag on the uniform of the nurse doing the most glaring:

'Mrs B. Speers, RN – Supervisor.' He gulped. His father actually refused to put his dentures in for this woman? The phrase 'no-nonsense' was probably invented just to describe B. Speers, RN. He smiled feebly up at her.

'You let him go,' she growled. 'You let him get away.'

'I did not!' Henry tried not to squeal.

'Let him get away *in my car.*'

Henry felt a surge of hope: someone was having a day at least as rotten as his own. If Ronnie had stolen my Taurus, I'd have thrown myself under the wheels to stop him. Life without access to an airbag is not worth living. 'Well,' he said. 'He looked like a pretty good driver. I'm sure things will turn out—'

'Ronald James,' she interrupted, bringing her reddened face down to his own, 'is ninety-three years old, senile, and has a glass eye!'

'Really,' said Henry. 'Which one? Whoever fit him for it did a remarkable job.' My crown work should blend in so well, he thought in a moment of jealousy.

Mrs Speers sputtered something, then turned to her staff. She clapped her hands. 'All right, everybody, back to your posts. Cindy,' she said, zeroing in on a panicked young nurse trying to melt into the background, 'Ronald was yours today, I believe?'

'Yes, Mrs Speers.'

'In my office and wait for me there. I'll deal with you after I call the police. Think about the implications of that, Cindy, and its effect on what remains of your nursing career.'

Yikes. If she delivers any lines like that to me, I'm back in my Taurus and gone. He watched as the rest of the staff practically carried the limp Cindy back to the building.

Mrs Speers slowly turned to him. 'And just who are you and what are you doing in that wheelchair?'

Henry decided to go on the offensive, since his defense seemed indefensible. 'I'm Henry Miles and I was semi-attacked by one of your patients, one of your *unattended* patients, which makes for a very interesting potential legal situation in my view, Mrs Speers. And I think you should consider yourself and the corporation that runs Fox Glen exceptionally fortunate, from my potential legal standpoint, that the only damage that crazy old man is likely to cause is to your Buick.'

Mrs Speers's lower lip quivered. 'My Buick,' she whispered, gazing off into the distance.

Henry stood up from the wheelchair. Gee, maybe I was a little rough on her. Bringing her Buick into it was a low blow. 'Did it have an airbag?' he inquired gently.

'Yes,' she said. 'And I never got a chance to use it.'

'Oh, I'm sure you'll get your chance,' he said in comforting tones. 'I'm sure the police will bring both your Buick and Ronnie back safely.'

She nodded mutely and the two of them stood together, staring off into the distance as if there still was something to see. 'Yes,' Mrs Speers said finally, 'the police. I better go in and alert them.' She turned and looked hard at Henry, a realization just dawning on her. 'Henry Miles, did you say? Stuart Miles's son?'

It took everything he had for Henry to nod in the affirmative.

Chapter 4

It had not been June's intention to drive over to Henry's office to confront him. Her first impulse, after hanging up on Margo, was to march outside, grab Jeffrey Lyons by his T-shirt and drag him into the house for a nice long fuck on the living-room carpet. She had actually gotten as far as the edge of her yard where she could just see Jeffrey in his driveway working on his motorcycle. Look at him there, all innocence in his white T-shirt. She saw him then, as Henry might, her long association with a dentist shaping the image before her. Young Jeffrey in white looked as clean and healthy as a baby tooth. His muscles bulging here and there were the cusps and ridges of a molar. Lurking in her yard, June felt like a clump of oral bacteria on the prowl. She stepped back. I will not be the cause of that boy's decay. This was not the way to get Henry, my rotten tooth of a husband. So, what does one do with a hopelessly rotten tooth? Yank it. Which is just what I'll do, she thought, hurrying back into the house for her car keys. Yank Henry right out of his little office and scrape the rot off of him.

June started up her Nissan Sentra, the sound causing Jeffrey to look up from the driveway next door and give her a cheery wave. You don't know how close you came, she thought. A pity. It might have been lovely. Certainly more lovely than Henry getting ministered to by Lotty Daniels in the front seat of a Ford. It's not fair. Henry goes crazy for her and all I'm good for is flossing. Jeffrey was saying something as he waved. She rolled down her window. I'm trying real hard to do the right thing. So don't tempt me, boy. Don't even give me the eensiest of openings or I will hop out of this car and drag you inside to my carpet. I am a dangerous and conflicted woman.

'Excuse me, Jeffrey. What?' She felt her tongue rise to her lips and lick back and forth. She stopped herself.

Jeffrey advanced a few steps. 'I said, glad to see you looking so good.'

Her tongue licked again. She smiled in disbelief. All right, so I *will* do Jeffrey Lyons on the carpet. That's morally OK, right? The boy wants it, I want it. I need it. It's just a coincidental adulterous situation, in no way related to my husband's scummy behavior with Lotty Daniels. Our lust is pure and private, not grotesque and public. And Jeffrey is seducing me. He knows what I need and haven't been getting. I'm no Henry, soliciting sex from a roving automobile. Well, I am sitting in an automobile, but that's it, that's all Henry and I have in common. Her tongue slid across her lips once more, this time nervously.

'I look good? How do you mean, Jeffrey?' How evva do you mean? She felt like she'd given it a southern lilt, Vivien Leigh coming on to Marlon Brando. He was a big T-shirt wearer too. Hmmm. Vivien hadn't come out so hot in that one. In fact, didn't they take her away and lock her up? Her foot moved toward the accelerator.

'Better, I mean.' Jeffrey stood on the edge of his driveway, a big metric wrench gripped in his hand. Behind him, his motorcycle. He looked like a poster adorning the bedroom walls of a twelve-year-old girl.

Or the fantasies of a soon to be divorced woman in her late thirties. But wait, 'better', he said. Not, 'looking good', but 'better'. That's a step or two down the stairway of lust, isn't it? 'Sorry, Jeffrey, I don't quite follow,' she called to him.

'Than this morning.' He tapped a finger to his head. 'Your migraine.'

She tumbled all the way down the stairs and hit bottom. End of lust. This time when she brought her tongue out, it was too dry to make it across her unpuckered lips. Oh, yeah. The migraine: my first unsuccessful rendezvous with Jeffrey. And now this, my second failure. 'Pretty much gone away, thanks,' she said wearily. 'Just on my way to the drugstore to get more

Excedrin in case it, you know, comes back.' She felt a sharp pulsing in her brain. Two failed attempts at adultery, Henry getting sucked off on the corner of Cedar and Park thereby forcing me to kill him, no ideas in mind for the twins' supper and no way will they eat meat loaf for the third night in a row. Yes, I'd say the migraine was due to reappear.

'Guess you'd better get yourself some of that extra-strength stuff, because really, Mrs Miles, you didn't look so hot earlier in the house.'

All right, already, Jeffrey. Rub it in, why don't you? 'Thanks for your concern, Jeffrey. So long.' She rolled up her window and backed out of the driveway. I'm a thirty-eight-year-old, cheated on mother of two, who doesn't look so hot. She glanced in the rearview mirror. Is that why Henry did it? The issue here is hotness? I don't generate the heat required to start his engine? Now Lotty, that oversized oral deviant, she certainly puts out the heat – I can't be expected to compete with her ability to burn calories. Or consume them. Or consume my husband. In a Ford. On the corner of Cedar and Park. Which is right where June suddenly found herself. At the scene of the crime.

She pulled the car over, stopped and got out, shaking. What did she hope to find here? Evidence to corroborate Margo's telephone testimony. Certainly Henry should not be convicted by Margo's words alone. Margo, queen of gossip, empress of hearsay and sleaze. What evidence could there be? Not panties tossed out of the car in the heat of the moment, because the activity witnessed by Margo was not of the panty-tossing variety. June clutched herself and looked around. An ordinary street corner, a stop sign, a mailbox, a street lamp above her. What could there be? She stood beside her car and stared at the asphalt. Maybe weird tire marks from the Taurus – didn't Margo say the car was jiggling? And with Lotty's added weight . . . No marks. Nothing, of course. June got back in the car and clutched the steering wheel.

What was she really going to do when she reached his office? She hit the ignition and inched forward, thinking. Do I want to make a scene? Henry really hates a scene. Let him have it right in front of his patients, in front of Rita and Jennifer. Jennifer. June went heavier on the accelerator. Wasn't Jennifer the one Henry was supposed to be doing it with? I mean, when dentists cheat, don't they usually cheat with their cute dental assistants? That was a scenario June could understand – not this Lotty thing in the front seat of a car. I could at least wage some sort of battle with Jennifer. She'd be a threat I'd understand. But Lotty? It's crazy. You can't fight crazy.

She cut over to Yale Avenue and then headed down Morton. She drove fast, then slow, then fast again, thinking. A guy in a BMW finally swerved around her and gave her the finger. She smiled. Not at the driver, whom she only dimly perceived, but at a thought that suddenly emerged from the small part of her that believed in Henry. Could it be that what he did with Lotty was not really an act of sex, but a cry for help? Why else would he have chosen a woman as gross and obvious as Lotty? He wanted to be seen. He wanted to get caught.

Henry's in trouble. That's got to be it. June screeched on to MacDade Boulevard. I'm coming, Henry love. Juney June will save you. She shot through a red light. He wasn't right this morning, why didn't I see it? He woke up in that spooky trance of his . . . What did he say? 'Are you ever filled with dread, June?' Wasn't that it? Dread. Poor Henry, I'm coming, what is it you dread?

She remembered to stop at the next red light. In the distance June could just make out Henry's sign, lit even in daytime, sitting atop his office. Lit for me, Henry, a beacon guiding me to you. A blue Buick sedan jerked to a halt in the lane beside hers. She glanced at it, then stared hard. There was no driver. No, wait, there was – something moved. The reflection on the glass made it difficult to see. She squinted. A tiny person. A very old tiny person. He turned his head quick like a sparrow and stared back at her. His next move was even quicker. He scooted from the driver's seat to the passenger side, closer to June, and pressed his little nose to the window. He wiggled his white eyebrows at her and grinned. He was back in front of his steering wheel in an instant, just as the light turned green. He gunned his engine like a teenager in a drag race, waved once to her and sped off.

Did that just happen? she thought. Behind her, a red car honked. The Buick drove into the distance; her eyes followed it until it disappeared beyond Henry's office. She shifted her gaze to Henry. The car honked again and she moved forward. Must not be diverted from Henry, who needs me, who will be able to explain away Lotty, so that I can go home again where it's safe, where there are no tiny men leering at me from blue cars.

June turned into the asphalt entrance shared by Dreami Donuts and Henry. The Dreami lot was filled with cars. In Henry's lot, there was only one, and it wasn't Henry's. Odd. It's not quite lunch, and Henry never leaves for lunch this early. Ever. That's Jennifer's little Mazda, isn't it? And she's leaving before noon and where's Rita's old Chevy Nova? Jennifer started up her Mazda, began to pull out, then abruptly stopped. She laughed and swatted at the arm of a man sitting next to her and laughed again. June could not believe it. She eased her car into the end slot as Jennifer began to back out again. She opened her car door as Jennifer drove by. Jennifer waved gaily to her but did not stop. Did she even recognize me? No, she was too busy laughing and cavorting. Jennifer cavorting? She was up to something steamy in that car, June was sure. She walked toward the obviously deserted office. What's with cars and sex today? She rattled the handle of the locked glass door. Jennifer engaging in foreplay in hers, and Henry – no foreplay for him. She kicked the metal door frame. No, no, Henry skipped the foreplay and went right to the blow job. She kicked again, because now she knew Margo had spoken the truth. Car sex, all around her. She turned and glared at the cars lined up in the Dreami Donuts lot. They looked like a row of beds to her, ready to receive naked cavorting bodies. 'Closed for the day' read the handwritten note taped to Henry's office door. She kicked one last time at the door and the glass cracked. A thin jagged break sliced between the 'Miles' and 'DDS' of the painted letters 'Henry Miles, DDS.'

'Closed for the day, are you, Henry?' June hissed. So you can drive around all afternoon picking up women on street corners? So you can perform your oral exams on them, that right, Henry? And after a day of that, you expect to come home to me. June hugged herself and leaned against the broken door and faced Dreami Donuts. Our life together has always been so untroubled, why would you do this? Not for sex, not you, Henry. And with strangers? No, you're too nervous for that. Sex with strangers is dirty, exciting and dangerous. And requires passion and you might rumple your clothes and get musky smells all over you. Will they let you run to the shower after sex, Henry? That's what you've always done with me. And afterwards, when you come out of the shower all pink and satisfied, will they do that one last thing for you, will they do what I always do, what you taught me to do? Oh, Henry, will they floss you? June brought her closed fist to her lips and stifled a sob, then tortured herself with one last thought: and will they use peppermint waxed?

June continued to hold her hand to her mouth as she squinted at something in the shadows around the side of Dreami Donuts. By the dumpster. Someone moved, a man. She realized he'd been there all along, watching her. Some sort of bag person checking out the contents of the dumpster? Do we have bag people in this town? Homeless people, I mean. Everyone she knew had a home, even two, if you count vacation places. The sun was in her eyes. He was wearing some kind of hat, it looked like. Men don't wear hats any more. Normal men, anyway. What's he doing? Coming this way, waving at me and coming this way. She was tensing herself for a run to her Nissan Sentra when he called out to her.

'Mrs Miles!'

June froze. When he moved out of the shadows, she recognized him. Marty Marks. The sugar king. That's what Henry calls him. He's always been civil to me, though, the few times we've spoken. Didn't he even give me two complimentary donuts a year or two ago? Yes, one of the times I came to meet Henry for lunch. He was handing them out as a sales gimmick and he went out of his way to come over to Henry's lot to give them to me, even knowing who I was, who I was married to, or used to be married to, since I'd say my marital status is up in the air at the moment. She smiled at Marty and waved back to him.

'Hello, Marty,' she called over to him. 'You kind of startled me at first, over there in the shadows.' Look at him in that Dreami Donuts cap. Silly-looking thing. I guess, though, it takes a sort of courage to put it on.

Marty stood in front of Henry's two-foot-tall yew hedge. 'Didn't mean to, Mrs Miles. Sorry about that.' He took a step or two back, then skipped forward and leaped over the hedge. The paper cap slid down over his eyes and he quickly readjusted it.

Who does he look like? thought June. I know – Dabney Coleman. A cross between Dabney Coleman and G. Gordon Liddy. But a nice G. Gordon Liddy. Good strong mustache. Henry tried to let his grow one time, on vacation, and it never really filled in. Looked fussy on him. The little prig.

Marty said, 'Saw you standing here.' He was in front of her now. He smiled, then suddenly grimaced and touched the side of his face. 'Sore tooth. Loose crown, actually. More than loose, I'd say. Missing entirely. Hole so big my tongue could curl up and sleep in there. If you know what I'm saying.'

'Big hole.'

'Yeah. Exactly. And real, real sore.'

'Mmm, I bet,' said June. Up close, Marty looked a bit disheveled and a little sweaty. Hauling too many stale donuts to the dumpster?

'Your husband deserted me,' he said suddenly, his face darkening.

June stared at him. Disheveled and sweaty. Had Henry, in his crazed sexual state, sought a hurried encounter with Marty as well? How many of his victims would she meet on this day? Henry bisexual? He didn't have enough sex in him to dole it out to two genders. Did he? Who was this man she'd been married to for sixteen years? By day a dull dentist, by night . . . no, she had it backwards. By day a scheming sex machine, by night, with me, a dull dentist. Marty looked eager to give sordid details. Well, give them to my pal, Margo, she always enjoys a bit of gossip.

'Well, Marty,' she said, starting to make a move for her car, 'this must be my husband's big day for deserting people. Guess we ought to form a club.'

Marty looked at her, puzzled. 'Club?'

'Club. I figure, I'm his wife, so I get to be president, since he deserted me first and everything. What do you want to be? Vice-president? Treasurer? Can't wait to meet the other members. Can you?' June was standing by the car now and Marty had turned his head to follow her as she talked.

He said, 'I don't really get you about the club. I'm talking about a tooth situation here, my crown. Dr Miles refused to see me. Just got in his car, not a half hour ago, and sped off. I chased him, too. Left me in the dust. Look at me, I'm a mess.'

'Sped off?' Not sexual. Dental desertion.

'That's right. Look at me.'

'Did he say why he wouldn't see you?' I mean besides hating your guts for being a sugar pusher.

'An emergency, he claimed.'

An emergency. Emergencies came to Henry, he didn't go to emergencies. 'Um, did he say what kind, exactly?' A crotch emergency.

'Frankly, I didn't believe him and I said so.'

Told him off, good man, Marty. A good man is hard to find. June felt a strange shiver work through her.

Marty said, 'I watched you a minute ago. You kicked your husband's door. You broke it, too. That'll cost him.'

You bet it will, thought June. 'You make a habit of watching women, Marty?' Her voice took on a slight huskiness.

'Oh, no, never. Well, I mean, not how you're thinking. I was just out back,' he pointed across the lot to his Dreami Donuts, 'you know, recuperating from chasing after Dr Miles.'

June touched his arm with her finger, then slowly removed it. 'It is tiresome chasing after Dr Miles, isn't it?'

Words rushed out of Marty. 'Mrs Miles, I'm trying to put two and two together here, if you don't mind. Maybe I'm getting it wrong, but, I mean, your husband roars out of here leaving me in the dust. Next thing, I see you drive up, get out your car and start kicking at his office door. And then you say this is your husband's big day for deserting people.' He paused. 'Am I seeing what I think I'm seeing?'

You bet you are. June Miles is, as of this moment, up for grabs by the first man who comes along and that's you, Marty. No, actually Jeffrey was the first man. The first boy. And June can't have boys, so maybe you will have to do. Did you read your horoscope today, Marty? Did it say, 'Today is your chance to offer the dentist's wife something sweet'? She smiled. Yes, of course. He was perfect. He was sugar coated. 'Marty, I guarantee you're seeing what you think you're seeing.'

Marty yipped like a puppy. 'So he *is* quitting dentistry! I'm sorry, Mrs Miles, it must be terribly disappointing for you, but for me it's a Dreami Donuts come true! I'll be able to expand my business now: buy Dr Miles's office, add on to my building, put in more parking spaces. I'll be bigger than any franchise on this strip. The little man will win for once.' Marty hugged himself. 'Oh, Mrs Miles, let me go get you a free half-dozen box, how about it? Jelly? Cinderella Cinnamon? Chewy Choo-Choo Chocolate?'

June shook her head. 'No, Marty.'

'No to donuts? No one says no to donuts. Except your husband. But now that he's out of dentistry, maybe even he will . . .'

'No, no,' June repeated. Marty must've slipped and put a hole in his own head this morning when he was putting holes in his donuts. Henry leave dentistry. She laughed out loud.

Marty smiled uncertainly at her. Her husband suddenly up and quitting his job – she's getting hysterical. Better get some donuts in her, quick. 'Mrs Miles, how about—'

'Never, never, never,' June said, cutting him off. 'Henry would never quit dentistry.'

Marty's voice kicked up an octave. 'But you said . . . He *is* quitting, you said so!'

'You thought I said so.' Oh dear, look at his face.

'But he zoomed off in his, in his car,' Marty stammered. 'And you kicked his office door . . .'

'Marty, are you going to cry?' She moved a step or two toward him.

Marty couldn't meet her eyes. 'I think I might,' he said. 'Excuse me.' He sniffed and dragged a hand roughly across his closed eyes. 'It's the tooth. And your husband driving away from me like he did. And my dream of expanding the business almost coming true. My Dreami dream,' he whispered.

June rested a hand on his arm. 'I'm sorry,' she said. 'About your crown and your dream and everything.'

'It's not your fault,' he said in a low voice. He fingered away a lingering tear.

They looked at one another then, in a moment of shared recognition. Marty slowly reached over to where June's hand rested on his arm and covered it with his own. June felt a slight metallic click as Marty's wedding band came into contact with her diamond ring. Not our fault. His fault. Henry ran out on us.

Marty was trembling. 'He shouldn't have done it,' he said.

'He shouldn't have done it,' June echoed.

'I feel an overwhelming need for revenge,' Marty whispered, his voice close to her ear.

'Here I am,' June said, opening her car door and pulling him in.

Chapter 5

It seemed like years since Henry had first spoken to Mrs Speers on the phone. He wished it had been years. But it was time for the encounter with his father, Stuart Miles, Daddy. When in full control of his mental faculties, Daddy would not have been caught dead without his dentures, brilliant white and minty fresh, firmly in his mouth. He pampered those dentures like other men might pamper an antique car. He soaked them and probed them and brushed them. He buffed and whitened and polished. The old man was never embarrassed that he wore dentures. He reveled in them. From the first, his smile doubled in size so that he could show them off, his lips opening like puffy pink curtains to reveal to the world the pearly treasures within. And now they were trying to cajole and threaten, even drug this man into putting them in his mouth?

Truly, Daddy had begun his downward slide and Henry did not wish to witness it. A broken hip which hadn't healed well had necessitated this move to Fox Glen. But the hip had not fundamentally changed him, nor even had the death two years ago of Lucy Miles, his wife. No, the slippery slide downward began this morning when Daddy decided to let his dentures remain in their bedside glass, soaking in water turned rejuvenating blue by two Polident tablets. This morning, Daddy chose not to be rejuvenated.

'Yes,' Henry quietly said in reply to Mrs Speers's question. 'I'm Stuart Miles's son.' He sagged before her.

Then brightened. Because what if the dentures were simply uncomfortable, suddenly ill-fitting! A common complaint of many denture wearers. Yes! Perhaps, for reasons unknown, he'd been unable to communicate this to the staff and they'd pounced on the poor old man. Yes, yes! There might be an easy explanation for all of this. An out! Daddy remained Daddy, perched safely again at the top of the slippery slope and not careening down it. OK. Simply patch things up and be on my merry way. Hell, might even make it to the diner in Morton for French fries after all.

'Excuse me?' said Mrs Speers, an odd look on her face. 'French fries?'

'What?'

'I thought I just heard you mumble something about French fries.'

Henry's hungry stomach gurgled an admission of guilt. 'No,' he said. 'I'm sure I didn't. I never eat French fries. Cholesterol, you know.' He cleared his throat loudly several times to mask another eruption of gurgles.

'Yes, I've always felt they were poisonous. If I had my way, I'd burn every McDonald's and Burger King in this fat-saturated country of ours to the ground.'

Righto. And I'll torch all the Dreami Donuts. You and me, Mrs Speers, purifying the teeth and blood vessels of America. Burn baby burn. A health crusade and nutritional witch hunt all in one. Take over where Jane Fonda left off. How about we jump in my car and go right now, Mrs Speers? Daddy can wait.

'But about your father,' she said abruptly. 'I was hoping to nip this in the bud, which is why I called you over an hour ago.' She arched an eyebrow.

'I was delayed,' said Henry.

'For an hour,' repeated Mrs Speers. 'An hour where I had to continue to focus my energies on your father, when I might have spent more time with the other clients.'

Clients. Henry hated the euphemism.

'Like Ronald James,' she added, in case he didn't get it.

So it's my fault that geriatric con man escaped from your little prison, is it, Warden Speers?

'Had you gotten here in fifteen minutes as you promised, my morning might have gone quite differently,' she continued. 'And now this,' she waved in the direction of the departed Ronnie, 'and that.' She pointed toward the cluster of white brick buildings that housed one Stuart Miles, troublemaker.

Hey, you think you're the only one who's taken it on the chin this morning? Don't sing your song of a.m. woe to me. 'I did try to get here sooner,' he said. 'Really.' Henry loathed himself.

'Well, what's done is done,' she huffed, and led him toward the white brick buildings.

He trotted along beside her like a small dog trying to keep up. 'What's done? What do you mean?' Several drops of sweat spiderwalked down his back.

'I mean your father is quieter now.'

Needles. Restraints. Big orderlies. 'By himself?' Henry asked, with no hope.

Mrs Speers pushed through a set of glass doors and Henry skittered in after her. 'By himself what?' she said over her shoulder.

The sweet smell of the nursing-home corridor crawled into his nostrils. Tons of floral air freshener trying to smother the smell of fecal incontinence. This mix of shit and flowers is not something God could have intended. Henry said, 'By himself did he calm down?' He thought he heard her release a derisive and ill-concealed snort.

'Hardly.'

Oh, Daddy, I'm sorry I signed the papers that put you in this place. Actually, he hadn't signed them. Stuart, brimming with mental clarity, signed them without coercion. 'I need more care than you can give me,' he'd said matter-of-factly. 'And besides, I want to look at the nurses' asses.' Henry and June had been incredibly relieved.

'What did you do?' he asked Mrs Speers. No, don't piss her off by pointing the finger at her. 'What did he require?' This woman was in charge of Daddy's daily fate, after all. Don't bite the hand that has the power to overmedicate him.

'To be blunt, when you failed to show up, I found it necessary to have the boys restrain him. And then I injected him with a sedative.'

Needles. Restraints. Big orderlies. Am I going to get even one break today? Will everything that I fear might happen, happen? Henry felt all his juices rise. The sweat popped out above his lip, in his armpits, his crotch. His stomach acid bubbled and hissed. His mouth filled with saliva, his eyes watered, he needed to pee. His pores and sphincters and glands snapped open and shut as if a drunk was at the controls.

He trotted along the corridors just behind Mrs Speers, unable to keep up with her quick and efficient strides. He wanted to duck into one of the rooms, lie down on a bed and pull the covers over his head. All the doors to all the rooms were open – you couldn't even fart in this place without all your neighbors knowing it. He imagined a good deal of farting went on around here. He bobbed and weaved past oldsters roaming the halls in walkers and wheelchairs, or clutching the wall railing with both hands as if the corridor was the deck of a fiercely rocking ocean liner. He smiled at each and every one of them, hoping to lock on to something positive, something to quell his rapidly escalating sense of doom. You people, he wanted to shout, you people, show me the good news, give me something to take to my father. Give me a reason he should put his dentures back into his mouth today and tomorrow and tomorrow.

As if in answer to his silent plea for guidance, a particularly old oldster stepped in front of him on wobbly legs. Henry paused in trembling anticipation. Will you tell me, ancient one? Will you give me a reason which I might take to my father, so that he will have cause to pop his choppers back in place and rejoin the ranks of the living? Henry had never seen such a wise-looking old man, his eyes cloudy but alive with intelligence, his ring of white hair encircling his skull like the crown of Solomon. Henry leaned down to hear the man's words.

'Weenies and cabbage.'

'What?' said Henry.

'Weenies and cabbage,' were the old man's repeated words of wisdom. 'My favorite. That's what they're serving for lunch.' He worked his way around Henry. 'Pardon me, bud. Don't want to be late for this one.'

Henry watched him shuffle down the corridor, elbowing past the others on his way to the dining room. So Daddy, Henry imagined saying to his father, it comes down to weenies and cabbage. You have to put your teeth in because without your teeth you can't eat your weenies and cabbage. Turns out, Daddy, weenies and cabbage is the essence of life, is our reason for being. Down at the end of the corridor Mrs Speers was waiting for him to catch up. She stood in front of 414D, his father's room. He walked slowly toward her. Weenies and cabbage, he repeated over and over, a mantra.

Mrs Speers halted him just outside the door. 'I am sorry your father's behavior warranted the use of interventions. But I acted within the medical and nursing guidelines established by this nursing home for the protection of its clients.'

Weenies and cabbage.

She went on. 'Throwing food trays and vases, and tipping over bedside tables, I'm sure you'll agree, is unacceptable. While this behavior is unacceptable, the underlying reason for it is something that concerns me much more. Up until this morning when we could not persuade Mr Miles to put his dentures in, I found him to be an essentially pleasant and predictable client. He was neat and clean in his habits, and cheerful. This morning he ceased to be predictable or neat or clean. As a dentist, you know how important self image is, especially to the denture wearers among us. I have found, over the years, that when a client makes the decision not to wear his dentures, when he suddenly alters any important habit, he is preparing to give up on life.'

'Teeth are life,' said Henry excitedly. My God, he thought, she knows, she understands. He wanted to hug Mrs Speers. More than that, even. He wanted to have this woman right here in the corridor outside his father's room. He wanted to nibble and gnaw on her, to chew and graze on her parts, show her just how much a part of life teeth really are. He stepped toward her.

She eyed him. 'I know this is very upsetting for you, the family member.' She moved back ever so slightly as she spoke.

'Teeth are life,' Henry said again, ready to pounce.

'Teeth are shit,' mumbled someone from behind the half-open door of room 414D.

Daddy? Of course Daddy. And here I'd been about to attempt a sexual act with a strange woman practically right in front of him. He looked guiltily at Mrs Speers. She glared at him, then brushed past him without a word and entered his father's room. Henry shuffled in after her. When he reached the foot of his father's bed, he clamped his eyes shut in a final effort to delay the inevitable. Closed, his eyes could not yet displace the vision of Daddy he always carried with him: neat, tidy and toothsome.

Stuart Miles, sedated and restrained in an upright position in his bed, also had his eyes closed. The orderlies were no longer in attendance.

'Teeth,' Stuart mumbled again. 'Shit.'

'Dr Miles,' said Mrs Speers, after waiting one toe-tapping minute. 'Open your eyes, please.'

'I'm not a doctor,' said Stuart, his words slurred by drugs and toothlessness.

'I was talking to your son.'

'You think so?' said Stuart. 'They drug you, too?' He smiled gummily.

'Dr Miles, open your eyes, please, and help me stop this nonsense.'

Henry was unable to open his eyes, or even speak for that matter. He remained paralyzed at the foot of his father's bed. Daddy all tied up. No, he was not ready for such a sight.

Mrs Speers did some more toe tapping, then leaned close to Stuart and addressed him. 'OK, Mr Miles, then you open your eyes. Please.'

'Oh,' said Stuart, screwing his eyes shut in defiance, 'so it's "Mister" now. Can't make up your mind, eh?'

'You are wasting my time,' said Mrs Speers loudly, lurching

for the door. 'You have been wasting my time all morning!' She huffed out of the room.

'Good!' Stuart attempted to spit in the direction of her departing voice, but since he was doped up and lacking teeth, the spit fell short and landed thickly on the toe of Henry's shoe.

Henry felt the gob strike his shoe and was further convinced that it was not a good time to open his eyes. He dragged his toe back and forth on the thin industrial carpet. The life of a nursing-home carpet could not be a happy one, he mused.

'Who's that scratching around in here? I hear you, don't think I don't,' Henry's father called out, working his mouth to spit again.

'Daddy,' Henry whispered. 'It's me.'

The two men faced each other, blindly.

'Son?' Stuart tried gamely to open his eyes. They fluttered and squinted open for a second, then dropped closed again. 'Doped,' he said. 'To the gills. But I guess you can see that for yourself. Look pretty bad, do I?'

'Actually, Daddy,' Henry began. Come on, you gutless wonder, take a peek. He popped his eyelids open and shut, and the bright fluorescent light that bathed the room hit him like a camera flash. A square of white, the retinal residue of his glimpse at his father's bed, danced and glowed behind Henry's darkened eyelids. The image of the bed seemed to float in deep space as if on a long celestial journey. Daddy on his heavenbound bed.

When Henry was silent for too long, his father said his name again. 'Henry? You looking at me? You're not looking at me, are you?'

Daddy knew him.

'You're still doing that, huh?' His voice trailed, then came back again. 'Did it as a kid. Closed your eyes at the scary parts. Sorry about all this.' He pushed against his restraints. 'Chained down like King Kong. Course, you don't remember that scene in the movie because your eyes were closed.' He chuckled moistly, his tongue slipping around on his toothless gums. He fell quiet, then his breathing grew heavy as if he was falling asleep.

But it's a complicated sort of scary, thought Henry. His father was not exactly right in this instance – he had had his eyes closed for much of the movie, but he had mistakenly thought it would be all right to look when Kong was safely chained and displayed on that stage. It turned out to be scary in a way that Henry had not anticipated – restrained, the creature became an object of pity. It frightened him that things could change so fast: one minute you're the king of the jungle, the next minute you're Daddy chained in bed. At least Kong retained his fangs. There is nothing on this earth scarier than a fangless Daddy.

'Henry!' the old man cried out. 'You there?'

Trying to be, Daddy. He opened one eye and kept it open. 'I'm here, I'm here.' Fifty per cent here, anyway. One-eyed, he moved to the side of the bed and reached out to give the old man a comforting pat. But his depth perception was off and his hand came to rest somewhere on Daddy's lower midsection. Somewhere like where his pecker should have been. Oh Jesus. Henry was about to jerk his hand off the blanket, but the tactile information coming to him through his fingers indicated that something extraordinary in the pecker department resided between Daddy's legs. Henry rifled through his mental filing cabinet until he got to the folder labeled 'Pecker: Father/Son Encounters.' The folder was exceedingly thin, due to Daddy's physical daintiness (no casual naked strolls to and from the bathroom) and young Henry's typical filial awe, embarrassment and confusion concerning matters genital. And now, it turns out, in awe for a good reason! What was this thing beneath the blanket? Henry did remember a long ago camping trip, staring at his Daddy's equipment as they mutually relieved themselves on a pine tree, deep within the privacy of the forest and well away from Mom. Sure, it was big, but naturally, attainably big, of a size Henry could reasonably hope to some day achieve in the hazy post-pubescent future.

'Henry?'

But this was altogether monstrous, this thing. As thick as a baseball bat and solid, hard. Not the fleshy rigidity of a normal erection. Better suited to King Kong. No wonder his father had gone bonkers. What had caused it? Aging? Some sort of steroids slipped to him at mealtime? Were they experimenting on the population here at Fox Glen? Sure, why not – an endless supply of guinea pigs. Daddy, forgive me, I'll get you out of here right now, break your chains and carry you in my arms out to my car. But let's not get rash here, he thought. Better check just once more before causing a scene. I sure do hate a scene. Maybe I'm getting carried away. He girded himself and gripped the beast again.

'Hey, for Chrissake, Henry! What are you doing to my urinal?' The old man twisted around in his bed. 'Sheesh.'

Urinal. Grabbing urinals, open both your eyes, idiot. Which he at last did, stammering, 'Daddy, I'm sorry . . . you see, what I was trying to . . .'

'Most sons shake their father's hands.'

He should never have provided Daddy with this opportunity. Doped, he was still a killer. I'll be hearing about it for the rest of his . . . Henry looked hard at his father, taking him in fully for the first time. Just how long would the rest of his days actually be? Without his teeth, Stuart Miles looked like a man collapsed in on himself. Not simply his face and cheeks, but all of him, deflated, caved in, like the rest of his days might include this afternoon and maybe tomorrow if he was lucky. How'd his skin get so papery and pale, his hair so thin? They had to drug and restrain this man? Henry, too, felt drugged and restrained.

Daddy lifted his head and let it drop again back on to the pillow. The evil-looking vest they had tied across his chest gave him little room to move. Henry moved quickly to help, but the best he could do was fluff and prop the pillows. They had Daddy where they wanted him.

Daddy sighed and wearily looked up at Henry. 'You know how many times in my life I've had occasion to use a urinal? I'll tell you. No times. I never even saw one up close before. Other fellas around here use them, but not me. I don't piss where they have to have somebody haul it away for me.'

'I know, Daddy.' Henry swallowed.

'Now they tie me up and I have no choice. One of the lovely little dignities of this place. Urinals, for God's sake.'

Henry eyed a drying spot of red beside Daddy's head on the pillow. And there was another on the corner of the sheet. Hit the orderly with his lunch tray, isn't that what Nurse Speers said? Wow. A scene. He and his father abhorred scenes, their vulgarity and chaos. And danger. Daddy, a retired college librarian, was not given to solving a problem physically. The most violent muscular act Henry had ever witnessed was the time Daddy threw a Roget's Thesaurus at the TV during the Bush inaugural ceremony. Daddy fighting for his life with a lunch tray, fending off the invading hordes. But why? For the right not to wear dentures, when for all those years he'd loved wearing them? What had Nurse Speers said about a change in predictable behavior?

Daddy blinked several times, then stared hard up into Henry's eyes. 'Son,' he said. 'I want to go to Disney World.'

Henry clutched the bed rail. This wasn't just a change in predictable behavior, this was demonic possession. Disney World: the homogenized shithole of modern civilization, to quote Daddy precisely. And he was not one to use dirty talk loosely. Henry could see it: wheeling Daddy, black plastic Mickey ears sprouting tumorously from his grey head, through the land of Pluto and Snow White. A lifetime of perusing the library stacks of academia, and now he wants to go see Goofy. Why?

'Because,' said Daddy, as if he plucked the unspoken question from Henry's brain, 'I'm dying.'

Have I been doused with a bucket of water? thought Henry, reeling. No, it is only the incessantly dripping sweat of my ever present floating anxieties giving way to the full-blown torrential sweat of my fear of death, my own in particular, and the death of my loved ones in general. Daddy, no.

'And in this great country of ours,' continued Daddy, 'the dying go to Disney World.'

'Dying children.'

'Well, I've always been a child at heart. You gonna deny this little boy his dying last wish?'

'You're not dying.'

'You got both your eyes open now, Henry. What do you see?'

'I came here about dentures, Daddy. Not dying.'

'Surprise.'

Henry blurted out, 'But I didn't bring you here to die!'

'You want to say that one again, son?'

'I know, I know. I mean, I know that's what happens in this place, but you're only here because of your hip. For extra care. I'll straighten out this denture thing and you'll be fine again. People don't die of denture problems, Daddy. We'll fix the teeth, then board the next plane south for Disney World. Epcot Center, too, if that's what you want.'

'Henry.'

'And they have some kind of new movie theme park, and all those sea world places. Take you down, me, you, Juney and the twins. It'll be great!' The room tilted and Henry's knees buckled slightly.

'Henry. Sit down and put your head between your knees, you look faint.'

'Right.' He dropped into the armchair beside the bed and tried to catch his breath.

Daddy regarded Henry silently for a moment. His eyes were open wider now, more alert. 'I don't really want to go to Disney World.'

Henry looked up. 'So you're not . . .?'

'No, I am dying. But I don't want to go to Disney World. I only said that to get your attention. Always been hard getting your attention, since you were a kid. Henry,' he said, forming his words slowly and carefully since he had no teeth, 'I have a big favor to ask.' He paused. 'Can you hear me, son?'

Not really, no, Daddy. Henry stared out the window at the

landscaped green surrounding the low brick buildings of Fox Glen. He felt suddenly sleepy. He'd like to lie down on that expanse of green. Catch some shut-eye, drift away . . .

He finally said, 'I heard you, Daddy. You don't want to go to Disney World.' Now Henry felt like *he* was in Disney World, on some wild ride where your daddy's trying to die on you and your patients are chasing you and you never get to eat lunch. Jesus, he wanted those French fries and there was no way he was ever going to get to them.

'Henry,' Daddy said, trying to shift himself against his chest and hand restraints. 'Think maybe you could loosen these a bit? I'm less than comfortable here.'

Henry's eyes opened wide and he tightened in his chair. 'Uh, Daddy. They have some pretty explicit rules, you know, sound medical reasons, and I really shouldn't, um, intervene here.'

'Well, you're a medical man too, aren't you? Don't they refer to you as Dr Miles at your place of business? I'd sort of be under your care while you were in this room.' Daddy made a clucking sound with his tongue and nodded his head theatrically as if remembering something. 'Oh yeah. Right. You're not actually a medical man, but a dental man.'

Dentist Man looked sourly at his father.

Daddy continued. 'So they call you doctor, but you're not in fact, as I understand the term, really a doctor.'

Dentist Man let out a slow hissing breath like a deflating balloon.

'MD-wise, I mean,' Daddy added for his zinger. 'So I can see how you'd feel medically uncomfortable loosening these straps a notch, you not being in medicine, after all.'

Don't rise to the bait, he's a desperate, doped and dying old man, you are better than he, Dentist Man. Henry brooded for several seconds. When he spoke, he tried to keep the boyish whine out of his voice. 'Daddy, as I have told you a thousand times over the years, dentistry is a branch of medicine, like you have eye doctors and bone doctors, you have tooth doctors.'

'So where were you when they were handing out the MDs? In

a corner with the podiatrists, I guess. Excuse me, I mean foot doctors.'

'OK, Daddy, you win, I'm not a doctor. Happy?'

'No, I'm not. I'm roped and tied like a steer and I was hoping my son was up to doing something about it. But I guess he's not. And look at me with no teeth spitting all over myself when I talk, it's pathetic.'

Henry stood up from his chair. 'I'll get Nurse Speers.'

Daddy motioned him back down with a wiggle of his fingers, the only part of his hand that was free to move. 'Goddamn it, Henry, no. She's the enemy! She gave the attack order to those two goons.' He glared at Henry. 'She's already done what she's gonna do. The question I'm posing is: what are you going to do?'

Do? Do. To do or not to do. Henry sat on his hands. Henry squirmed in his chair. If I loosen those straps, there'll be some kind of scene, or I'll get in trouble, maybe they'll accuse me of practicing medicine without a license. But I *do* have a license and it is a medical license no matter what Daddy thinks. It's better than medical, it's a license to be: Dentist Man! Yes, that's who I am, that's what I do. Do? Fix his dentures, that's what I'll do. He felt his chest swell and his muscles grow taut. DDS and proud of it. Goddamn, I wish I'd remembered to bring my white coat. He rose up out of his chair and bellowed to his father, 'Your dentures. Tell me where they are and I will fix them. That's what I'm going to do!'

'Henry, you nincompoop, get away from me.' He twisted his head from side to side, as Henry, one knee on the bed, tried to peer into his mouth.

'Daddy, hold still, will you please?' Too bad they didn't restrain his head while they were at it. Sure could use Jennifer right now. 'I need to have a quick peek, make sure there are no ulcers on your gums or anything. That can make wearing dentures very . . . Daddy!'

Daddy chomped down on Henry's probing forefinger with a

gummy ferocity. If he'd been wearing his dentures, Henry's finger would have been chewed to the bone.

Henry went white and whimpered. Daddy continued to clamp down on the finger, which was in no real danger beyond receiving a good bruise. Henry remained absolutely still until at last Daddy spat the finger out of his mouth like a bad cigar. Tears of relief sprang to Henry's eyes – he would not be practicing four-fingered dentistry after all. He brought the throbbing appendage to his lips and kissed it tenderly.

'What's with you medical types?' Daddy growled at him. 'Coming at me all the time, thinking you have some sort of right of access, sticking and poking and tying me up. Make me sick, every one of you.'

'Sorry, I was only . . .'

'Trying to goddamn help. All of you, doing what's best for me. Did it ever occur to you I might know what's best for me?'

'But,' said Henry, 'I'm a tooth expert. Daddy, you helped put me through college to make me one, remember? And I was just,' he felt himself choke up, from the pain in his finger, from his failure to help Daddy when he was really trying to, choking up on the unending fiasco of his day, 'I was just trying to give a little something back to you.'

'Henry. Son. It's not about dentures. OK? Which brings me back to the favor I—'

Henry cut him off. 'But you loved them. You were so proud of them. And now – this.' He gestured at the restraints.

'I still love them, Henry. You did a great job. You did. They fit like a dream.'

'Then why . . .?'

Daddy closed his eyes and slowly opened them again. It seemed to take him a moment to find Henry. 'Because if you don't have your dentures in,' he said, 'it makes it harder for them to do mouth-to-mouth. To resuscitate me, Henry.'

'Why? Why would you want to make it harder?'

'Suicide,' said Daddy. 'They stopped me before I really got a chance to get started. They're like you, think I just have denture problems. What's that joke? "The operation was a success but the patient died." Well, they think by tying me to my bed they performed some sort of successful operation, but I guarantee this patient is still going to find a way to die.'

'Die? Suicide?' said Henry frantically. He peered down at Daddy's straps to make sure they were nice and tight. 'Two weeks ago you were still ogling the nurses and chowing down on the grub. Now it's suicide?'

'Things changed, what can I tell you.'

'What changed? In two weeks, what? The nurses? The food?'

'My outlook, Henry.'

'In two weeks?'

'I'm eighty-three, it was bound to happen. When the time comes, it comes.'

'Who told you it was time? How do you know? Voices in your head?'

'You're scared, Henry. I can see your eyes wanting to close.'

King Kong wants to kill himself, you're fucking right I'm scared, thought Henry. And I thought it was scary when they chained him down. Now he wants to blow himself away onscreen? He said, 'If I'm scared, you should be terrified.'

'I want to go, Henry.'

'Would you quit saying that. How do you know?'

'You know when you're hungry, don't you? Or when you gotta take a shit? Well, in the last two weeks, at eighty-three, I know. My body's been talking to me.'

'Why all the talk? Why didn't it just go ahead and do it?' The last time he came to visit, hadn't they just discussed baseball or something? He should have taken control of the conversational agenda the minute he walked in here. Should've brought Ed or Fred. Daddy would've never pulled this death stuff on them. Surely there might have been some way to avoid all this.

'The luckier ones do just go, Henry. Leonard Haines, down the hall in 426, had a stroke at dinner last week and died with a forkful of *au gratin* potatoes in his hand.'

Potatoes. French fries. Henry's stomach grumbled mournfully.

He got so hungry when he was upset. He spied half a banana wrapped in plastic on Daddy's chest of drawers. How could he get to it? He had a thought then. What was Daddy doing saving bananas from breakfast when it had been his intention to be dead by lunch?

Daddy went on. 'I started thinking, what if I don't go quick, like Leonard? What if it takes me a month to die? They'd ship me to the county hospital, they always do, and God knows how much time that would add on to it, how many tubes in my arms and up the ass. Not for me, Henry. Not for me.'

'I wouldn't have let them, Daddy.'

'You'd have panicked, son. Most do and then it's tubes and machines all the way.'

Henry whispered, 'But what do you know about suicide? Who told you about taking out your dentures?'

Daddy, glancing quickly at the door, whispered back, 'You won't tell?' He raised an eyebrow and smiled, inviting Henry into the conspiracy. 'The enemy,' he jerked his head at the door, 'must not know.'

The enemy. They drugged and restrained Daddy, of course he was on the old man's side. Wasn't he? Henry cut his eyes to the banana. If he could just have a little bite. Something to sustain him. He moved casually in the general direction of the banana as he talked. 'Tell? The enemy? Me?'

'You have to pee, Henry? You're doing a lot of pacing. You used to do that as a little boy, too. Pace when you had to pee.' He closed his eyes a moment. 'You haven't answered me, either, don't think I didn't notice.'

Henry snatched up the banana while Daddy wasn't looking. 'Maybe I shouldn't know,' he said over his shoulder. 'Maybe this is on a level beyond the normal, the reasonable, I don't know, beyond the safe sorts of things I should be having to cope with.' He turned and looked at his father. The banana was in Henry's coat pocket. He was trying to pick off the plastic wrap secretly and with just one hand it was not easy. There. Almost. 'To tell you the truth, Daddy, I'm feeling a little overwhelmed.'

Daddy tapped his fingers on the bed and looked away. 'Right. Right. You're a frail boy, Henry. Always were, always will be. But you're the only one who can do this favor for me.'

Dentist Man's not so frail. But Daddy wouldn't understand the concept of Dentist Man, how powerful I am back at the office, my domain, where I command when the world will rinse and spit. 'I'm tougher than you think, Daddy,' he lied. Sometimes, maybe. 'So, OK, so tell me about this, this suicide thing.' What favor does he keep trying to ask and why won't I let him? Henry felt frail.

Daddy nodded. 'OK.' He was whispering again. 'There's a book. We just got hold of it.'

'A book?'

'And we've passed it around among us. Among the inmates.' He laughed quietly. 'A how-to book. Called *Special Deliverance*.'

A how-to book passed among the inmates. Henry's stomach went crazy and he was so sweaty he was about to die and if he didn't eat right then and there ... He turned and crouched, popped a broken-off end of banana into his mouth and chewed it frantically. There may even have been a piece of plastic wrap stuck to it, but he didn't care. He was well into the act of swallowing when it suddenly hit him, why Daddy saved the banana from breakfast to eat at lunch even though he expected to be dead by lunch. The banana! The instrument of Daddy's suicide! He'd laced it with something, the powdery insides of pilfered pills, or the other inmates had set it up for him, got it from that how-to book. Step one: take out your dentures. Step two: spike a nice soft banana with a killer dose, then gum your way to the heavenly beyond. And I've taken a bite, death is halfway down my throat, the Special Deliverance Banana Splitsville, so long, Henry, one tiny bit more of a swallow and the poisons are in your stomach and off to your bloodstream.

Oh my. Henry floated out of himself for a moment and considered the possibilities. Hadn't he always assumed he'd die in some ugly, violent and accidental manner? Auto, fire, crime victim, some horrible thing from The List? Banana death. It was so easy. Easy? He was *there*. No agonizing preparation, the time was now, the smallest muscular movement, a mere twitch of the esophagus, and it's good night ladies. Bye-bye, so long, Daddy, whose dying I do not wish to become involved with, so long, cavity-ridden, fecal-breathed patients of mine, so long, June and Ed and Fred and Rita and Jennifer and all of you who elicit powerful and burdensome emotions which plague me and which make me feel so terribly sleepy. Sleepy, so tired, maybe a little of the sedative is leaking from the banana chunk, Lord, it's easy. All my sorrows soon be over, I feel for the first time since this morning, since the moment of my birth, so calm, so peaceful, farewell, farewell, Dentist Man bids you all—

Jesus Christ! A surge of panic brought the slimy lump of banana retching upward, up up up and out, Henry coughing and spitting into the palm of his trembling hand. Die? Me? Now? Am I getting it all out? He spit into his brimming palm until his saliva was banana free. Let me live and suffer no toxin-induced neurological deficits and I swear to you, Almighty Lord, that I will work one Saturday a month in a free dental clinic, tending to the poor and disenfranchised. Well, maybe not that, but I will try to keep my prices within ten per cent of inflation for this fiscal year. And I'll let June drive my Taurus sometimes, so she can have the benefit of the airbag. And I'll try not to let the twins get on my nerves as much as they do. His heart was pounding, but he seemed to be moving into the plus column of life. I will be a good guy, thank you for giving me this second chance. I will cut back on my high-fat diet. I will floss nightly – wait, I already do that. I will . . .

'What's wrong over there, Henry? You got hairballs? I never heard such a commotion. Sound like a dying cat.'

Dying? Not me. Now where am I going to dump this poisonous crap? Banana spit was beginning to ooze through his fingers. Is there a bathroom around here? Daddy's giving me the eye.

'Henry? You all right?'

Against all his principles concerning the proper disposal of oral waste, Henry emptied the contents of his hand into his coat pocket. A wave of nausea passed over him – guilt, disgust, and perhaps a trickle of banana poison.

'You look a little green around the gills. Something you ate?'

Wait a minute. Daddy looks a bit too concerned. Something I ate. He knows exactly what I ate. He left it there for me to eat. It was a set-up. Henry's eyes went wide and another wave swept over him, of fear this time. Daddy tried to murder me. His denture escapade was a ruse, a scheme to get me here, in proximity to the banana, the banana he knew I'd eat because he purposely interrupted my lunch hour, and he knows how cranky I get if I miss lunch. Twisted old coot, look at him there in his straitjacket, which I plan to make sure he never gets out of. Daddy, you kill me. Or at least you tried, didn't you? Offing your offspring – is there a more heinous crime?

Father and son regarded one another. Henry began to feel a little gulpy. But why, Daddy? Wasn't I a good boy? I never, ever caused you trouble. Rarely naughty as a child, hardly rebellious as a teen, went to an affordable state college to keep expenses down, and then a dental degree, marriage, grandkids (all right, so you couldn't tell them apart either, is that my fault?) and finally, this lovely nursing home. My life was dedicated to your ease. And a lethal banana was my reward? He glanced down at his coat pocket where the sticky mess was beginning to seep through the seersucker. Should have worn my polyester dental top. Damn. And damn him, too. So I didn't get an MD. Every other father in this country would kill to have a dentist son and my father has a dentist son he wants to kill.

'Why, Daddy?' Henry got the question out.

'Why what?'

'Why the banana? Why me?'

Daddy studied him. 'Is that Socratic or Aristotelian? Philosophy was never my strong point.'

'This is funny to you?'

'Well, it's odd, anyway,' said Daddy.

'Daddy, we're talking murder!'

'No, son. We were discussing suicide, as I remember. Before

your coughing fit – you ought to have a doctor check that out for you – yes, suicide, which we better discuss faster because the enemy will be back in here before too much longer. They never let you be.' He crooked a finger at Henry. 'Come closer,' he said. 'It's all in the book. One: take out your dentures. Two: make sure your baggie has no holes in it.'

Henry raised his hand to stop him. 'Wait, wait. Baggie. What baggie? What are you saying?'

'The baggie,' whispered Daddy, 'is the key. A big baggie is how you do it.'

'The banana is how you do it.'

'You got yourself a book, too? I'm not familiar with the banana method. How's that one work? Ah, well, never mind. I was all set up for the baggie, which they say is a remarkably gentle way to go. I was going to be the first one here to give it a try.'

The banana wasn't poisoned. Henry stared down at the ruinous ever-enlarging stain on his coat pocket. Stan, of Stan's Kleen 'n Go, is going to have a conniption. Better take it to Morrison's Dry Clean over on West Chester Pike. They don't know me there. Stan takes stains so personally. Dry cleaners made Henry think of those big clear plastic bags everything comes back to you in. He had a vision of the motorized hanger rack in the back of Stan's place with all the residents of Fox Glen hanging from it, each individually wrapped in a clear plastic bag. 'Come in for your father, did you, Henry?' Stan would say, hitting the button and bringing Daddy whirring toward him on the rack.

Henry shuddered and looked around the room for Daddy's hidden baggie. His stomach rumbled again and he was sorry he had so foolishly disposed of the banana.

Daddy watched him silently for a time. At last he spoke. 'It's in my drawer, Henry. Along with two sleeping pills I'd saved up. No reason to hide it, since I wasn't suspected of anything.' He took a long breath. 'But circumstances have changed. Henry, come over here. Please. Come sit on the bed with me a minute.'

Henry did so, feeling curiously reversed: how often, when he was a small boy, had Daddy come into his room and sat on the side of the bed, when he was ill, or at bedtime before turning out the light? And now, thought Henry, it's my turn to sit on Daddy's bed. He let his fingers briefly brush Daddy's restrained hand where it rested on the blanket, then shyly pulled back again.

'Henry, I have this favor I have to ask of you. Kind of a big one, son.'

'Anything, Daddy.' And as he said the words, he believed them. Your father, who sat on your bed, who fed and clothed and loved you as best he could, who had not intended to murder you after all (Henry blushed with guilt), your father asks a favor, by God, you grant it. 'You want these damn restraints off, I'll make them take them off.' He was already reaching for the nursing call light fastened to the side of Daddy's bed rail.

'Stop a minute, put that down. Forget the restraints. They may take them off while you're here, but believe me, they'll pounce on me the minute you go. I'm a marked man.'

'I'll take you home. That what you want? Not right away, though. I mean, I'd like to, but I can't. We have to make room, shuffle things around a bit. Take a couple days, if you can just—'

'Henry, I'm not asking to come home with you.'

'But we'd love to have you. And the intergenerational family thing's real big right now – be good for the boys to have you around. Now, June might take a little convincing, she can be fussy about upheaval in the home.' Henry patted Daddy's hand. 'Not that you'd be upheaval, I don't mean it that way. It's just that June's a bit of a queen bee when it has to do with the running of the house – you know, like I'm kind of the king bee around my office.' Henry paused. 'Are there king bees?' he asked.

'If there are,' said Daddy, staring at him, 'then I'm sure you're one.'

'Right. So you get the picture. Give us some time, we'll get you out of here.' He couldn't shut up. 'But first we have to get those teeth back in and forget all this, this baggie stuff.' Why couldn't he shut up? 'Now, where are those darn dentures, the cause of so much trouble this morning?' He couldn't shut up because he knew he didn't want to hear the favor Daddy was about to ask. 'Yeah, boy. Let me at those dentures, those gosh darn dentures, those . . .' He trailed off hopelessly.

'You finished, Henry?' Daddy asked gently.

Henry couldn't look at him.

'I don't want to come home with you. I thank you, but I don't. And I don't want to stay here at Fox Glen, although it's been an essentially pleasant experience. Except for this morning, of course. What I do want, Henry, is to move on, to listen to my body and just, move on. OK?'

Henry sat very still. 'OK,' he said.

'Good. Thank you.' He breathed deeply. 'And now the favor. As far as Nurse Speers and the rest of the staff around here are concerned, I'm a wacko, an old guy who's over the edge. They don't know what I was up to, the suicide, they just know they'll have to watch me.'

'They'll watch you,' Henry repeated dully. He struggled to keep his eyes open. He wanted to lie down on the bed beside Daddy and take a nap.

'Yes. So, Henry, I'm going to need a little help.'

Just curl right up beside him on the bed. Wouldn't that be nice? Did Daddy just say something? I couldn't quite hear. Been such a busy day. Need a little help. 'Sure, sure,' Henry murmured, yawning. And he might even have yawned himself into a denial-induced narcoleptic slumber but for the undeniable words Daddy spoke next.

'Henry, I want you to do me in.'

Ding ding ding ding! exploded the alarm clock in Henry's head. He jumped up from the bed. So he had been half right with the banana after all. There really was murder in the air. Daddy not kill Henry. Henry kill Daddy. Police catch Henry and lock ass in jail. No French fries for ever and ever, unless he gets murder one and they let him order French fries as his last meal. A vicious anxiety hunger gurgled upward from his poor belly. He was so hungry now that the thought of a last meal didn't sound half bad.

'Kill you?!'

'Hey, pipe down, will ya,' Daddy said, glancing at the door. 'The walls have ears. I prefer "do me in", if you don't mind.'

'Well, I prefer murder, because that's what we're talking about.'

'Such a flair for the dramatic.'

'No no. You got that wrong.' Henry paced back and forth. 'What I want here is undramatic. Like your teeth back in and everything the way it was yesterday.'

'Yesterday, I was planning for today.'

'Well then, two days ago, dammit, Daddy.'

'Do me in.'

'You do you in,' Henry snapped back.

'I tried,' he said quietly.

Try again. Was he really about to say that? Now I'm pissed at Daddy for not successfully killing himself. He's got me coming and going, the wily bastard: his suicide is now something I prefer. To murder? Yeah, I'd say so.

'How do you want me to do you in? Hold a baggie over your head? Jesus, Daddy.'

Daddy hesitated. 'Quite honestly, Henry, I'm not sure how to proceed now. I kind of blew phase one.'

'So let's forget the whole thing, how about it? No phase two. Especially if it involves me. I got a family to consider, you know.'

'Didn't that used to include me?'

'Daddy, please.'

'Do me in.'

'I can't.'

'You have access to drugs. You could inject me. Or stand by to make sure I inject myself properly.'

Henry stopped pacing. 'With what? I have access to Novocaine. You want me to numb you to death?'

'Hey. Death and numbness – not so far apart.'

Henry reached for the nursing call light and pressed down hard on the button. 'This has gone far enough, Daddy. I'm leaving.'

Daddy stared at him. 'When I start to go downhill, they'll take me to County Hospital. Then it's machines, Henry. Machines.'

Where was Nurse Speers? He tried not to think of Daddy hooked up to machines.

'My teeth, Henry,' Daddy said suddenly. 'My dentures.'

Are we back to that? thought Henry. What's he trying to pull?

'Over there next to that jumble of stuff on the dresser. Those incompetents didn't even put them back in my denture cup. Get them, will you, boy. Quick now, before they come.'

So now I get to put them back in for him, after all this. Gee, Daddy, why didn't we do this before the mental anguish, the bite on my finger, the permanent banana stain on my seersucker coat? Playing hard to get? Or trying to work on my sympathy: if I let you put my teeth in, then you have to promise to kill me, sort of thing. Sounds like an even trade to me, Daddy. He walked toward the bed, dentures in hand, ready for the next command.

'Take them home,' Daddy said.

'I can't take you home,' said Henry, thinking he hadn't heard right.

'Them. Not me. The teeth.'

'Home?'

'So you'll remember I'm here.'

'I'll remember.'

'Take them, they'll be like a dog biting you on the ass, reminding you what you have to do.'

'What I'm not going to do, you mean. Here.' He held them out to Daddy, forgetting that he was restrained.

Daddy shook his head. 'You don't take them, the minute I get a chance I'll step on them.'

Henry gasped and clutched the dentures to his chest. 'You

wouldn't.' He would, I can see it in his eyes. 'Imagine what that would do to me,' he said.

'Imagine what you not helping me die does to me. Machines, Henry. I'll be waiting for you,' he whispered.

Footsteps outside the door. Daddy closed his eyes and Henry quickly dropped the dentures into his coat pocket, the one not filled with banana glop. Henry sniffed. He was beginning to ferment.

Mrs Speers marched into the room. She surveyed the scene. 'Well. Everyone's eyes open? Well, at least yours are open,' she said to Henry. 'I never saw such nonsense.'

'Me neither,' he said, working his way around her toward the door. 'There's nothing I can do here, I'm afraid, Mrs Speers.'

She looked down at Stuart. 'No, I suppose that's probably true.'

Henry stood in the doorway, awash with guilt. I have to leave you, Daddy. 'I want those restraints off him as soon as possible. Can we have him watched closely? I'll pay extra if need be.'

'Certainly we'll watch him,' said Mrs Speers.

'And forget the dentures for now, OK? We'll worry about them later.'

'As you wish. You're the dentist, after all, Dr Miles.'

She emphasized the 'Dr' just like Daddy. All the world hates a dentist. Henry sighed. 'I'm sorry about this, Mrs Speers. Believe me, I am. I'm sure everything will straighten out.'

'Oh, it will. I'm absolutely certain it will.' She smiled. Dangerously, it seemed to Henry.

He stood a moment in the doorway. Waiting for a secret blessing from Daddy? It would not come.

'I'll be in every day,' he said, shifting his eyes to Mrs Speers.

'Fine,' she said.

He turned to go, then immediately turned back again. 'Mrs Speers?' he had to ask.

'Yes?'

'Your car. Ronald James escaping in your car. The police come up with anything yet?'

'Not yet.'

Behind them, Daddy's old white head shifted on the pillow. One eye popped open and then closed again. No one noticed.

Chapter 6

'Marty,' said June. 'Don't look so panicked.'

Marty was looking over his shoulder out of the back window of June's Nissan Sentra, as his Dreami Donuts receded in the distance, his life preserver floating out of reach. 'They saw me,' he said, straining to see. But there was nothing left to see. He turned and stared out the windshield. He recognized nothing, although he'd driven to work on this strip for over ten years. 'Everyone in my Dreami Donuts saw me get into this car with you. Lou the cashier saw me, Frank behind the counter, every single solitary customer with a donut in his mouth saw me. Saw us.'

June patted his knee and he flinched. 'Guess there's no turning back then, huh?' she said.

'My managerial career. My marriage of twenty-one years. Over. Gone.'

'Don't be silly. This is merely an interlude, a positive wrinkle in what was surely going to be another dull day of donut drudgery.'

'My job is anything but dull,' said Marty defensively. 'That's a common misconception. Each and every day brings a new challenge.'

'Great,' said June. 'Then just think of me as today's newest challenge.' *Why am I trying so hard?*

'But it's not a donut challenge. I'm out of my context.'

'I don't know,' said June. 'This is a kind of donutty situation.' She smiled wickedly at him and lifted an eyebrow. 'I mean, what I'm offering comes with a hole and is very sweet.'

Marty blanched. 'Oh my God,' he said. 'Oh my God.' He glanced at the car door and wondered if he would be killed if he threw himself out of it.

June snapped, 'You wanted this, remember, Marty? I believe you said, and I quote, you had "an overwhelming need for revenge". I am right that those words came out of your mouth five minutes ago?' Or did they come out of my mouth? What exactly is my need? Is it you, Henry, I need?

'But I didn't say an *immediate* overwhelming need. I mean, I could've waited a day or two.'

'Fate has thrown us together, Marty,' she sighed. 'Fate doesn't wait a day or two.'

'Why did fate have to throw us together right in front of my place of business?' He took his paper cap off his head and fidgeted with it in his lap.

'Oh, nobody saw you.'

'The place is all glass. It's a window to the world.'

'No one was watching. They were too busy stuffing their faces with your donuts.'

Marty brightened. 'You think so?' he said. 'You really think so?'

Oh, brother. Why couldn't fate have put me in Jeffrey's arms? Why did he have to be eighteen and living next door? Why couldn't he have been older and wearing a Dreami Donuts cap? She looked at Marty and tried to transform him. Then she answered him. 'Yes, Marty, I think so. Every one of your customers munching away.'

'That's a double positive, then.'

'Sorry?'

'The first positive is everyone eating my donuts with such pleasure and concentration. You know, I personally make at least one kind of donut every single morning. This morning, for instance, I made Rah-Rah Raspberry. And the second positive is that you, a potential customer standing outside, could observe with such clarity the activities inside the building. That's the psychology, you see, the reason for all that glass. So you, the potential customer, can look in and develop an acute craving for the donuts.' Marty couldn't stop smiling. He placed his paper cap back on his head and tilted it at a jaunty angle.

'Hey, Marty,' said June. 'You know what?'

'What?'

'I'm one up on all those other potential customers.'

'How's that?'

'I didn't just get the donut. I got the donut maker.' And if I close my eyes, he doesn't look too bad.

Marty shivered in his seat and stared out his window for a moment. Then he said, 'This is kind of a secret, but do you know what I call myself sometimes? When I open up the store in the morning, when I'm alone real early back in the bakery, firing up the big ovens and the deep fryers, slinging around those heavy flour sacks, mixing everything together in those giant bowls. Gosh. You've never seen so much butter and so many eggs. And the sugar, oh, the sweetest whitest purest sugar in all the world. Mixing it all up. Pouring out the donuts, the heat of the ovens and the fryers, the smell of all those sweet ingredients, bringing it all together, making something so powerful and tempting. And it's a good temptation. Because it's a temptation a person with forty cents can satisfy! I don't just tease – I deliver. And I do it over and over, a million times a year. I'm the man behind it all, the man behind a million donuts. Mrs Miles,' said Marty, his eyes flashing at her, his body emitting a sudden rush of heat as if from some tremendous internal oven, 'Mrs Miles, I am Donut Master!'

June swerved into the oncoming lane, then jerked back out of it again. Marty bounced around in his seat, his cap sliding down over his eyes. June's heart pounded. Donut Master. I'm dumping Dentist Man for Donut Master. And my next superhero, who will it be? Master Plumber?

'You all right, Mrs Miles? I guess I got a little overexcited there.'

'It was pretty strong stuff, Marty. I'm very impressed.'

'If you want, you know, you could call me by my secret name. Just work it into the conversation sometime. No one's ever really done that before. Not even my wife. She thinks it's . . . well, she thinks it's silly. She just doesn't get it.'

'Oh, but I get it . . . Donut Master.'

Marty sucked in his breath and looked quickly away. 'Wow.'

They were still driving on MacDade Boulevard. June had not yet turned off, committing herself to a definite direction. She could do a U-turn right now, zoom back to the parking lot, dump Donut Master and be home in fifteen minutes. And then do what? Sit on her ass until Dentist Man decides to show up? She looked over at Donut Master and sighed. Oh, well, a superhero in the hand . . .

'Marty,' she said.

'Yes, Mrs Miles?' he smiled.

'Right or left?' They were stopped at a red light.

Marty's smile faded back into his face. 'Aren't you in charge of that?'

'Well, physically, yes, since I'm the one steering the car. Beyond that, however, I think we have a fifty-fifty thing going here.'

'Can't we just keep heading straight and see where we end up?'

'Well, Marty,' she said, drumming the steering wheel with her fingers, 'MacDade will eventually take us to I-95 South, and if we keep going on 95 we should hit Florida in two days, and beyond that comes the Atlantic Ocean. Are we talking about going for a swim here?' The light turned green.

'Go straight a minute,' he said. 'Let me think.'

'Think away.' Was Lotty this ambivalent in her encounter with Henry? She thought of Lotty making the Taurus jiggle. Rhythmically, Margo said. No ambivalence in rhythmic jiggling.

Marty cleared his throat. 'Um, Mrs Miles, I got a kind of a question, if you don't mind.'

June turned her head and looked at him. He had his Dreami Donuts cap in his lap again, playing with it. She was picking up his body language. Cap on, Marty was Donut Master, in control, potentially daring. Cap off, he didn't know what the hell to do. She saw it then: he'd have to wear the cap in bed or he'd never get it up.

'I don't mind at all. What's your question, Marty?'

'Well,' he said, tracing his finger along the Dreami Donuts logo on his cap, 'well, what I'm not real clear on is why exactly you're here in this car with me. I mean, what it is your husband did so that, you know, here we are, you and me suddenly like this. You were really kicking at his office door back there, I mean really kicking.'

'That's a fair question.' June set her jaw and stared straight ahead. 'Without going into the lurid details, I found out that this morning, on his way to work, my husband had a public sexual encounter with one of his patients. An oral public sexual encounter.'

'With a patient?' Marty breathed.

'Yes.'

'But that flies in the face of professional integrity! Individuals like Dr Miles and myself, who occupy positions of responsibility and authority, are morally obligated not to exploit those who rely on us. I have never, and would never, touch a customer of mine. Dr Miles should not have touched one of his patients.'

'Touch is hardly the word I'd use to describe it.'

'Mrs Miles, touch is the only word you need to describe it. Anything beyond "touch" is practically criminal.' Marty jammed his cap back on his head.

'I was entitled to kick his office door, then?'

'You were entitled to burn his office to the ground.'

'Hmmm,' said June.

'Two crimes in one day.'

'What's that, Marty?' She had been imagining the flaming scene. Henry's beloved office burned to the ground. She grew warm thinking about it.

'Two crimes. Touching one patient and abandoning another. Me. Me and my poor aching crown. Your husband has lived some evil hours this May morning.'

'And he still has the whole rest of the afternoon ahead of him.'

'Mrs Miles, I have to ask. Have you ever come into my

Dreami Donuts? Have you ever, as best you can recall, been a customer of mine?'

'Never. You think Henry would have let me?'

'I had to ask. You understand that.'

'I understand and even appreciate it. Donut Master.'

Marty bit down on his lower lip. The pleasure of it, the pleasure of it. Donut Master. Who would've ever thought he'd actually get to hear someone call him by his secret name? Judy, his wife, never did. Said it was dirty, because he wanted her to whisper it to him while they did it. And now he was about to do it with Mrs Miles and he could almost feel her hot breath in his ear as he sat here thinking about it. Yes, there was absolutely no doubt she'd whisper his secret name. Maybe repeatedly. Maybe all she'd have to do was whisper it, over and over, and that would be good enough, they could lie there fully clothed and whispering is as far as it would go. He wouldn't be cheating on his wife in a technical sense. And hadn't she really been the one doing the cheating – cheating him out of a tiny harmless pleasure, the whispering of two words? Donut Master.

'Mrs Miles. Your husband deserves what we are about to do to him, doesn't he?' He looked straight ahead as he spoke.

'Yes, Marty, I believe he does.' And I deserve something, too. Something more than Henry gives me, something he so readily gives to others. I really deserve Jeffrey, but you'll do for now, Marty. You'll do for now.

'And my wife will never find out about this.'

'Never.'

'And this thing we are about to do, we will never do it again. Right?'

'Right.' But who really knows? She felt light-headed and suddenly hungry. So hungry she might have to do it again and again. Henry, stop me.

'I have a score to settle and you have a score to settle.'

'Right, right, right. We agree on all points,' said June. 'We agree about the need to score, but what we need to decide now is where to play the game.' Stop me.

Marty squinted. 'Video camera,' he said suddenly.

June pursed her lips. 'I don't do kinky,' she said evenly.

'Do you have one?'

'Did you hear me, Marty? Weird's not for me.' June's skin prickled. He's one of those psycho guys you read about. Someone you think you know: the donut thing and the silly paper cap are used to lull you, and suddenly he's in the car with you, talking about kinky sex in front of video cameras. They'll find my body somewhere. They'll find me in the dumpster behind Dreami Donuts, filled with Boston Creme and coated in powdered sugar, and then won't you regret Lotty Daniels, Henry? Won't you? A scream was working its way up out of her lungs when Marty quickly spoke again.

'No, no, no, Mrs Miles. Not for weird, for proof.' He saw the panic in her eyes, and he began to panic too. 'To show Dr Miles, don't you see? How's he going to know we've settled our score unless we show him? Wouldn't that have the greatest impact, actually seeing the two of us together? Do you think he'd ever molest another patient? Do you think he'd abandon another poor guy with an aching tooth? He'll come back to you, Mrs Miles, a humbled man. He will come back to you on his knees.'

June took a deep breath and let it out slowly. So Marty wasn't going to sprinkle her with sugar and dump her. 'Video camera, huh?'

'It's revolutionizing the way this country perceives reality.'

'It would certainly revolutionize Henry's reality.' Me with the donut man. Maybe she *would* have Marty sprinkle her with sugar, then have him slowly lick it off. That ought to make Henry think twice before he lets another patient suck his lollipop.

'Do you have a video camera?' asked Marty. 'I'm afraid they're still a bit out of my range.'

'Actually, we have two of them.'

'You have two video cameras.'

'Yes, I'm not really sure why, even,' she said vaguely. 'Henry said something about it being good to have a spare.'

Marty looked at her in disbelief. 'What kind of monster buys a second video camera for a spare!'

June spoke sharply. 'Hey, Marty, he's a monster for having sex with a patient and a monster for leaving you to suffer with your bad tooth, but I really don't think you can say he's a monster for owning two video cameras.'

Marty was silent.

'Besides,' she said, 'one of them is broken and in the shop right now. So does that make you feel better about a spare?'

'It's not fair,' said Marty.

'What's not?'

'That a man who's acted the way he has today should get to own multiple video cameras. To be awash in video cameras.'

'So tell him so while we do it in front of one of those cameras. Pile it on. Sic 'im, Marty. Go get him, boy.'

'You're making fun of me.'

'No, I want to make fun with you,' she said, running a finger down the side of his leg. 'So now we know where we're going, right? To the land where video cameras grow on trees. My house. We've decided? Yes?'

'I guess we have. You're right.' Marty touched his cap but didn't take it off.

June watched him. Phew, that was close. Now if she could just get him all the way home, out of the car and upstairs to the bedroom with that cap still on his head, she'd have it made. Wouldn't she?

Chapter 7

Henry bounded out of Fox Glen. His Ford Taurus seemed miles away in the parking lot. He ran toward it, panting. When he finally reached it, he dropped his keys twice before he managed to unlock the door and throw himself inside. He did not immediately start the car. Instead, he let his head drop slowly forward until it came to rest on the padded rectangle in the center of the steering wheel. He closed his eyes and imagined that the airbag had inflated itself for his safety and comfort, that his head was now engulfed in its pillowy softness. Ah, yes, like a woman's breasts – June's; finding comfort in the large and welcoming swell of her flesh. It was so warm. No one could get to him, no one could make him do anything he did not want to do. June's bosom would enclose him, would always be there for him, hidden in his steering column that would protect him from the crash of life.

He kept his eyes closed. It sure was warm. June's breasts, his daddy's dentures, nothing made sense. Why was it so warm? Henry slowly, dopily, opened his eyes. The hot May sun had been baking the car for over an hour. What was it, a hundred-fifty degrees in here? He rolled down both front-seat windows. The cool air sucked over him, reviving him. Somewhat. He'd almost ended up heat dead, like one of those dogs people are always leaving in summer parking lots. Dogs? Hell, children these days. He shivered, despite the heat. Had that been his intention, to end up dead, to use his beloved Taurus as a final resting place?

Hey. He looked out the window at Fox Glen. Do Daddy in right here, in the Taurus? Tell Nurse Speers he was taking him out for a day trip, get him in the car and then just walk away. It would be Daddy's decision after that. Either roll up the windows or not roll up the windows, it's up to him. I don't know, though – what would Daddy dying in here do to the upholstery?

I'm doomed. Doomed. Henry started up the car and headed down the long tree-lined drive out of Fox Glen. I knew I was doomed the second I opened my eyes this morning. But I know that every morning. Yes, but that's just my daily doom, doom I'm pretty sure I can handle. Today's doom is way out of my league. This morning Daddy was partway down The List. And now he's number one, right there at the top. Well, he can stay at number one, because I am never crossing him off, I'm not doing it.

I need to do something life affirming right away, he thought, as he came to the end of the driveway. The world stretched before him, chock full, he was sure, of things that were wonderfully life affirming. Only he couldn't think of any. He didn't have to go back to the office for the rest of the afternoon, that was sort of an affirmation right there. Wasn't it? Then again, working on patients might well have taken his mind off Daddy. Why did I tell Rita to cancel everybody? Maybe I'll run into a patient, like this morning with Lotty Daniels. I guess I could always repair Marty Marks's crown. He thought of Marty running down MacDade Boulevard after his car, spewing expletives. No, I'm not that hard up yet, let the little weasel suffer. Lotty, though. I could always make a house call. Henry thought about it. Then he decided no, bad precedent. Very, very bad precedent. He'd be hopping around from house to house for the rest of his professional life, tending to invalids and shut-ins. Not that people like that didn't deserve good dental care. But it would just be too distressing for him, too strange, the alien decor, the unfamiliar odors. Shut-ins have piles and piles of newspapers stacked to the ceiling and too many cats. They'd have big glowing stand-up radios blaring out shows that didn't exist any more. Too creepy. Besides, what was he thinking? Dentists don't make house calls. So why am I feeling so guilty? He was still paused at the end of Fox Glen's long driveway. Because of Daddy. He's going to taint everything. I'll never have a life-affirming moment until I give him his death-affirming moment. Which I refuse to do, so I'm fucked until he dies of natural causes, which will never happen because the minute he starts to slip, Nurse Speers will ship him off to County Hospital to be put on life-support, and then I'm triple-fucked because, like Daddy says, I won't ever have the guts to tell them to turn the machines off.

June, save me. Hold me. Let me rest my exploding head on your gentle airbag breasts. Henry turned on his left turn signal. Left will take me home to my wife, to my affirming partner who stands by me in all crises. Had they ever had to endure a crisis together before? Well, the twins, they were an ongoing crisis. No, I guess they were more of an intermittent hardship. Dental school was certainly a rough period, June working as a secretary at that Toyota dealership, her boss pinching her ass all the time. But that was more an ordeal than a crisis. Henry listened to the blink-blink of the turn signal. So, OK, this Daddy business was their first full-fledged crisis. The bonds of their marriage were about to be truly and severely tested. They would be tested and they would survive, the marriage would emerge stronger than ever. Henry got a little gulpy thinking about it. He thought of June all safe and snug and innocent at home, no idea of what was about to hit her. It will ruin her day, no doubt about it, jar the serenity of her domestic rhythms. But she will make it, I will make it, *we* will make it. This Daddy thing is almost a blessing, if you look at it that way. He's forcing us to grow, to face the unfaceable. Together. June and I. As one.

The turn signal blinked. Still Henry did not move. Hmmm. So I'm bringing June into this. Henry and June kill Daddy together. That would certainly test the marriage, now, wouldn't it? Better yet, what if he could convince June to kill Daddy all by herself? Henry licked his lips. For the first time since running out of Daddy's room, he felt a tiny surge of hope. Be still, my heart. Sure, it's slightly loathsome to consider asking June to do the deed. But if you think about it dispassionately, it makes perfect sense. Emotionally as well as financially. If I kill my own father, my flesh and blood, I will suffer deep psychological trauma, the whole Oedipal thing, and I may well never recover. June, on the other hand, will find it deeply upsetting, but she'll snap out of it eventually. So, trauma versus upset, she's obviously a better candidate for the job. And, in terms of preservation of the family unit, it's best I don't get directly involved. I bring in the lion's share of the income. Sure, June chips in with her three days up at the mall, but the burden of keeping the family afloat rests on my weary shoulders. And if I go down, the twins will follow right behind me. If it goes wrong with Daddy, if I get caught, if they give me – oh God – the electric chair, the twins might as well be sitting on my lap when they strap me in and pull the lever. But if it's June who gets caught – tragedy, yes, but financial ruin, no.

I'm a pig. Henry clicked off the turn signal and slumped back in the driver's seat. Daddy, look what you've done to my marriage. You've got me trying to figure out a way to get my wife to take my place on death row. I can't go home, not yet. If I go home, I know I won't be able to keep my mouth shut, I know I'll try to bring June into it. Why am I so weak? Why can't I kill my own father all by myself?

Hey, how about the twins? Henry flinched, but couldn't stop himself. If the twins help, they'd only be charged as minors and serve a stretch in reform school. Stop, Henry, stop. Protect your ears from Satan's whisperings.

What was Satan doing to his stomach? He felt his insides gurgle and flip, acidy twinges snake-licked the lining of his stomach. He had to get something in there right away or his body would begin to digest itself. Eat first, then go home. He looked at his watch. One-thirty. I deserve a little something after the morning I've had. A late lunch at Rio's in Morton, a big greasy burger with some life-affirming French fries. And after I get something in my belly, maybe I can think straight.

He suddenly sniffed the air around him. What a stink. The banana, he'd forgotten about it. When he began to wriggle out of his stained and redolent coat, his father's dentures clattered out of the other pocket and fell into his lap. He looked down at his crotch in horror. The dentures appeared ready to chow down on his manly parts, the upper teeth resting on one side of his fly, the lowers on the other. Daddy, no. Henry swatted at them and they bounced over on to the passenger's seat. He gunned the engine and screeched out on to Ripley Road.

He was nearing the outskirts of Morton before he was able to look at the dentures again. The best part of Daddy was lying there on the seat beside him. Even if they had attacked him. Well, they were just doing the bidding of their master. A flash of sunlight sparkled off one of the molars. Henry wondered if the dentures, his creation, were something immortal. After the winds of time blow away the dust of Daddy's bones, will the dentures remain? My work lasting longer than the Lord's, think of it. If the Lord had used polymers instead of tissue and bone, I might've been out of a job.

Rio's Diner. Henry pulled into the municipal parking lot just beyond it. He hesitated, then reached over and picked up the dentures, fitting the uppers and lowers back together. He placed them in the palm of his right hand and lifted them to eye level. He regarded them silently.

'Daddy, Daddy, Daddy,' he finally whispered.

The dentures smiled at him.

'What are we going to do with you?' We? June and I? Me and the twins? 'What am *I* going to do with you? Just me, by myself. Nobody else involved. You're my responsibility and no one else's.' Unless, maybe, someone else volunteers to help me. That wouldn't be my fault, would it?

The dentures smiled at him.

'Speak to me, Daddy. Let me off the hook. Tell me you plan to die peacefully in your sleep this very night.' Henry stared at the dentures. They smiled back at him – and then they began to do something more. Henry leaned closer, squinting, unsure. The dentures seemed to twitch. It felt like he was holding one of the twins' gerbils. But he didn't drop the dentures (as he had accidentally dropped the unlucky gerbil into the garbage disposal). No, he kept his hand steady and waited for what surely would come next. As Henry stared, a small gap began to appear between the upper and lower sets of teeth. The gap widened, the dentures slowly began to open. Really? No. They were opening, yes, to speak to him! To provide further guidance? To retract Daddy's demands? What? What? Or perhaps Daddy is dead, has just this moment died. Don't spooky things like teeth talking usually happen at the moment of someone's death? Here it comes: release me from my filial duty, O teeth of Daddy. Say I don't gotta do it. Talk to me, talk to me . . .

'Talk to me, dammit!' Henry shouted at the dentures.

Tap, tap, tap.

Morse code? thought Henry. Are his dentures going to chatter the message in dits and dahs?

Tap, tap, tap. 'Hey, buster. Yo,' came a voice outside the car.

Henry jerked around as a female hulk in a blue uniform tapped his window again.

'Yo, in there,' she said.

He clamped his hand over the dentures and quickly lowered them out of view. Then he slowly rolled down his window. 'Yes, officer,' he said, barely getting the words out. God, Daddy, you already got me in trouble with the police and I haven't even killed you yet.

'Not "officer", strictly speaking,' said the woman in uniform. She was trying to look past him into the car. Henry kept the dentures out of sight. The woman said, 'Senior Meter Reader Johnson.'

'Senior Meter Reader.'

She scowled at him. 'You got some kinda problem with that?'

'No, oh no. No problem with that, officer. I mean, Senior Meter Reader Johnson.'

She scowled some more. 'I seen them teeth. I seen you talking to them.'

'I can sort of explain . . .'

'I don't want no kind of trouble, of a tooth nature or otherwise, in my jurisdiction.'

'Your what?' said Henry.

'My jurisdiction, which is to say, this parking lot.'

Henry glanced around him at the parking lot, looked back at the imposing and glowering Senior Meter Reader Johnson and then out again at the parking lot. Were those rows of parking meters, or the tombstones of unlucky motorists who had crossed this hulking woman? He could feel her breath on his cheek. He could smell it, too. Abscessed gums, acute gingivitis?

He said, 'I assure you, I'm not someone who causes trouble.'

'You're someone who talks to teeth. And that sure looks like trouble to me,' she said. She pushed up against the car as she spoke. Henry could hear the metal of his door begin to buckle.

'As I said, I can explain—'

'Tell you something else that's trouble,' she cut in. She pointed at the parking meter in front of Henry's Taurus. 'You ain't put your dime in.'

Henry stared through his windshield at the blood red VIOLATION flag filling the tiny window of the parking meter. 'But I just got here. I didn't have time to put a dime in,' he squeaked.

'You had time to converse with your teeth,' she said.

'They're not my teeth.'

Henry watched as SMR Johnson's hand slid down to a canister attached to the side of her big black leather belt. My god, Mace. She's going to Mace me.

'Whose teeth you got there?' she said, real slow.

'My father's teeth. Not his real teeth. His dentures.'

'Where's your father?' She scanned the interior of the car.

'He's still alive,' Henry almost shouted.

'Who said he wasn't?' said SMR Johnson cautiously. She was slowly pulling the Mace out of its leather loop.

'I mean of course he's alive. And well, too. Very well and very alive. He's at Fox Glen. He's alive and he's at Fox Glen and he gave his dentures to me. Really, he did.'

'Don't he need 'em?'

'Just exactly what I said to him. "Daddy, you need your dentures." But what could I do?'

SMR Johnson was silent. Her fingers drummed the side of the Mace canister.

'And I'm a dentist,' Henry went on. 'So what you saw me doing in here was inspecting his dentures. For problems, you see. Maybe there's something wrong with them. That's why he gave them to me. To inspect and fix. Then I'll give them back to him and everything will be hunky-dory.'

'Let me see your license.'

'My driver's license,' he said, reaching for his wallet.

'Your dental license.'

'My dental license? It's not like on a little card or anything. I have a diploma on my wall at the office. And a framed thing from the ADA saying I'm a member in good standing.'

'Hmm,' she said, drumming her fingers. 'I don't know.'

'Wait, I can prove it!' cried Henry. He pointed up toward her frowning mouth. 'Something's wrong in there, isn't it? In your mouth. You're in pain right now. Am I right, am I right?'

SMR Johnson's hand came up from the Mace canister and touched the right side of her jaw. She wasn't scowling now. She was obviously impressed. 'Damn,' she said. 'How'd you know?'

'Because I'm a dentist. I can spot the signs.' Henry felt his chest swell. Ah, Dentist Man, ever vigilant.

'What'd you spot?'

He had her. 'Actually, it was more smell than spot. Your breath – now, how shall I put this – has the aroma of infection.'

SMR Johnson nodded gravely. 'Yeah, it's been real funky lately.'

'And something hurts. Tooth? Gum?'

'Both, kind of. Bleeding when I brush, too.'

'Mmm hmmm,' nodded Henry. 'Not good, not good. Do you floss?'

'Not lately. On account of the pain.'

'Better let me have a quick look-see.'

'Right now?'

'Sure. You need attention. I could not truly call myself a dentist if I did not render my assistance in a dental emergency.'

He thought of Marty Marks. Fuck him, the little car chaser. 'Come on now, don't be shy. Lean close here a minute.'

'If you say so. Doctor.'

Henry stuck his head out the window and SMR Johnson leaned close, very close, her big face so close to Henry's that Margo Zimmerman, who had just parked her car several spaces away, couldn't believe it. Believe her luck, that is. She could certainly believe that Henry Miles was making the moves on another woman from his Ford Taurus, because she had seen him do the same thing with Lotty Daniels less than four hours earlier. It was not as if she'd been following Henry, either. Out doing a little shopping and here he is again, about to do it with the meter lady. Margo had a sudden chilling thought. Is he somehow following me? Is he some kind of weirdo exhibitionist who is going to perform sex acts in front of me all day? Am I a victim? The gossip in her said stay and watch, the victim in her said go. She started up her car and backed out. She was frightened and happy. She had to get to a phone to call June. She had to call lots and lots of people.

Henry glanced up as a vaguely familiar red minivan sped out of the parking lot, then he returned to his inspection of SMR Johnson's oral problems. Jesus, she stank. Her breath was of the rancid canine variety. Reminded him – isn't it funny how a smell transports us? – of Punky, an old collie that had lived in his neighborhood when Henry was a child. Punky was the only dog he knew of that had been put to sleep because of the foulness of its breath. Mind on your job, Henry. He peered into the wide-open mouth before him.

He found himself wandering again. All these open mouths. How many have I looked into over the years? It's too much of too little. My world measures two inches wide, two deep, two tall – the size of a clenched fist. His own fist remained clenched around Daddy's dentures. Henry could feel the teeth beginning to bite into his palm. Daddy gnawing at him. He stared into SMR Johnson's mouth, into the familiar terrain of his world. He saw her open mouth before him and then saw all the open mouths of all the patients he'd ever worked on. Thousands of open mouths, a great chorus of open mouths. Ready to sing his praises, or release in unison a single howl that would shatter him? Henry trembled. Do they hate me or love me? Or not even care enough to do either? I am merely the instrument for their release from pain and decay. Chew me up and spit me out. Daddy, maybe *you* should kill *me*.

'What do you see in there?' said SMR Johnson, her words garbled. 'My tongue's starting to dry out.'

Henry peered dutifully into her rank cave, squinting as she breathed in his face. Punky the collie lived, reincarnated as a meter reader. When SMR Johnson spoke again, Henry heard the words come barking and growling out of her.

'Woof woof,' she said. 'Bow wow wow.'

'Uh huh, right,' said Henry. 'I think I see something.'

'Woof?'

'Yes. At the edge of number twenty-two, your lower right molar. Reddened at the gum line and a bit of drainage.'

'Bow wow, ow ow ow.'

'Yes, I'm sure it really hurts.' He gazed up from her mouth and into her eyes. SMR Johnson was not really Punky the collie. She's a human being. My patients are open mouths with human beings attached to them. I must remember that. I am not jaded, I am merely having a bad day. Tomorrow I will be happy again. I will love my patients and my patients will love me. Why wait until tomorrow? I will declare my love for SMR Johnson this instant and turn my day around. He smiled at her. He loved her.

'You're smiling at me,' she snarled.

'Yes.'

'I hate it when dentists smile at you.'

'I'm smiling because I . . .'

'Because I'm in pain.' She stepped back from the car.

'Oh, come on. Not true.'

'True.'

'That's a cliché. Dentists aren't painmongers and sadists.'

'Sure they are.'

'I want to help you. That's why I asked to look in your mouth.' Look how big she is. Muscly big and wearing a uniform and I'm pissing her off and I really don't want to. 'Please,' he whispered plaintively.

'You were diverting me.'

'No.' Squeak.

'And I don't intend to be diverted.'

Henry watched as her right hand moved slowly down to her leather belt again.

SMR Johnson said, 'I'm going to make you pay for this.'

'Please don't.' Would she beat him senseless with the Mace canister and then spray him, or spray him first and then beat him? She'll overdo it with the Mace and I'll be permanently blinded. Henry closed his eyes and waited for the blows to rain down on him.

'Begging won't help.'

Henry listened for the poisonous hiss from the Mace canister. Instead, he heard a rustling of paper. He sniffed the air gingerly. Still no Mace. He opened one eye. He opened both eyes. SMR Johnson was scribbling something on a pad. She tore off the sheet of paper and thrust it through the open window at him.

Henry read it. 'A citation,' he said.

'Meter violation, code 352-B. That's five dollars, Dr Dentist. You were too cheap to pay a dime, now you're gonna pay five dollars.'

'A citation,' he said again in happy disbelief.

'I wish I could write you another one for trying to bribe a meter reader with offers of free dental advice.'

'But I just looked. I never got to the advice.'

'Smart-ass dentist.' SMR Johnson jammed her pad back in her pocket and stood back from the car.

Henry kept his mouth closed.

'All right,' said SMR Johnson. 'There's one more thing I gotta say. The meter reader code of personal conduct requires that each reader will end his or her encounter with a member of the public with a statement of courtesy. It's required, understand what I'm saying?'

Henry nodded mutely. He tried to meet her eyes.

'So I'm gonna do it,' she went on. 'Because I obey the rules, whatever they are. Not like you, too cheap to pay your dime. So here it is, Dr Dentist. As required of all meter readers in the municipality of Morton, Pennsylvania, I want to say to you, Have a good day.'

Henry smiled weakly. It was over. But instead of leaving, SMR Johnson marched closer to the car and practically entered it through Henry's window. Their noses almost touched.

SMR Johnson whispered ominously, her Punky the collie breath watering Henry's eyes as her words blew into his face. 'That's what they make me say, but I'm gonna add this, coming personal from me, Gladys Johnson, to you. I hope you don't have a good day. I hope your day is shit with flies all over it, you understand? I hope your day crawls up your tight ass and lights itself on fire. I'm saying to you I think you're a crook for not putting your money in the meter, and a sonofabitch for tricking me into opening my mouth right here in the parking lot so you could laugh at me. So don't you even think of having a good day, Dr Fucker Dentist.' She slowly pulled her massive head back out of the window. Then, as Henry watched in terrified paralysis, SMR Johnson reached down to her leather belt and removed her Mace canister. But she did not lift it to his face and release its blinding spray into his eyes. No, she did something much, much worse.

'No!' Henry managed to cry out.

SMR Johnson smiled as she pressed the metal canister hard against the door of his brand new beloved Ford Taurus and scratched a thick line through the blue paint.

'Oh,' whispered Henry.

SMR Johnson continued to smile as she said, 'Have a bad day now, you hear?' and strolled away from the car and disappeared across the parking lot.

Henry hopped out of his Taurus and dropped to his knees in

front of the injured door. He traced his finger back and forth along the wound. He was proud of himself for not bursting into tears. If his very bad day was going to bring on tears, it would be now, at this moment. O dear little Ford Taurus, that any harm should come to you. You who exist only to protect me from vehicular death. I should have stopped her somehow, placed myself between you and that meter monster. But I was afraid, forgive me. I'll take you to Auto Body Magic on Baltimore Pike and get you touched up. And if you say that's not enough, I'll replace your door with a new one. He leaned over and lightly touched his lips to the scratch, then slowly raised himself. My bad day is so bad, I've become dangerous to my significant others. Is it mentally stable, Henry wondered, for me to think of my Taurus as a significant other? Is it mentally stable for me to think my father's dentures were about to open up and speak to me? Henry locked the car door and advanced toward the parking meter, its little red VIOLATION flag sticking out at him like a tongue.

'You and I both know,' he muttered to the meter, 'that I was going to put a dime in, that all this was completely unjustified.' He reached deep into his pocket and pulled out a fistful of change. He began pressing coin after coin into the meter. Henry was buying time. Lots of it. When the bloated meter wouldn't accept any more, he stuffed the remaining change in the two meters that faced the empty parking spaces on either side of his Taurus. He was not taking any chances.

It was two o'clock in the afternoon. He advanced towards Rio's Diner. He was battle-scarred and weary, but he was going to get his lunch. Lots and lots of lunch. Maybe that's all he'd do for the rest of the afternoon: sit on his ass in a booth in Rio's and eat lunch. Henry almost smiled. Hey, he thought, brightening, how bad can my day be if I can almost manage a smile? Zippity doo dah, up the stairs and into the diner we go. Yum, smell that grease, listen to those burgers frying on the grill. I love this place. Oh boy, an open booth and there's Gloria, my favorite waitress.

'Hello there, Gloria,' Henry greeted her, as he worked his way toward the booth.

The waitress stared at him blankly as she wiped her hands on her smeared smock. She lifted a thin finger, the fingernail of which was crusted with either old blood or ketchup, and pointed to a plastic name pin which hung akimbo above her left breast.

Henry tilted his head sideways to read it. The name on it was 'Janice'. 'Wow, you and Gloria really look alike,' he said. 'Sisters?'

Janice snorted. 'You sure you're in the right diner?'

'Well, Janice, you're probably new here,' said Henry. 'I'm kind of what you'd call one of the regulars.'

'And I'm kind of what you'd call the same waitress that's been working here for the last ten years.'

'I guess we're just two ships that keep passing in the night, then,' said Henry cheerily as he lowered himself into the booth.

'Whatever,' said Janice. 'You know what you want yet?'

Henry stared at the dishes and debris still sitting on the table. 'Actually, you think you could tidy up here a bit first?' he said.

She flipped her pad closed. 'I'll be back when you know what you want.'

Henry watched in disbelief as she moved down the crowded aisle to another table. *You're no Gloria, that's for sure. Gloria would've had this table sparkling clean. Only Gloria didn't work here, but that's not the point. The point is service, respect for the customer. Twice in the last ten minutes I've been abused by women who scribble things on little pads. What did it mean?* He stared at the mess in front of him. Ketchup everywhere, dripping off half-eaten onion rings, oozing out of a hotdog bun, congealing on the dishes and table. *This wasn't a meal, it was a murder scene. The person who did this didn't even finish his French fries, what a criminal. Ordered French fries* and *onion rings. This guy has a habit. An ugly habit.* Henry couldn't look at it any longer. He got up and eased himself over to an empty stool at the counter. *I could've made a scene with Gloria or Janice or whatever she calls herself, but I'm scened out for the day. I'm in* the right, but it doesn't matter. I was in the right with the meter reader too, and look how well I did with that one. The pad scribblers rule the world. Henry watched Eddy at the grill, tending to burgers and cheese steaks, checking the deep fryer hissing and popping at his elbow. After a minute, Eddy turned and surveyed the row of customers facing him along the counter and zeroed in on the new face, Henry.

'Janice get your order?'

'Eddy,' said Henry. 'How's it going? No, she didn't get me yet.'

Eddy came slowly over and leaned on the counter opposite him. 'Name's Bert, pal. What can I get you?'

Bert? Janice? 'Is this Rio's Diner?' asked Henry.

'That's the name above the door, pal. Look, I'm not feeling so good here, you know? Stomach virus or something, so I'm not really in the mood for the name game. You want to order something?' Bert grimaced as he spoke and rubbed his belly through his T-shirt.

Bert's face looked pale green. Sweat dotted his forehead. Or was he splashed with fat globules from standing over the grill all day?

'You really do look a bit under the weather.'

'You oughta be a doctor.'

'Well, I am a doctor. A dentist, actually.'

'Great, you're a lot of help to me then.' Bert winced again, burped in Henry's face, then gripped the edge of the counter and closed his eyes.

I'm going to let this fellow prepare my meal? Henry considered leaving, but his hunger was making him swoony. Besides, he figured, everything he wanted was fried, so that should be enough to kill this guy's germs. Jesus, though, look at him.

Bert slowly opened his eyes. It was obviously an effort for him to focus on Henry. Finally he whispered through his gritted teeth, 'What'll you have, pal?'

'Baco-cheeseburger with a double order of fries,' Henry said quickly.

Bert nodded, groaned, then turned back to the grill.

'Bert doesn't look so well, does he?' said an old fellow with a careful part in his white hair, sitting on Henry's right.

Henry nodded, 'Gee, I'll say.' Come on, Bert baby, just get my burger on the grill. Just get my order of fries and then you can go home for the day. Bert was moving very slowly. It was taking him for ever to get the wrapper off the hamburger patty. Come on, come on, drop it on the grill. Atta boy. A waft of greasy smoke enshrouded Bert's green face.

'I think maybe he's got that pig disease that was going around a couple of years ago,' said a guy wearing a Phillies cap on Henry's left.

'Swine flu,' said Henry, watching Bert pull the fryer basket out of the hot grease and begin to pour a bag of frozen French fries into it. Henry salivated.

'Yeah, right, swine flu,' the Phillies guy chuckled. 'Phew, I'll tell you.'

Don't tell me. Bert began to sway visibly as he lowered the basket of frozen fries into the boiling grease. He stood there looking down into the pop and hiss of the deep fryer. Then he closed his eyes. Henry tensed.

'I'll tell you, when I had that ol' swine flu,' continued the chuckling Phillies guy, 'I turned green just like ol' Bert there. And the thing was, I didn't have like a fever or the runs. But boy, I'll tell you what I did do. Every ten minutes for that first day I'd turn green and grab my guts and lean over whatever was handy and just—'

Vomit. Which was what Bert proceeded to do, into the only receptacle in sight: the deep fryer. Bert went up on his toes, then folded over and retched long and hard into the container of hot oil. The oil erupted in hissing protest, then slowly settled again as Bert staggered backward and slumped against a refrigerator.

Henry sat absolutely still.

The Phillies guy let out a whoop, jumped off his stool and slapped Henry on the back, as if in congratulations. 'Your

French fries! Right on top of your French fries! Can I call 'em or can I call 'em?'

Henry listened to the sizzle of the deep fryer.

'Watch out they don't try 'n charge you extra,' the guy said, jostling Henry with his elbow.

Janice hurried over and hustled Bert away. The rest of the customers were whispering excitedly, pointing to Henry and then over to the grill area.

The old fellow with the careful part in his hair had watched the entire episode in silence, too. Finally he turned slightly toward Henry and, dabbing his lips with his paper napkin said, 'You know, I believe I'd stay away from the French fries if I were you.'

Henry turned his head in the old fellow's direction.

The old fellow said, 'I'm a tuna salad man, myself. With just a dollop of mayonnaise. On pumpernickel, with a pickle on the side.'

'Sounds good to me,' said Henry numbly. He rose from his stool and prepared to exit. Nothing sounded good to him, especially if it was prepared at Rio's Diner.

'You're leaving?' said the old fellow. 'Lunchless?'

'Well, I've had a rather bad experience, don't you think?' Henry took another look at him. The face. Oddly familiar.

'Offputting, yes. I'd have to agree. Bert makes such a tasty tuna sandwich, though.'

Henry sniffed the air. The deep fryer continued to cook away. Who would turn it off? Who was in control here? Who, for that matter, was in control of his day? And who was this old fellow? Henry stared openly.

'Guess.'

'Sorry?'

'Who I am. You're looking at me, trying to.' The old fellow stood up and reached into his pocket for his wallet. He carefully pulled out four dollar bills and fingered around in a palmful of coins. 'Say, do you have a dime?'

'Sure.' Henry patted his pockets. 'Uh, actually, no. I used them up out there on my meter.'

'No matter. I'll use a quarter, though I hate to overtip. It's like being overlavish with praise. Doesn't build character.' He lined up his money on the counter. 'Figured me out yet?' he said over his shoulder.

'No, not yet.' Former patient? Henry tried to see into the old fellow's mouth. He often forgot faces, but never dental work.

The old fellow took hold of Henry's arm. 'I'll walk you out.' He pushed something crackly into Henry's hand as they walked. 'Here,' he whispered. 'Got you a couple of crackers for your lunch. Go ahead, take them.'

Mortified, Henry looked around him, then slipped the cellophane packets into his pocket. Hell, though, he thought, sticking out his chin, this place owes me a few crackers. He glanced back at the deep fryer. It had begun to smoke. He moved a little quicker toward the door. The old fellow was slowing him down. Henry tugged him along. I may be having a bad day, but I sure don't plan on having it end in flames here in Rio's. Should he warn the other diners? He stepped out into the safe, open air, the old fellow still hanging on to his arm. Sure, they all laughed at me, but do they deserve to burn for it? Probably not. How about just a few of them? Fire suddenly erupts and I rush back in and rescue the ones closest to the door. Not too dangerous for me and absolutely fabulous in terms of publicity. LOCAL DENTIST RISKS LIFE AT RIO'S ROAST. Photo of me, make sure I get them to mention my office address. The TV ghouls would probably show, too, if it was bad enough. Uh oh, what's that? He watched through the window as Janice hurried into view and snatched the fryer basket out of the smoking oil. Well, he thought. Too much to hope for.

'OK, here's a hint,' said the old fellow.

Henry had forgotten about him. 'A what?'

'Hint. A clue.'

'Were you a patient of mine, sir?' Henry really wasn't in the mood for hints and clues.

'You a doctor?'

'Sure. Well, yeah, you know, a dentist.' Why do I put myself through this?

'A dentist is certainly a doctor in my book,' said the old fellow. Henry looked at him. 'Really?' he said. 'You really think so?'

'Think so? I know so. You perform a laying on of hands just like an MD, only you do it in a more concentrated area.'

Henry beamed at him. 'Yes! That's right, I do!'

'Like a brain surgeon for the mouth.'

'Yes, yes!'

The old fellow let go of Henry's arm and took a step or two back. He cleared his throat and hummed once or twice, searching for his range. Then he took a breath and began to sing, 'Oh you are – who you think you are. Just hitch your dreams – to the nearest star.' He stopped suddenly and grinned at Henry. 'That's it,' he said. 'That's the clue.'

Henry raised his hand to his open mouth. He was six years old, sitting on the living-room floor in front of his parents' mammoth black and white TV. It was eight-thirty in the morning, he was tense with happy anticipation. A strum of music from the TV and then – that voice. 'Kids, what time is it?' Henry would answer that sweet voice right back with his own little voice, piping, 'It's time for *The Tommy Tooly Show*!' And Tommy would step on to the screen and sing, 'You are who you think you are.' And when he was done, he'd smile and say, 'I wonder what Bubbles and Zeke are up to?' And Bubbles and Zeke, the brother and sister marionettes, would come hopping on to the screen, followed by Bingo, their marionette dog. Henry would stare unblinking for the show's half hour, bathed in TV magic, stunned, his mouth hanging open – as it was at this exact moment.

'Now you know, don't you?' said Tommy Tooly.

'Is it you? Is it really you?' whispered Henry.

'Sure it is. You bet.'

'But you were canceled when I was twelve. I still remember that terrible day. My friends had stopped watching by that age, but not me. I never left you, Tommy. I don't think I ever would have.'

'Very sweet of you,' said Tommy Tooly.

'And then you were canceled,' Henry said again in a drifting voice. He had cried, when Tommy failed to appear on that awful Monday morning long ago. It was Henry's first experience with death. For surely Tommy had died. That was the only explanation for his sudden and terrible disappearance. Henry's TV daddy – dead. His real daddy, Stuart, tried to explain it to him.

'His show was canceled, taken off the air, that's all,' Stuart said. He looked at his son in exasperation.

'But where'd he go?' Henry asked plaintively.

'I don't know where they go.'

'Heaven?'

'Henry, I told you, Tommy's not really dead. You're twelve years old, you should be able to understand the concept of a canceled TV show.'

'But Tommy was with me all my life. Always,' whimpered Henry.

'The show was for six-year-olds. You should've stopped watching a long time ago.' Stuart lifted his newspaper to his face.

'But I loved him.'

'Jesus,' said Stuart from behind his paper.

'And he's gone, they killed him.'

'Oh, I see. He's not just dead of natural causes. They killed him, is that it?'

'And what about Bubbles and Zeke? What about little Bingo? Daddy, who will feed Bingo? Tommy always used to give him a snack on the show.'

'The dog was a marionette, son,' said Stuart, lowering his paper to stare at Henry. 'He was a puppet.'

'But he ate snacks.'

'Did you ever see him actually take a snack in his mouth and swallow it? No, right? Because he's a puppet.'

'I'm going to leave snacks out for Bingo every night in case he comes here.'

'Why would he come here?'

'Because he knows I love him.'

'Tommy Tooly's gone, son. Canceled. Let it go.'

But Henry wasn't listening. 'And Zeke and Bubbles. They'll be hungry, too. I'll have to leave lots of food in case they come around.' Bubbles, Zeke's marionette sister, was the one Henry was especially interested in having come around. Henry was hot for Bubbles. It had begun a few years earlier when he began to notice she looked really good in her costume. For reasons never explained on the Tommy Tooly show, Bubbles wore the form-fitting sequined outfit of a trapeze artist. Zeke wore a safari hunter's clothes. Sure, Henry knew Bubbles was made out of wood and she had lots of strings attached, but she had beautiful skin. Mahogany. And a pair of bright blue eyes and curly golden hair (his TV was black and white, but he was sure about the blue and the gold). The more interested in Bubbles he became, the lower down his perusing eyes wandered. Her little wooden breasts, so firm beneath the sequins, her curves, the astonishing swell of her backside. Zeke, the dumb cluck, never looked at her. OK, so he was her brother. But still. And Tommy was always the perfect gentleman. The perfect daddy. Not like his own real daddy, who thought he was a dimwit for leaving snacks out for Bingo. Which is what Henry did, for about a week, until it all began to fade – leave bits of broken cookies out on the back porch steps for Bingo and the corners of his peanut butter and jelly sandwiches for Zeke and Bubbles.

Henry looked at Tommy Tooly. So old now. How old was Bubbles? Fifty-five? Sixty? No, wait, marionettes don't age, do they? She was still the same, the sequins, the firm wooden breasts. She had waited for him. He cleared his throat. 'Say, uh, Tommy.' He looked down, pushed at some loose pebbles with the toe of his shoe.

'What can I do for you?'

That voice, that voice. It tugged at him still. 'Well, I was wondering . . .'

'Wonder away. The world is full of wonder, son,' Tommy said.

So up on life. He was then and he still is. He's the real thing. And look, his teeth. They're still real, too. My TV daddy has real teeth, my real daddy has fake teeth. What's it all mean? 'Well, Tommy, what I was wondering – this is silly, one of those memory lane things – but what ever happened to the marionettes? Bingo and, uh, Zeke and the other one, what was her name?' Bubbles, Bubbles, Bubbles, you filthy-minded liar.

'My lovely Bubbles,' said Tommy. His voice caught.

Henry glared at him. Say it isn't so, Tommy. Your interest in Bubbles was something more than fatherly?

'Lovely Bubbles in her lovely costume.'

Henry blushed, imagining it: Tommy reaching his fingers up under Bubbles's costume at the end of each show.

'You want to know why she was dressed the way she was?' said Tommy. 'That's one of the questions folks always ask when they run into me.'

No, I don't want to know, you puppet-pinching pervert. Henry nudged pebbles with his shoe again. I worshiped you, Tommy Tooly.

'Had to do with my sister,' said Tommy.

Oh, this should be great, thought Henry.

'I couldn't talk about it for years, but now I can.'

So go on the Oprah Winfrey show. Don't tell me your slimy secrets.

Tommy's voice went soft. Henry found himself straining to hear the words despite himself. 'Evelyn, little Evelyn, my sister, died when she was ten. Polio. I was just starting out on stage, you know, doing small town shows, putting together my variety act. I was twenty, Evelyn was ten.' Tommy's voice misted.

Henry looked away. Shame, shame, shame on you, Dr Henry Miles.

'Everything went on hold when Evelyn got the polio. My brothers and I stayed at her bedside night and day. Evelyn was so sure she was going to get better. On good days, she'd laugh and tell us stories, or talk about places she wanted to go, things she wanted to be when she grew up.' Tommy took a long breath. 'I can hear it now, her sparkly little laugh rising up out of her iron lung. I remember the way her golden curls would jiggle when she'd laugh, the way her blue eyes would shine so bright.'

Oh God, God, thought Henry.

'Evelyn loved the circus,' said Tommy, looking into the distance. 'She'd been only once in her life, we were so poor, you know. But boy oh boy, when she saw the lady on the flying trapeze, sparkling in her costume way up high – that was it, that was just what she wanted to do when she grew up. Join the circus, slip into that beautiful shining costume and fly.'

Stop. Please, please stop. I'm sorry I ever suspected you of puppet fondling and incest. Henry's eyes were filled to overflowing. He snuffled loudly.

'Well, in her own way, I suppose Evelyn finally did get to fly,' continued Tommy Tooly. 'If there is a heaven and angels have wings, then Evelyn got her wish. I hope they're golden wings, with lots of sparkles.'

'So Bubbles,' said Henry in a hoarse voice, 'is little Evelyn. Little Evelyn all grown up and turned into the lady on the flying trapeze.'

'Bubbles is Evelyn.'

Which means I spent all those years lusting after a ten-year-old girl in an iron lung. Henry, is there no end to your depravity?

'Yes, Bubbles was a great comfort to me.'

'Was?' Surely he still had her.

'Gave her away long ago. To a young girl in a foster home, after a charity show. It was her tenth birthday, you see.'

'You gave Bubbles away,' echoed Henry.

'Life is letting go, son. Letting go and moving on.'

If I live to be a hundred, I'll never be as wise as Tommy Tooly. He knew just how to put a thing. He zinged you every show with some little insight, some moral observation he'd slip inside your brain while he introduced cartoons or clowned around with Zeke and Bubbles and Bingo. Oh Tommy, why weren't you my real daddy? You'd never ask me to kill you. You'd never even want to die, I bet. When Tommy does finally die, he'll do it with pep and zest, maybe right in the middle of one of his charity shows. Sure, I bet he does shows for nursing homes. He'll be up there in front of all those wheelchairs, showing them how to wring the last precious drop out of life, telling jokes, doing a little soft shoe – and then he'll suddenly stop, clutch his chest, give them one last smile and a wink and keel over dead.

'Tommy, you know everything there is to know, don't you?' said Henry. His eyes were wide and his mouth was open, as if the Tommy he was staring at was coming to him from the screen of a TV.

'Less than you think,' said Tommy. 'Less than you think. For instance, I don't even know your name.'

'Oh sorry, right, sure.' Henry held out his hand. 'Henry Miles,' he said.

'*Doctor* Henry Miles,' said Tommy. 'I do know that.'

Henry shook his head and smiled. 'See that? You instinctively know how to make people feel good. You're wise and you're good.'

'Piffle.'

'Not piffle. I was at my best when I was watching your show. I loved you.'

'Hey, Henry,' said Tommy, 'that's why I quit doing the show. I decided it wasn't such a good idea for children to be loving me through a TV set.'

'You were canceled,' said Henry slowly.

'No, no. I quit.'

'No, you wouldn't suddenly strand all those children like that.'

'How else was I going to do it, Henry? Say goodbye to each kid, one show at a time?'

'It killed me. I worried so much about Bingo getting his snacks.'

'Bingo wasn't real.'

'You were my TV daddy.' There, I said it.

'Henry, Henry. See? That's why I quit. I was like Bingo. I wasn't real, either. Didn't you have a father of your own?'

'Sort of.'

'Sort of? You mean yes. And he was the real thing. Not like me.'

'You were wise and funny and nice.'

'Sure, for a half hour a day. It's easy to be anything for a half hour. You mean to say your own father didn't manage to give you a half hour a day of wise and funny?'

'Not like you.'

'You took me too seriously, Henry.'

'Just what my father said the day you were canceled. Quit.'

'Those were wise words.'

'OK, so he squeezed out a few words of wisdom every now and again.'

Tommy Tooly looked at Henry silently. He shook his head. He sighed. 'The unresolved father thing. I should never have gone on the air. Henry, I wasn't anybody's father. Not even off camera in real life. I never even married.'

'Sure you were. You were Bubbles's and Zeke's father. And mine.'

'You had your own father, Henry. I'm sorry it didn't go the way you wanted it to. I'm sorry he passed away before you got a chance to resolve . . .' Tommy stopped when Henry cleared his throat and kicked hard at a pebble.

'Um,' said Henry.

'He's still alive,' said Tommy.

'You know the unresolved father thing?' Henry said, the words of confession rushing out of him. 'My father is in a nursing home and he wants me to resolve him and I want to keep him unresolved. Unresolved is really best, I think.' See, you would never have put me in this position, Tommy, if you were my father. Henry blinked, getting it now. Which is why, he thought, Tommy looks so good compared to Stuart. You never have to resolve your TV daddy. The perfect eternal father. Stuart, on the other hand, Stuart who has not really been such a bad daddy

– his only crime is that he's real and that he demands resolution.' Henry lifted his eyes to Tommy, looking to him as he might have thirty years ago, waiting for Tommy's guiding TV voice to enter him. Speak, Tommy. Henry heard himself ask in a twelve-year-old voice, 'You always know best, Tommy. Tell me what you think I should do.' Speak.

'Well, I'll tell you, Henry. Now, this is just one old man's opinion, but unresolved is never best.'

Henry thought he might faint. He could barely get the words out of his dry mouth. 'Are you sure? I mean, resolving Daddy seems so, seems so . . . dangerous.'

'Resolution is risky, yes, maybe even like you say, dangerous. Not resolving, however, is fatal.'

Doesn't he have it backwards? Henry felt his brain contracting and expanding within his skull.

'Go to your father,' said Tommy, placing a hand on Henry's trembling arm. 'Go to him as soon as possible and do whatever it is you have to do. Confront your fears, do what may even be dangerous to do. Resolve the situation.'

Tommy Tooly wants me to do it. Stuart Miles wants me to do it. My two daddies want me to do it – what son on this earth could be expected to resist the compelling force of two daddies wanting resolution? The pressure inside his skull suddenly eased. I'm there, thought Henry, floating upward. I'm going to do something. I'm going to take charge. This day has always been waiting for me. My life has been a list of unconfronted terrors. Yes, The List! Growing every day, waking up to it, going to bed with it, my list of fears, the things I could never do anything about: urban decay, Aids, toxic waste and, today, the toughest of them all – Daddy. But this time, by God, I'm going to do something. I don't know how, but before the sun goes down on this day, I will do something. I'll make my daddy proud. Dead, but proud. Tonight I come home to my wife a man. A true Dentist Man – and every other kind of man you can think of!

Henry wasn't nervously pushing pebbles with the toe of his shoe any more, he was pawing the asphalt parking lot like a bull.

'Yes, Tommy, I'll do it! You are absolutely right. God, I feel like a million bucks.'

Tommy stepped away from him. 'Atta boy, Henry. You've done the hard part already. You've made a decision.'

Henry grabbed Tommy's hand and shook it hard. 'I gotta run, Tommy. I gotta get moving on this thing.' He turned toward his Taurus.

'Wow,' Tommy marveled. 'Resolution is the key. Go ahead, boy. Resolve it.'

Henry shouted over his shoulder, his closed fist punching the words upward to the sky, 'Resolve! Resolve! Resolve!' He didn't even notice the long scratch on his car as he hopped inside and raced off into a world that was finally and utterly in his control.

Chapter 8

June and Marty did not speak for the fifteen minutes it took to drive from MacDade Boulevard to June's house on Dickinson Avenue. June was too busy concentrating on the logistics. Marty was simply too petrified. June glanced at him every so often to make sure he was keeping his Dreami Donuts cap on his head. He was.

'Listen, Marty,' she said, when they were about to turn on to Dickinson.

He almost yelped when she broke the silence. He hadn't been looking at her and she hadn't spoken for so long he was hoping she had somehow vanished. He'd made a big mistake getting into the car. It all happened so fast and it had a perverse and driving logic to it. One minute I'm chasing the husband's car, the next minute I wind up in the wife's car. There were a thousand details to this thing and he couldn't seem to think fully through a single one of them. Like, what if Dr Miles suddenly comes home? He's out there somewhere, a rogue dentist roaming the town in search of sex acts. And, Jesus, what if he's *not* roaming and he's home and we walk in on him? And what about my wife, what if Judy finds out? Everybody at Dreami Donuts saw me climb into this car. This is beyond me, this is not how I spend my day, this is not batter and raspberry filling and vanilla icing with chocolate jimmies. And on top of everything, I am expected to perform with a woman I don't even know – on camera!

'Marty, you with me?' said June.

On camera. I can't even work up a proper smile when Judy tries to snap me with the Instamatic. Ten minutes from now I'm supposed to get an erection with a zoom lens aimed at my penis? Not only is this whole enterprise fraught with danger, but I'm about to be humiliated on the most basic male level. As if on cue, Marty's penis began to contradict him. He stared down in amazement at the sudden bulge. The thing felt huge, his pants could not possibly accommodate it. Whose penis was this?

June stared where he stared. 'What do you think you're doing?'

Marty covered himself with both hands. 'I – I don't know.'

'Well, get rid of it. Nothing happens until the camera starts rolling.' *I am not into car sex like Henry.*

But still it grew, as if the mention of video performance gave life to it. *Has this been my calling all along,* thought Marty, *and I never knew it? Porno film performer? What if my erection grows and grows like Pinocchio's nose, what if it never goes down and I wind up seeking treatment in an emergency room somewhere? Is there a treatment? Will it require a scalpel?*

June squinted through the windshield. 'All right. We have to get you into the house without being seen.'

He instantly wilted, maybe even shrank a size or two below what he'd started out with. The danger part. They were already at the danger part. 'Without being seen,' Marty mumbled numbly.

'That's how these things usually go, I think,' said June.

'Please,' said Marty. 'I'm out of my element. Sneaking around – it's something you read about, or see on TV . . .'

'It's something you better do right now.' She placed her right hand on the back of his neck and forced him down in his seat.

'What are you doing!' He struggled, but she held him down.

'Calm yourself. This is my street, Marty. We're coming up to my house. You think I want to get caught with the Donut Man? Master, I mean.' *It's Dentist* Man, *Donut* Master. *Mustn't bruise their fragile egos, in the heat of passion call out the wrong name. Heated by whom,* she thought. *Because of Henry I'm here with Marty who should be Jeffrey. Or Henry? Henry, will you and I ever touch again, let alone generate heat? Even before all this, we never exactly scorched the sheets.* She bit her lip. *We could have rekindled something, there were enough sparks there to* start a small fire if we'd really tried. But you let Lotty Daniels's hot mouth raise the temperature of your thermometer. June's mercury rose thinking about it. I'm going through with this, Henry. You started it.

Caught, thought Marty frantically, she used the word caught. Criminals get caught, not law-abiding donut makers. Is that what I've suddenly become, this one short car ride has turned me into a criminal trying not to get caught? But I haven't committed a crime. Yet. He stared at a section of his zipper. The thing seemed to grin up at him with its notched silver teeth. 'I don't want to get caught,' he pleaded. Her hand was still pressing down hard on his neck.

'You won't. Just keep like you are until I pull into the garage. When I close the garage door, we can slip into the house straight from the garage and never be seen.'

Slip into the house. Never be seen. Caught, caught, caught. Marty blurted from his hunched over position, 'I'm not the criminal, your husband is!'

'Don't shout, Marty. You want someone to hear you?' June rolled up her window as she pulled into her driveway. Next door, in his driveway, Jeffrey Lyons still worked on his motorcycle. Sweat glistened on his broad young back. June looked down at Marty in his donut cap, cowering in the seat beside her as she waited for the garage door to open. She looked across the way at Jeffrey again. To think her morning had begun with fantasies of Jeffrey's T-shirts, that at one point she'd actually had Jeffrey in her house. Marty twitched and trembled beside her. And now I've ended up with this donut. Curled over on himself, Marty did seem to be turning into a donut.

'Are we in the garage yet?' he whispered. 'Can I sit up, my back's killing me. I've got a slipped disk.'

Of course you do, Marty, of course. Jeffrey has the most fantastic back on the planet Earth and you, my little Donut Mouse, have a slipped disk. 'Hold on, we're almost in,' she said out the side of her mouth so no one would see her speaking.

And once in, of course, he'd never get out. Marty tried not to hyperventilate. She's got to let me straighten up, he thought dizzily. I need to get some oxygen to my brain. I've got to tell Mrs Miles to turn this car around and take me back to Dreami Donuts. But when he straightened up to speak, he saw the garage door slide closed behind the car. All was darkness. Marty was afraid of the dark. He groped for June.

June slapped at his hands. 'Hey. Nothing happens 'til we start the camera rolling.' She scooted away from him. 'The stupid light's supposed to come on in here when the garage door opens. Never does, though.'

Marty held his breath until she opened her car door and the overhead light blinked on. He began to tremble when she got out of the car.

'Take me back,' he called to her.

She poked her head inside the car. 'Say that again?'

'Back to where I belong.'

She saw then that his Dreami Donuts cap was in his lap. Uh oh.

'I don't belong here.' Marty stared at her. June's face was lit by the overhead car light, but the rest of her body was out there somewhere in the vast darkness of the garage. She was trying to tempt him into the darkness with that body. He whinnied like a frightened pony.

She resisted an overwhelming urge to throttle him. 'Marty, put your cap back on. You'll feel better.' It was not as if they had all day to do this dance. It was three p.m. Ed had baseball after school and Fred had band practice. So she and Marty had been handed a little time, but not much. She put one knee on the driver's seat and reached for Marty's cap.

Her lunge toward him from out of the dark was too much for him: Marty closed his eyes and screamed.

June froze, her hand hovering above his cap. Then she snatched it up and crammed it on top of his head. 'Marty, Jesus, what are you doing?' If he opened his mouth to scream again, she'd belt him. Who had heard?

There was a great banging on the outside of the garage door. 'Mrs Miles, you in there? You OK?'

Jeffrey Lyons had heard. She cupped her hand over Marty's mouth. Jeffrey to the rescue. God, how she wished. 'Hi, Jeffrey. I'm OK in here. Don't break my door down, please.'

Marty sat rigid in his seat. The banging had stopped, but it still rang in his ears. It sounded like a gorilla on the other side of that garage door. He understood now that there was no escape, he'd have to go inside the house with Mrs Miles. If he didn't, the gorillas on the other side would get him. He tried to speak but she still had her hand over his mouth.

June whispered to him. 'Marty, you scream again and you're a dead man, got it?' When he nodded yes repeatedly, she said in a loud voice, 'Just bumped my knee on the lawnmower, Jeffrey. Didn't mean to carry on like that. But I'm fine now. Really.'

'You sure, Mrs Miles? I'll be glad to help.'

'I'm sure. See you, Jeffrey. Thanks for being a good neighbor. Bye.'

There was a pause. 'OK then. Bye.' Another pause. 'But call across the way if you need me.'

I need you, Jeffrey. 'All right. I will. Thanks.'

'Bye, Mrs Miles.'

'OK. Bye.' She listened as Jeffrey walked off. She waited another minute, then released Marty.

He clawed for the door handle. 'Take me inside. Please. Now. Quick.'

Bingo. Wearing that cap does it every time. Maybe I should staple it to his head. 'All right, Donut Master,' she said. Must remember to call him that. The things we do for love. 'All right, follow me, Donut Master, around the car, watch out for the work table, that's it.' She guided him through the dark. He bumped and stumbled toward her, trying to see by the dim light coming from the interior of the car. The ordinary objects in the garage looked to Marty like demons crouching in the dark, waiting for him to lose his way. At last he reached her. He wrapped himself around her, his heart thumping wildly in his chest.

'Mrs Miles.'

'Marty. Off.' She peeled him off. 'Follow me.' She found the entrance door from the garage to the house. Light blazed into the garage. She stepped into the house, pulling Marty in after her. 'That stupid garage light. I'm gonna kill Henry when he gets home for not taking care of it.' She considered what she had just said. 'Of course, I'm going to kill him when he gets home anyway, aren't I? I don't think there'll be enough hours in the day for the number of times I plan to kill him,' she said. Then added, 'Do you suppose he will come home?' What if he did? What if he didn't? Were those the only choices? She wanted another one. She wanted the one she couldn't have: the clock moved backwards to this morning, to breakfast with her family, to a world with people and rules she understood. She stared at Marty as he walked stiffly around her kitchen afraid to look at or touch anything. Who is this person? she thought. What are the rules? The rule is, no rules. She felt her skull open and her brain float up and away. This morning, breakfast with my loved ones. This afternoon, fucking on videotape with a stranger. Margo, my gossipy friend, I am sorry you are not here to witness what I'm about to do. If you watched, then went home and called me on the phone to tell me what you just saw me do, I wouldn't believe you. And if I didn't believe you, that's because it couldn't be true, yes? So Marty, go home, it is not possible we are going to fuck. It's not true. Go away, shoo, out of my kitchen, enough of this.

'May I have a drink?' said Marty. He shifted back and forth from one foot to the other.

Shoo, thought June.

'Drink?' Marty tried again. She was looking at him weirdly. He tried to imagine her as she would be ten minutes from now. Naked. He couldn't make his mind penetrate her clothing. Well, that's because this has to do with justice, he reminded himself, not sex. Did he hear his penis snickering up at him from behind its zippered door? But if I can't imagine this woman naked, I must be right. Justice will prevail. Either way, though, we still wind up in bed together, don't we? He swallowed thickly. 'Drink,' he repeated loudly.

June came to. 'Drink, oh right, yes. Drink.' She moved for the refrigerator. 'OJ? Hawaiian Punch? Prune juice?'

'No, real drink,' said Marty stiffly. 'Drink of alcohol.'

'Oh,' she said. 'Not too early for you?' She smiled vaguely. 'What am I saying? Today we break the rules, right? Everybody gets to break the rules. Beer, Marty?' She started for the refrigerator again. 'I believe my former husband drinks the occasional Rolling Rock.'

'Hard stuff,' he said like a robot. He hadn't drunk the hard stuff since college. He hadn't slept with another woman besides his wife since college, either. He tried to recall if hard alcohol and women besides his wife had been fun in college. Why didn't it feel like it was going to be fun now?

'Hmm. Hard stuff, huh? Boy, you really do want to break the rules.' She put a finger to her lips. 'I think we only have some vodka, or maybe a little gin. Henry's the kind of guy who likes to remain in control, you know? Sexual control, though, I guess he was willing to make an exception there, right? Right. OK, follow me to the hard stuff. Better look for the video camera, too.'

They moved into the living room. Marty walked carefully, not touching a thing. Fingerprints. His. Criminal. Police. Jail. No donuts in jail. Suicide. Where was that vodka? Could he drink from the bottle without getting his fingerprints on it? Maybe if he held it with his elbows.

June searched a small wooden cabinet in the corner of the living room. 'Voilà! Vodka. This is your lucky day, Donut Master.'

He wished she wouldn't call him that any more. It was obvious to him now that he was master of nothing – especially not his own fate. That's why Judy refused to call me Donut Master. She saw me for what I am. Donut Dupe. Here I thought I was about to get revenge on Dr Miles and it's he who's still getting me! I'm trapped in his house. There are gorillas patrolling outside. My own penis is laughing at me. This is revenge, this is justice? He snatched the bottle of vodka from June and lifted it to his upturned mouth. Fingerprints be damned! He drank mightily.

June stepped back, her eyes wide. When he finally lowered the bottle, she said, 'Guess you'll pass on a glass, huh?' She squinted at the bottle. He'd emptied it. 'You just finished half a bottle of vodka. You sure they don't call you Vodka Master?'

The Dreami Donuts cap had slipped forward on Marty's head and now partially covered one eye. He lifted the bottle again and held it above his open mouth. The remaining drops slowly fell on to his tongue and mustache. He gulped hungrily, then lowered the bottle and searched the room with the eye that was not covered by the cap. 'Got any more?' he said.

'Marty, you just drank more than my husband puts away in a year.'

'Priming the pump.' He blinked his one eye at her.

'No more primer for you.'

Marty belched. 'Now I have room for more.'

'That was vulgar. Vulgar does not appeal to me. It's important that you appeal to me, at least marginally.'

Marty nodded without hearing her. 'I'm ready.' He stepped toward her, then stopped. He looked down at his feet. *Are those my feet? They seem very far away.* He lifted one foot tentatively. *They seem to be connected to my legs, though. If these are in fact my legs. Vodka is very tasty. Vodka would be very tasty in my donuts. Vanilla vodka creme. Be a big seller. I would buy them. If these aren't my feet, then whose are they?* 'I'm ready,' he repeated, only now he wasn't quite sure what he was ready for. *To find his missing feet?*

'Oh, that's a lovely line. "I'm ready." Is that the one you use on your poor wife?'

Marty blinked. 'My wife? She's just there. We don't talk, we just do it. Know what I mean?' Marty knew what he meant, for about ten more seconds, then he didn't know what anything meant. A great uncentered warmth rushed through him.

'You are grotesque. My husband was right to abandon you. At first I was feeling sorry for both of us. Now I'm feeling sorry just for me. I don't think I want . . .' She stopped and watched Marty. He slowly sank to his knees in front of her. 'Begging won't help,' she said uncertainly.

Marty lifted his face to hers. It seemed to him that she was a building, a female building, a great big female building and he could barely see to the top of her. He looked up at June's breasts hovering way above him, only he didn't know they were breasts. He thought they were some kind of overhang, some kind of ledge on this great big female building. If he could just reach up to that ledge, if he could get a grip on it, he would be OK.

June slapped his wiggling fingers away. 'Hands off, asshole!'

Marty nodded gravely at her. A look came over him, an understanding of something he had to do. He brought both of his hands to the side of his head and removed his Dreami Donuts paper cap. Then he folded it as best he could and laid it gingerly on the rug to the left of June's feet. He stared at the cap a moment, then fell face forward on to it and rolled on his side with a deep groan. He did not move again.

June nudged him with her toe. 'Marty?' She nudged again, harder. 'Donut Master?' He smiled once, but that was all. 'Marty, you've passed out on my rug. You can't do that.'

Marty lay as inert as a boulder in the center of her living room. In fact, he was a smallish sort of man, but passed out on the floor he seemed positively geologic. So now what do I do? She continued to nervously nudge him with her foot. Guess I could still get the video camera out and tape him. Boy, that would shock the pants off Henry, now wouldn't it? A tape of a sleeping donut maker. Some revenge. Some wild afternoon fling. And won't it be fun explaining all this to the twins? She nudged Marty a hard one and he flopped over on to his back. His eyes flickered and he mumbled.

June went down on her knees behind Marty's head, placed her hands under his armpits and lifted. She could do it. She could drag him out to the car. And then . . . who cares? Drop him off behind Dreami Donuts? Sure, next to the dumpster. That's where I first spotted him, that's where I'll put him back. The video camera was a wonderful revenge, Marty, I'm sorry we don't get to use it.

Wait. June started to pace on the rug in front of Marty's body. Wait, wait. She smiled. God, this can still work. Yes, it's much better! They do it all the time, don't they, actors on camera? Fake the sex. Marty's body is here and that's all I need. Simulated sex, no need to protect myself from the Donut Master's creme filling. I didn't want to do it with him anyway. Or, I did and I didn't, but it's all moot now, isn't it? Except the part where I teach Henry a lesson. She trotted upstairs to get the camera.

June found the video camera, then moved quickly into their bedroom. She was flushed and excited. She was about to do something wicked downstairs, wicked and sexual, but of course not sexual at all. What if Marty came to while she was writhing away on top of him? Too wild. She shivered. Should she be on top, or on bottom? Which would pain Henry more, his wife being dominated, or his wife dominating? Hey, dominatrix. Should she wear leather? Ooh, God, listen to me. But all I have is that floor-length suede coat Henry gave me last Christmas. Must keep this simple and to the point. OK, what do I need? She grabbed a handful of underwear from her dresser. Scatter it around, make Henry ponder the sexual chaos that took place in his living room. On the rug. In the daylight. She grabbed a sheet off the bed and hurried downstairs.

Marty hadn't moved. June's skin prickled. Breathe, Donut Master. Come on, inhale. He drank that vodka way too fast. She moved closer. They can die doing that, go alcohol toxic. Shit, gotta get my story straight. He burst in here. No, wait, he kidnapped me because my husband wouldn't give him an appointment – breathe, Marty, come on – kidnapped me, and Jeffrey Lyons's my witness because he heard a commotion in the garage and tried to come to my rescue. Then what? Then Marty forces me inside and I grab a bottle of vodka and whack him over the head with it and . . . and his mouth is open and a lot of it winds up going down his throat. At that moment, Marty jerked his leg and smiled stuporously, as if in response to June's ridiculous scenario. She wanted to hug him in relief. No, Marty Master, I'm going to do something even better, although you'll never even know it happened. She dragged an end table to within a few feet of him, then put books and magazines under the camera (Henry's books and dental magazines) until she was at the right height and angle to focus on Marty's sodden, inert mass. Zoom in a little, oops, go back. Perfect.

Now what? She still clutched the underwear. All right, have to spread this around. She tossed the underwear into the air, and the wad bounced off the ceiling and landed in a pile directly on Marty's upturned face. He made a low sound and began to munch softly in his sleep. June watched as he pulled a pair of her pale blue panties into his mouth like a goat. She leaned over him to snatch the pile off his face. She got everything but the blue panties, which Marty clenched tightly in his teeth. She tugged. Marty, though unconscious, tugged back. It continued this way until June put her foot beside his head and jerked with all her might. She tumbled backwards clutching the panties. She held them up. Daylight shone through a gaping hole. She watched his lips close over a ragged piece of blue as he continued chewing, until at last he swallowed with a thick gulp. Donut Beast.

She dropped the panties back on to his face. This time he did not react. Good, I'll be safe. Now how do I do this? How much nakedness would this involve? She spread the sheet over Marty. Too high – it had slipped over his face. She studied the effect. She'd changed Marty from a partner in a sex scene into a victim at a crime scene. Even when she pulled the sheet away from his face, he still remained corpselike. Oh well, I've slept with worse, right, Henry? She tugged the sheet completely off him. Guess I better undress him. She unbuttoned his shirt and peeled it off of him. This was the first man since her marriage to Henry she'd touched with sexual, or even simulated sexual, intent. She felt no thrill, however, only a faint anatomical curiosity.

Now me. She looked over her shoulder at the video camera, its one eye open and gazing directly at her. She turned away shyly. The thing wasn't even on yet – would she be able to perform when it whirred to life? She had to. She did a 360 of the living room. Curtains closed, no peepers that she was aware of. She cleared her throat nervously and began to unbutton her blouse.

'Marty?' she whispered, hesitating at the last button.

Marty licked his lips as if in anticipation, but remained otherwise unresponsive.

June let the blouse slide off her shoulders to the floor. She knelt beside Marty in her bra and slacks. Maybe this was naked enough. She looked back at the video camera. It seemed to raise an impatient eyebrow over its waiting eye. All right, already. She sat back on her bottom, lifted her legs in the air, and wiggled out of her slacks. She trembled in the suddenly cool air. Or was it hot air and she was shivering with fever? No, it wasn't hot or cold. Still, she was shaking.

'This is silly,' she said out loud. She reached for her pants, then dropped them back on the rug again. Perhaps she should just turn on the camera and lecture him. No, one picture is worth a thousand words, isn't that what they say? So that means one videotape must be worth . . . Oh, the hell with it, math was never her strong point. One videotape must be priceless, infinitely valuable in the payback department. Any time Henry thinks of cheating on me again, I'll just pop this video in the ol' VCR as a reminder. Hmm, thought June. A reminder? Does that mean I'm taking Henry back after what he's done to me, that I'll have him around to remind? Or do I break up the marriage, sentence the twins to shuttling back and forth between the divorced parents and sentence myself to (she shuddered uncontrollably) the dating life again? She looked down at Marty in despair, as if she was already on her first date and this was how her evening was ending, with her date drunk and snoring on the living-room rug. No way. I save the marriage, but this tape is Henry's punishment and his eternal education.

She reached her arms behind her and unhooked her bra. She slowly peeled it off. Marty moaned softly, as if he could see through his closed eyelids. The sound of him made June feel unclean. But this is what it's all about, right? Unclean acts.

Time to think mechanics here, June. Lights, camera, action and all that. Marty wasn't going to be supplying any of the action, that was for sure. It was up to her. She'd have to give the performance of her life. At least she wasn't totally unprepared. She'd had a little practice faking it, hadn't she? With Henry, the times he'd interested her about as much as Marty there, the times he was merely a body under her, or over her, and she'd had to pretend. She had to, or Henry pouted, or questioned her to death, as if the questions themselves, if he asked them relentlessly enough, would bring her to orgasm.

OK, thought June, I know what to do, but whether I can do enough for me *and* Marty is the question. He's going to look pretty lumplike. I'll just have to keep the audience riveted on me, go for an Academy Award. Make love to the camera, isn't that what they say? Oooh, she thought, curiously warming to the idea.

So. Turn on the camera. How? Marty's here, the camera's over there. I can't do it with my toe. And I can't just turn it on and run back to Marty. Or maybe I can, not run, but walk. Yes, my big bare ass will be the first thing the audience, I mean Henry, sees. It'll fill the screen, he won't be able to take his eyes off it, as I work my way back to Marty. And before he can get over the shock of my bare butt right there in front of him, I'll already be going at it with Marty. He won't even notice the transition, he'll just be sitting there with his mouth open thinking, That's June's ass, that's June's ass, there'll be a one-minute delay where I can start in with Marty, get the Donut Master looking like he's alive and participating, before Henry kicks into, Oh my God, she's fucking some guy, she's fucking some guy.

Right. So. Guess I have to take my underwear off to do all that. When my underwear comes off, I'll be totally naked. I'll have crossed the line. Or do I cross the line when I turn on the camera? Face it, June, you crossed the line when you first spotted Marty over by the Dreami Donuts dumpster and thought, there, he's the man. The deed was done and now this part is a mere physical extension of the thought. Off with the undies. She held her breath and stepped out of them. The house did not collapse, Marty did not move a muscle. And I'm not even really screwing him, so calm down.

June stood naked above him. She leaned over and adjusted the sheet, pulling it up to just above his pants. With his shirtless upper body exposed, he gave the impression of: Guy, naked, waiting to fuck your wife. She touched a hand above her left breast and felt her heart skip and pound. She hadn't felt this excited since . . . since that first time with Henry long, long ago. I'm getting a little confused here. Don't think. Perform.

Lights, she thought. Need more of it. She moved around the living room, turning knobs and flicking switches.

Camera. She went over to it and arranged herself so that her ass was two inches away from its ready eye. She had to half turn and reach behind her to get to the PLAY button.

And . . . action. She hit the button and felt an electric surge zing through her entire body, as if it were herself she had turned on. The camera clicked and hummed and adjusted itself as it came to life. The autofocus lens raced back and forth frantically attempting to get a fix on her ass. She envisioned Henry's frantic attempts to focus, too. The pink blur of me, thought June, and then my voice—

'Marty,' she called out loudly. 'You mean you want to do it again?'

Move, move. She got herself to step forward. Not like a robot, put some sex into it. She moved again, slowly rolling her haunches. Behind her the camera settled into focus. You see it now, don't you, Henry, your Juney June on display.

'But Marty, I don't know if I can. It was almost too much the first time.'

Was it worth this, Henry, your ten minutes in the Taurus with Lotty Daniels? Probably not, huh? She was bending over Marty now, her body still blocking the view. Here's the tricky part. Straddle him while keeping the sheet in place. This won't work. Too late now. Create the diversion.

She gasped. 'Jesus, it's so big! I think it's bigger than last time. Marty, you're not human!' She scrambled on top on him, a blur of movement and panting commotion. She yanked the sheet around her waist and began to bounce and sway. Her breasts lifted and dropped rhythmically – and that's what Henry will see. I did it, I'm there, sheet's got Marty's pants covered, mmmmm, and it's going, mmmm, well. She leaned forward and let her hair drop over on to Marty's face. His body was flopping and jiggling beneath her, in what she hoped was a vague approximation of physical response.

Wow, this is like aerobics or something, sex aerobics, I'm getting a workout here. She turned toward the camera and smiled through her pants and groans.

'Marty, Marty,' she chanted. 'It's sweet, Marty, it's so sweet.' Mmmm. Sweets for the dentist's wife. June bounced and pressed. This is so strange. Mmm. 'Sweet, so sweet!' What's he doing to me down there? He's barely alive and yet, and yet. She couldn't get that word out of her brain. Sweet. She bobbed and bumped to it. Sweet. Donuts. Cavities. Drills. Eclairs. What's he doing to me down there? What am *I* doing to me down there?

'Marty, unh, Marty, I think . . .'

I can't be. I'm supposed to be faking it. She twitched and shuddered. This is pretend. Sweet. Don't stop, Marty. 'Don't stop, Marty!' Stop what? It was about to happen – the sweet thing was about to happen.

June's flushed and sweaty face strained toward the camera. She thrust herself against Marty and went rigid. She yipped. She squeaked. Marty wasn't even at bat and he was about to hit the homerun of a lifetime. Who was at bat? June felt herself sail up and out of the ballpark, heard the crowd roaring in her ears, saw the lights and the green grass disappear below her. Up, up, up, until she had to stop it, this was too much, too much. MartyJeffreyHenry!

She looked down at Marty's face. His eyes were wide open. She screamed and rolled off him, toward the camera. He screamed and rolled the other way. She reached up with her foot and kicked the camera off the end table. End of scene. Cut!

Marty lay sprawled against the upright piano like a wind-tossed leaf. He cradled his spinning head in both hands and stared at June.

June lay on the rug in total relaxed collapse, her chest heaving. She wriggled her toes and fingers to see if she was still alive. Alive? She'd just been beyond alive, to some kind of sexual fourth dimension. She turned her head slowly and let Marty come into focus.

'Wow,' she said when she could speak.

'Mrs Miles,' Marty whispered over to her. He winced when he spoke. His eyes did not seem to be moving in unison. Vodka, he thought. Lots of it. 'Mrs Miles,' he said again, as if she was the only thing in the room that he could comprehend.

Hearing his voice brought her down a few notches. Her pelvic area throbbed happily. Henry, I forgive you, she almost thought. She went up on one elbow.

'Mrs Miles.' He tried to go up on one elbow too, but his head missed his hand and bounced on the rug.

June pulled the sheet over herself and sat up. 'Are you OK? Are you going to be sick on my rug? I just had it cleaned last week, you know.'

'Mrs Miles.' He drifted away, eyes slowly closing. He imagined that his brain had been replaced with Rah-Rah Raspberry filling. He imagined that his body was curling into an O. He had become the perfect donut. He smiled. Then he frowned. In the black distance, he could see a huge open mouth drifting toward him. There were many rows of teeth in the mouth. A face formed itself around the mouth. The face belonged to Dr Henry Miles.

Marty's eyes popped open again and he saw Mrs Miles in a bed sheet, advancing toward him. He cringed against the piano.

'You with me there, Marty?'

He nodded yes. He clutched his head again to settle the filling that sloshed against the inside of his skull. 'You were naked,' he whispered hoarsely. He looked down at himself. He was half naked. The important half still seemed to be clothed. 'You were on me.'

'It was perfect, Marty. And we got it all on tape.'

'All?' What had he done? Again he checked to see if he had his pants on. He did. 'I have my pants on.' If she agreed that he was wearing his pants then that would be a double verification.

She did not verify. She smiled glowingly.

Marty understood about glowing women. A naked glowing woman with a sheet casually draped around her meant that although he had his pants on now, he probably had not been wearing them earlier. He attempted to assess the status of his genitals with a moment of intense mental concentration, since he could not just drop his pants and have a peek. He did not feel post-sexual. The little testicular ache that always followed an encounter with his wife was not there.

In fact, he felt nothing at all. Marty's stomach did a little flip of fear. He was absolutely numb down there. What had she done to him while he was unconscious? Was she some sort of psycho avenging sex angel? He dropped his hand between his legs and gave himself a squeeze. He felt a wave of relief. He moved his hand quickly away, but she had seen the whole thing.

'You need to tinkle, Marty? My boys used to do that when they were small.'

'No, actually,' he said, 'I was just . . .' He trailed off.

June walked around him. What a fascinating creature. Absolutely repellent, yet with him she'd just achieved the most intense and astonishing orgasm of her life. And then he tugs and scratches at himself like a toddler.

Marty hugged his knees and looked up at her. His eyes still could not focus properly. He wished she would stand still. Or maybe she was and it was the vodka that caused her to orbit him.

'When Henry sees the tape,' said June, 'he'll understand what I'm capable of, what he and I have been missing.' It was a long moment before she was able to speak again. She stared at Marty. 'We exist only on tape now, Marty. We've done our job, much more than our job, and now it's time to get dressed. We'll dress ourselves and I'll drop you off back at your dumpster and I won't even wave goodbye, do you understand? We are video and nothing more.'

Marty nodded and shouted, 'Yes. Right. I agree. Dumpster. Let's go!' He attempted to jump up, but the vodka sent him wobbling to his knees. He grabbed the piano and tried again. He wondered if he could ask her to place him in the dumpster, rather than beside it. He would feel very much at home among the other refuse of this awful day.

'Can you walk?' she asked, hovering over him.

One of her breasts peeped out from the bed sheet. Marty closed his eyes. He wanted no more trouble. He wanted his dumpster. 'I'll be all right in a minute.' He lied. Maybe when she turned her back, he could crawl out the front door and disappear. So this was what adultery was like. And half the married people in America willingly engage in it? He peered at June as she started to pull on her clothes. Well, it had been good for her, anyway. He felt a sudden gripping pain in his stomach. He winced and belched. He worked his tongue around inside his mouth: he'd brought something up. He fished it out with his finger and studied it. A soggy bit of blue cloth. He popped it back into his mouth when June spoke to him.

'You want to shake a leg there, Marty?' She tossed his crushed Dreami Donuts cap and his shirt over to him.

He worked his arms feebly into the sleeves of his shirt. Why had he eaten a piece of blue cloth? What sort of wild sex had she forced upon his vodka-numbed body? What else had she made him eat? If they slit him open, stuff would pour out of him like the contents of a shark's belly: tin cans, candlesticks, potato-chip bags, bits of blue cloth. He was a living dumpster!

'Marty, would you hurry, please? It's after four o'clock. My boys will be home soon.'

He was on his feet in an instant. Boys home soon. And the roving dentist, he could show up at any time, too. Slit me open like a shark. No, dentists use drills, not fish knives. How long would it take to be drilled to death? He started a wobbly course across the living room toward the front door.

June took his arm from behind and swung him around. 'No, no. Through the kitchen, remember? Back out to the garage.'

No, he didn't remember. His mind, in survival mode now, was trying to black out everything that had happened to him. In fact, his mind was attempting to black out things that were still to come, like the ride back with her, and whatever else this day might do to him.

June paused in the kitchen. She had the videotape with her. Now she needed two more things. She found the duct tape in the drawer beside the refrigerator. Then she leaned over the kitchen counter, closed her eyes a moment in concentration, opened them again and began to write the note that would accompany the tape. Marty stood mutely facing the door out to the garage, waiting patiently like a dog, his mind dimming to minimal wattage.

'There,' said June. She gathered up everything, including Marty, and moved through the dark garage to the car.

Marty lay quietly out of sight on the rear seat for the trip back to Dreami Donuts. He spent much of the ride thinking about nothing, moving his tongue idly back and forth over his teeth. When June turned on to MacDade Boulevard, he realized his tongue had settled into caressing one tooth in particular. He smiled.

'Hey,' he said, sitting suddenly upright. 'Hey, you know my crown, the tooth that was killing me all day? Well, I don't feel a thing right now. It doesn't hurt me a bit.'

Chapter 9

So what was the plan? Henry glanced at his watch. Four-thirty. OK, the plan, the plan. He drummed his fingers on the steering wheel while waiting for a green light. The plan: kill Daddy and get home in time for a late supper. But was this realistic? Maybe it would be later than a late supper, like a bedtime snack type of thing. It would have to be more than a snack, of course, since I haven't eaten since breakfast. OK, whatever – I'll get some food in me at some point, that phase of the plan will take care of itself. He hoped. Nasty images of French fries danced in his head.

All right, the important part of the plan, phase one. Taking care of Daddy. His encounter with Tommy Tooly had given him the will but not the way. The light turned green. Henry moved the Taurus forward with determination, if not direction. He seemed to have spent the day in this car trying to figure out where exactly he wanted to go. Faithful wounded Taurus, you have stuck with me throughout these awful and interminable hours. I call on you for one journey more, back to Fox Glen for my rendezvous with Daddy's destiny, then I will ask you to take me home at last, to the welcoming bosom of my family. Can you do this for me? He stroked the steering wheel. The station wagon seemed to give a brave little surge.

Time for the ugly details, come on, Henry. How will you kill Daddy? If you decide how to do it, then you'll know what direction you want to go. He stopped at yet another light. Gun shop? Knife shop? Supermarket for a box of baggies? He glanced over at Daddy's dentures which he had placed, uppers and lowers clamped together in an inscrutable smile, beside him on the passenger's seat. Last time he'd tried to communicate with Daddy's teeth, he got abused by a pseudo officer of the law. No, the teeth would not speak to him. What could they say that Daddy in person had not already told him back at Fox Glen? 'Do me in,' had been Daddy's command. In other words, I don't care how you do it – just be a man and figure it out by yourself.

Fine. All right. Let's do this logically. Number one: I don't have a great desire to get caught. Number two: I would like to avoid mess and pain. Number three: I want to get it done as quickly as possible, i.e., in the next couple of hours. If I sleep on it, I'll never do it. Ah me, planning my father's murder. His suicide. A fitting end to the day. And the twins, years from now when they plan my murder, will they flip a coin to see who gets the job? Or will they come at me in tandem, one with a knife and the other with a pistol. Or one with the pills and the other with the glass of water to wash them down. At least they will have the comfort of a partner. I have no one with whom to mull over the details. Don't mull, Henry, he heard his father whisper (or was it his father's teeth whispering?), just do it. I am a prisoner in a nursing home until you free me.

Not the baggie and the sleeping pills, Daddy's way, nothing that can take time. Nurse Speers will be hovering. Henry's palms went slippery. The sweat slid over his entire body. How many times today had he soaked his clothes with his anxious juices? He would never be able to cleanse himself of the stink of this day. The Taurus trembled and sputtered as it waited at the light. Henry looked quickly at the dashboard. God, the fuel gauge was on the red danger zone past the E. He flushed with shame. Not only have I failed to feed myself properly today, but I have neglected the hunger of my Taurus as well. When the light at last turned, he managed to coax the car two more blocks to a Texaco station. He got out.

A blue Buick sedan pulled in on the other side of the pumps. Hey. He watched as Ronald D. James, the elfin escapee from Fox Glen, hopped out of the Buick. Henry crouched behind one of the pumps. Ronnie, even though ancient and tiny, looked more sinister now that he was a fugitive on the lam. Should I nab him? Henry closed his eyes to think. Sure, yes. He's only four feet tall, shouldn't be too dangerous. I make the collar, bring him and the Buick back to Nurse Speers and she's so happy she takes the pressure off Daddy and I get a little more leeway to kill him. She'll be so indebted to me, she'll look the other way while I do what I have to do. Hell, maybe she'll even give me some medication to do the job. Why not? Daddy's a pain in the ass for her now, she'd probably be happy to be rid of him. Henry smiled back.

'You're the fellow, aren't you?' Ronnie said in his high voice. 'The dentist fellow who helped me escape, right?'

'Helped you?' Henry bleated.

'Escape. Couldn't have done it without you.' Ronnie reached up, grabbed one of the gas nozzles, and dragged the long hose over to the Buick. Henry skittered along behind him.

'Hey. Hey now. I was not involved in your escape.'

'Son,' said Ronnie, pumping the gas. 'You were absolutely integral. Glad I have this chance to thank you. Wish I could repay you somehow.' Ronnie chuckled. 'Boy, the way you blocked those nurses with that wheelchair. I knew I could count on you the minute I laid eyes on you.'

'I didn't block anybody, I just . . .'

'I'd offer you money, but I only got enough for this gas.' Ronnie removed the nozzle and nudged past Henry to hang it back up.

Henry followed him back and forth. 'You stole this car.'

Ronnie looked at him slyly. 'I made an emergency acquisition.'

'You have to go back.' Henry moved a step closer, remembering his plan to nab Ronnie.

'To Fox Glen? Ha.'

Henry stepped back. Even a little guy, if properly aroused, could inflict wounds. 'What's so bad about Fox Glen?'

'Must have been something pretty bad about it, don't you think?' said Ronnie, moving off to the cashier's window. Henry had to trot to keep up with him. 'Must have been something pretty bad I went to all this trouble to escape. Don't you think?' Ronnie handed the cashier a twenty dollar bill and waited for the change. 'Gee,' he said. 'It's nice just to buy some gas, you know what I mean? It's nice to be back.'

'My daddy's there,' Henry said suddenly. 'They always treated him well.'

'That's right, Stu,' said Ronnie, moving fast back toward the Buick. 'Good man, Stu. Good poker player, too. Sorry I didn't get to say goodbye to him. Didn't get to say goodbye to anybody. No chance, had to make my move.'

'They always treated him well.'

'Oh, they treat you well, physically,' Ronnie said, opening the door to the Buick and climbing inside. 'They certainly care for you. I got no complaints about the maintenance.'

'Then what's the problem?' whispered Henry.

'It ain't the physical, son. It's the conceptual. They had my body, but not my head and my heart. I'm all gassed up now, ready to put some miles between me and the nursing home of the soul.'

Henry nodded. What could he say to that?

Ronnie eyed him. 'Stu's been in about a year now, that right?'

'Right. Yes.'

'A year, a year,' said Ronnie softly. 'A year's not much if we all live to be a million. But I guess we don't, do we?' He stuck a thin arm out and extended his hand. It barely reached out the window. 'Thank you again . . .'

'Henry.'

'Henry. Henry the dentist. Thank you for what you done for me and believe me, I intend to pay you back.'

'My pleasure, Ronnie.' Because now Henry had it in his mind that he had helped him escape, maybe a little, in some way. Just by not nabbing him now, he was assisting in his escape, right? And in another hour or so, I'll help Daddy escape, too. Daddy's just taking a different route, that's all. He's made his choice, Ronnie's made his and I'm just here to assist. He watched as Ronnie began to pull away from the pumps. It would be nice if Daddy was heading off into the sunset in a stolen car, instead of heading off into the Big Sunset with a baggie over his head, or whatever I come up with. But Daddy's not Ronnie and besides, he's no spry elf, his hip's no good, he hasn't got that kind of energy. He's just an old man who understands what the nursing home is doing to his soul. Henry waved to Ronnie, then filled his Taurus with gas. He pulled out his wallet as he walked over to the cashier. He stopped and looked closer. But he had a twenty in there, he remembered from this morning. No twenty. The cashier was waiting to get paid. Ronnie. Had used a twenty for his gas. 'Believe me,' he'd said, 'I intend to pay you back.' Henry whacked himself in the head.

'Fifteen-eighty,' mumbled the cashier.

'Um, you take plastic?' said Henry. Ronnie had left the plastic.

'You don't got cash? Plastic is paperwork. You sure you don't got cash? People give you plastic even when they got cash.'

'Hey, pal, I was just robbed, you mind?' Henry snapped, sliding him his Visa card.

'Sure,' said the cashier. 'I believe you.'

Of course Ronnie had robbed him. Ronnie was by nature a pickpocket and a car thief. And crazy, and I just let him get away when I should have nabbed him so I could use him as a bargaining chip with Mrs Speers. Should have stuck to the plan. The plan, the plan, the plan. Do Daddy in. No more diversions. Pain free, no mess, fast. Where do they sell that? Henry got back in his Taurus and slammed the door. He looked over at Daddy's dentures. What was it he'd said back at Fox Glen? 'You could inject me.' But what with? Dentists don't have killer drugs.

Henry froze. The lock box. The emergency medication kit every dentist is required to have in his office. Tucked away in a cabinet somewhere. Full of killer drugs. The plan! Henry pulled out of the Texaco station at full speed. A destination! My office. Pain free, no mess, fast – all inside the lock box. Injectable Valium, Phenobarbitol, Epinephrine, who knew what else. Make up a big lethal cocktail, hand Daddy the syringe and point him to a big vein. Henry bit his lip. And then step quietly out of the room. It's up to him from there. I can do no more. At last, Tommy Tooly, resolution is at hand.

Henry drove along, almost happy. It was a grim business and it might not end well for him, but so it goes. When you choose to battle The List, you enter the realm of chance and danger. And perhaps victory. But if you never do battle, as he well knew, you die a slow, sweaty, hand-wringing death.

'Sweat no more, Dentist Man!' Henry shouted, urging his Taurus into the fray. Beside him on the other seat, the dentures clattered and clacked as he sped along. If Henry had looked and listened, he would have had the distinct impression they were trying to tell him something.

He turned on to MacDade Boulevard, down the homestretch. Dentist Man should have known all along that the solution to his problem would be somewhere there in his office. His office had always been the place where the serious business of his life had been conducted. He could think in his office. And not just think, but do. At the office he got results. At the office he was in charge, the master of his own fate and the fates of others, too. And in the waning hours of this day, the office would affect the outcome of his father's fate. As it should be. Neat and tidy. He pulled into the entranceway he shared with Dreami Donuts. Even sharing an entranceway with Dreami Donuts seemed as it should be. Decay and degeneration on one side, health and hope and dentistry on the other. Yen and Jung. Chang and Eng? Whatever they call the harmonious balance thing. Me and Marty Marks, harmonious balance. We need each other. I should be nicer to him. He pulled into the parking space with his name boldly painted within its borders. Maybe I'll pop over there and take a look at his crown for him. Why not? Hell, why not? Take care of a little unfinished business of the day before I take care of Daddy. Besides, working in somebody's mouth would soothe me before my ordeal to come. Sure, I'll open up the office and give him a call. Henry paused beside his Taurus and scanned Dreami Donuts. His eyes lingered on something. Back behind the store, in the shadows, what was that? Slouched there against the dumpster, some sort of derelict. Give Marty a call, can't be having the store attracting riffraff to the neighborhood. Henry hustled up to the front door of his office and stopped dead in his tracks.

'Oh,' he said. 'Oh, oh.' He traced his finger along the long crack in the glass of his door. It went right through the lettering on his door, between 'Henry Miles' and 'DDS', separating Henry from the medical degree which allowed him to practice the profession so dear to him. Everything that is sacred to me, they have attacked this day. First, the door on my Taurus. Then this assault on the gateway to my profession. What next? The only things I value as much as my car and my job are my wife and kids. It was at that moment that Henry finally noticed that something else was not right about his door. Someone had duct taped a videocassette to the glass at exactly nose level. Beside it, also attached with a jaggedly torn piece of duct tape, hung a note. In June's handwriting.

Henry thought he was going to scream, but all that came out of him was another series of muted 'Oh, oh, ohs'. He had moved beyond screams to whimpers. A videocassette and a note. My car, my office and now they've kidnapped my wife. Henry's mind went immediately to the contents of the emergency medication kit. He would use whatever he found there on himself. He leaned close and made himself read the kidnap note. Demonically clever, making my wife write it so the FBI would be unable to scour it for clues.

'Henry,' she had written. 'Do not come home until you play this tape. Do it now. Your wife, June.'

Not 'Love, June', but 'Your wife, June'. She was obviously under terrible duress. The bastards. He imagined torturing them with excruciating dental procedures: extractions, root canals without the benefit of local anesthesia, soft tissue curettage. Let me have ten minutes with them before the FBI hauls them off. He sagged against the door. Is that what he was going to do now, go to the authorities? He removed the note and the videocassette. But his instructions were to play the tape, do it now. What would be on it? Further instructions, June duct taped to a kitchen chair with her masked abductors cackling insanely as they stood behind her? Did he have it in him to view the tape? He had to. And forget the authorities. On TV you never went to the authorities first. You do that and the kidnappers send you an ear or something. A tooth. They'd yank one of her teeth because they'd know just how to get to him.

Henry read the note several times. He turned the videocassette over and over in his hands. Why kidnap a member of my family? Revenge. An enraged former patient? Or money. I have a few stocks and bonds, a little gold. And those long term Certificates of Deposit I wisely locked in when rates were at an historical high. But I can't cash in my CDs without significant penalties. Surely June's kidnappers would understand that. Do they know about my whole life insurance policies? Please don't make me touch those. Say, life insurance. Hadn't he upgraded June's policy a few years back? Henry steadied himself. God forbid any harm should come to her, but if it did . . . he stood to make a boodle. Don't think like that. But he had to, for the sake of the twins. Yikes – the twins. Raising the twins by himself! He ran over to the Taurus and jumped in. Play the tape and figure out a way to rescue June, get her the hell home, preferably in time to feed the twins.

Henry raced back out on to MacDade Boulevard. OK, Daddy, got to put you on the back burner for a while here. Do June, then do you. Where? Where do I play this damn tape? June's instructions from the kidnappers were to play the tape, then come home. Are the kidnappers stupid enough to be holding her hostage at the house? The tape will tell. So now what, rent a VCR, take it back to the office? No TV at the office. So, rent a TV and a VCR? Then have to set all that crap up? I can't even plug in my own VCR – the twins have to set everything up for me. Should I pick up the twins at school, get them in on this? No, solve it on your own, Henry. Just like you'll solve Daddy. Solve everything, isn't that what the world wants out of you today?

Henry sped down MacDade. The stores zoomed by in a blur. Should I drop by a friend's house, somebody who has a VCR?

Hi, there. Sorry to interrupt your dinner, Bob, but would you mind if I pop my kidnapped wife's ransom tape into your VCR? Wouldn't that go over well? Besides, Bob's not that close a friend. Or, for that matter, neither are Bill or Raymond. I don't have the kind of friend I could kick back in front of the TV and enjoy a good kidnap video with. Ha ha. Shit. I can't involve any of those guys. The kidnappers would get wind of it, they always do, and start sending me June's teeth.

Where then? The stores whizzed by. Henry didn't see them, and then suddenly, he did. He almost braked to a stop in the middle of MacDade. A store, yes! A TV store. A mile or two up ahead: Circuit City TV and Appliance. He'd been in there the other day with June. With Juicy June – he gripped the wheel and swallowed back a sob – to buy a new washer. Which they hadn't delivered yet, come to think of it. Maybe while he was in there, he could nudge them along on that. Anyway, while she had lingered among the washers, he went over to the wall of TVs they always had going. Must've been twenty or thirty of them all tuned to the same show. But they were all hooked up to a central VCR, too. Henry remembered because a salesman came over with some customers and pushed in a cassette. He was a little pissed because he'd been watching *Jeopardy* and the cassette was *Fatal Attraction*, which he'd already seen and found so ridiculous – who could believe a guy could bring so much bad luck down on himself as a result of an insignificant adulterous fling? Sheesh. So what he'd do when nobody was looking – slip June's tape in that VCR, then take it from there. Perfect.

Henry had to will himself to drive the speed limit to Circuit City. Don't let a cop stop me, or next thing I know I'll be down at the station playing the tape for the entire police force. Then the kidnappers will be sending me all of June's teeth. He glanced over at Daddy's dentures, still resting on the passenger's seat. No dentures for June, keep it at the speed limit, Henry boy. And what about the twins, they'd be getting home soon. The after-school stuff should be over by now. Would they be walking in on the kidnappers, if the kidnappers really were at the house?

Christ, if he didn't hurry up with this tape, his entire family might be wearing dentures.

He skidded into the Circuit City parking lot. No parking meters, we're off to a good start. He grabbed the videocassette and ran into the store. Big damn place. Weren't the TVs back around there near the microwave ovens? Or over behind the air conditioners? So many electrical appliances, so little time. He wound his way through a maze of refrigerators. Like Stonehenge, these refrigerator monoliths. Who buys these monsters? Someone latched on to his elbow from behind.

'Hello there, sir. I see you're interested in our huge selection of refrigerators and upright freezers. I'm Lucien, how may I help?'

Henry shook loose and moved forward without speaking or turning around. Lucien, undaunted, squeezed between two freezers and jumped in front of Henry.

'I like that, sir,' said Lucien, smiling widely and brushing at his bright blue blazer with its Circuit City logo. 'A customer who knows precisely what he wants.'

Henry squinted at him. 'Your teeth are bad, Lucien. I wouldn't take a free refrigerator from a salesman with teeth like yours, got it? Now, out of my way. I'm here for the TVs and VCRs.' He tried to press on.

Lucien stepped in front of him once again. 'That's impossible about my teeth.' He ran a moist meaty tongue over them. 'I wore braces when I was thirteen. For two years, I wore braces and all the other kids tortured me. They called me Tin Grin and Metal Muncher. I couldn't chew gum for two years. I must have swallowed a pound of those little rubber bands. My teeth are beautiful. I did not suffer in vain.'

'If I had your teeth,' said Henry in a trembling low voice, 'I'd have every one of them ground down to a stub and capped. And even that wouldn't work. You have an alignment problem you couldn't straighten out with a sledge hammer. Now where are the TVs, pal?'

'What makes you such an authority on teeth, anyway?' hissed Lucien.

Henry stepped toward Lucien and went nose to nose. 'Because I am Dentist Man!' he screamed, as Lucien stumbled backward. 'Now where are the fucking TVs?'

Lucien clutched a deep freeze and pointed to the north end of the store. As Henry moved past him, Lucien whispered, 'Sonofabitch dentist.'

'Tin Grin,' Henry called over his shoulder as he hurried out of Refrigerators toward TVs. 'Metal Muncher, Brace Face!'

Ah, yes. Just ahead of him loomed an entire wall of TVs on racks. A sea of TVs. A world of TVs. All alike, all different. Were the huge sixty-inch front-projection TVs the mamas and papas of all the smaller TVs? TVs spawning more TVs? And each generation mutated in some way, different size screens, different types of controls. Who would stop this incessant breeding? And every one of them showing the exact same image. Henry felt like he had a fly's eye view of the world. He watched as thirty fires erupted on thirty screens. The evening news. Already six o'clock? A few shoppers moved about in front of the TVs, fiddling with volume and color controls. How do I get rid of them? Yell fire? I haven't got time to screw around. I'm just going to have to put the cassette in and let 'er rip.

Someone touched his elbow from behind. Lucien again? Henry whirled.

The woman in the blue blazer looked startled, then forced out a smile. 'Uh, sir, may I help you? My name's Sue Ann.'

Henry tried to smile back. He managed to raise his upper lip, which instantly bonded with his front teeth because his mouth was dry and sticky. He worked to get the lip back down. Finally he lifted his fingers and gave it a yank. The woman tried not to stare.

'Right. Yes. A VCR. That's what I want to see.' He was going to need this young woman's help with the machine, since the twins weren't here to guide him through the controls.

'Any particular kind? Two heads? Four? Stereo?'

She looked like a nice young woman. Sue Ann. He wanted to confide in her. He would explain to her that she was going to be one of the heroes in all this. When the FBI arrested the kidnappers it would be because of this tape, and Sue Ann here, with her lovely teeth, was going to be the hero who put it up on all those TV screens for me. He wanted to tell her that if it all went well, and he knew it would, this kidnapping would probably be featured on one of those Real Crime shows, and she would have a major, major role. Not quite as big as mine, of course. I'll be the star, if you could call it that, the dogged dentist in relentless pursuit of his wife's captors. Maybe the FBI would give me a break when they discover that I've also killed my father the same evening. A stress crime – I'm sure they'd be lenient. Yes, with Sue Ann on one arm and my rescued June on the other, they would have to be lenient.

'Yes, Sue Ann,' said Henry. 'There is a particular VCR I wish to see.'

'Great,' said smiling Sue Ann. 'An informed customer.'

Henry wanted to plant little kisses on her perfect teeth. Sue Ann, who will restore my family to me. Sue Ann, who had probably worn her teenage braces without complaint. No one called you Metal Muncher, did they? Your beauty could not be marred by dental appliances, only enhanced. Take me to your VCR, smiling Sue Ann. Rescue my Juney June. Rescue me.

Sue Ann was waiting patiently. 'Sir? Which VCR was it you wished to see?'

Henry cleared his head with a slight shake. 'Oh, I'm sorry, Sue Ann. I was just. Thinking.' He looked around. There, over there. That was the VCR which had transmitted *Fatal Attraction* to all those screens. Henry pointed.

Sue Ann's smile grew even larger. 'What a lucky choice!'

It is? A lucky choice! I've chosen the lucky VCR and I'm going to slip in the lucky tape from June and there will be nothing but lucky news on it. Yippee! 'I feel lucky,' said Henry to Sue Ann. He walked with her to the VCR.

'Excuse me, miss?' A woman in a green sweat suit tried to approach Sue Ann.

Henry stepped in front of her. 'She's busy with me. Wait your turn.'

The woman stammered something and moved away. The TV section suddenly seemed full of knob-twisting, button-testing shoppers. Well, he wouldn't let any of them near Sue Ann until she hit PLAY on the lucky VCR. 'I'm sorry, Sue Ann. You were saying?'

She looked a bit flustered, but she managed once again to get her smile in place. 'Just that, you know, you've chosen to see a quality model. Goldstar, actually. Four heads. MTS stereo.'

Goldstar. A name he could pronounce and understand. Gold. He understood gold. He worked with gold. Star. Lucky VCR, lucky star. He started to hum softly: When you wish upon a Goldstar. He stopped. Sue Ann was staring at him.

She said, after a long moment, her smile fading, 'And what's really lucky for you . . .'

'Lucky for me,' repeated Henry.

'Lucky for you, is we actually have this particular Goldstar all hooked up to those TVs. You get to actually try it.'

'Perfect!'

Sue Ann busied herself with the machine. 'Now, let's see. Where'd they put that demo tape? Here. *Fatal Attraction*. You know that one? Where the guy cheats on his wife and—'

Henry raised his hand to stop her. 'Actually, I brought my own tape.' He lifted it to show her.

She looked confused. 'Your own copy of *Fatal Attraction*.'

'Ha, ha. I don't think so.' His face went tight and he had trouble getting the rest of it out. 'It's a personal tape. Sort of.'

'Oh, right,' said Sue Ann, gently taking it from him. 'So you can see for yourself, make a comparison of how this tape looks on your old machine versus this new one. I've never had someone ask to do this before. You're a very savvy shopper, sir. I admire you.'

Henry nodded. He was unable to say any more words. He was

frightened and excited. Sue Ann was about to play the tape that would define his future. He pointed to the tape, he pointed to the machine, he pointed to the wall with thirty ready and waiting TV screens. Fasten your seatbelts. Pass the popcorn. It's showtime!

Rita Hoops, Henry's aging and bewigged secretary, perusing the CD player section, spotted her boss over in TVs. She had spent a long afternoon in search of the best deal and she knew that Circuit City was not the place that offered the best deals. She would warn her boss. Her job, after all, was to look after him and as she adjusted her wig and slowly approached, she could see that he certainly needed looking after. The bump on his forehead from this morning's fall in the bathroom had risen nastily, his clothes were in an unusual state of disarray, he appeared confused and unsteady. He was in no condition to make a decision about the purchase of a major household appliance. She reached the outskirts of TVs and Video, was about to call out to Dr Miles when she abruptly stopped and looked up at the long wall of TV screens.

In fact, every one of the shoppers, men, women, children of all ages, stopped and surrendered themselves to the visual pull of the thirty TV screens. It was an automatic human response to an alteration in video input. Sue Ann had just pushed June's tape into the Goldstar machine and hit PLAY. The instant the evening news suddenly clicked off and the hissy granulated snow of the tape's first few seconds appeared, everyone tuned in. Every brain in the TV and Video section of Circuit City simultaneously asked the same question: Gee, I wonder what's coming on next?

The blur of pink that suddenly jumped on to the thirty screens did not immediately answer that question. Directed by their confused brains, everyone, men, women, children, Henry, Sue Ann and Rita, took an automatic step closer to the TVs. The blur of pink kept zooming in and out of focus.

June's voice, loud and clear, suddenly called out from at least sixty sets of speakers, two per TV. 'Marty! You mean you want to do it again?' The blur of pink sharpened at its edges, as June moved forward, her now unmistakable ass filling the screens of two-inch Walkmans, twenty-seven-inch Zeniths and an assortment of sixty-inch front-projection TVs. To Henry, it was a revelation, June's ass spread out before him in infinite and erotic display. This deeply pleasant sensation lasted less than two seconds, as ego quickly asserted control over id.

That's June's ass, that's June's ass! Henry lurched toward the wall of screens as if he hoped to cover them all with his body.

June's voice boomed again. 'But Marty, I don't know if I can. It was almost too much the first time.'

No one moved except Henry. Sue Ann's hand was just beginning to think about making for the STOP button. Henry's nose touched June's naked body as he pressed against a twenty-seven-inch screen. His brain raced. What kind of kidnap tape is this? He was going to let the FBI watch it? 'Marty', she said? The kidnapper – Marty?

'Jesus, it's so big!' cried June, scrambling on top of . . .

Marty? Henry leaned away from the TV and squinted. Marty Marks, the weasel bastard. The little donut maker and Juney June.

Mothers and fathers, finally kicking into action, grabbed their small children and ran for the dishwashers and water heaters. Two or three grown men settled back to enjoy the show. A thirteen-year-old by the name of Jerry Franks watched open mouthed; he would remember this day fondly for the rest of his life. Sue Ann frantically hit all the buttons on the Goldstar VCR, but she couldn't seem to zero in on STOP. On thirty screens, June and Marty sometimes bounced merrily in fast forward, sometimes in reverse and occasionally they paused in jittery embrace.

The embrace is what broke Henry. He turned slowly and began a stony-eyed death march out of TVs and Videos back toward Refrigerators and Freezers. He did not stop to assist Sue Ann in her desperate effort to eject the tape from the VCR. She had hit so many buttons so fast, the machine simply ignored all input and began to play the tape in slow motion. June's breasts rose and fell like half-filled helium balloons. Her eyelids opened and closed in a dreamy blink. Her sighs filled the appliance store. Henry, as overloaded with input as the poor VCR, saw and heard nothing more as he moved toward the exit.

'Dr Miles.' Rita hurried to him and clutched his arm. He looked dully at her. She happened to be wearing a blue overcoat similar in color to the sales clerks' blue blazers.

Henry shrugged her off and said, 'No thanks, I don't want a refrigerator. No thanks, I don't want a VCR. No thanks, I . . .'

Rita waved a hand in front of his eyes. He stopped talking. 'Dr Miles. Wait here. Don't move.' She hurried back to TVs and Videos.

The minute her back was to him, he sprinted for the exit. He did not want to buy refrigerators or VCRs or anything from this woman, as strangely familiar and seductive as her voice was. He wanted to get the hell out of this store. He had something he had to do. Oh June, you naughty, naughty wife. As he ran, it clicked. The woman with the voice was Rita, of course. He looked over his shoulder. Rita, and she's just seen a tape of my wife mounting Marty Marks. He ran faster, bursting out of the store and into daylight, his trusty Taurus waiting in the distance for him.

Rita, capable, efficient, loyal Rita, stepped in between Sue Ann and the fractious VCR. Sue Ann gratefully submitted to the intervention.

'I can't seem to eject it,' she said in a panicky voice. 'It won't listen to anything I do.'

Rita nodded. She looked one last time at the slow motion efforts of June and Marty. She noticed something that none of the other viewers had, riveted as they were by June's vigorous performance. When the sheet covering Marty Marks (whom she knew and recognized) was jostled aside for an instant, she saw that he was wearing trousers. Marty was dressed under that sheet. How interesting.

She said in a loud voice to Sue Ann and the rest of the onlookers, 'Any of you people recognize those two?'

The onlookers, all men except Sue Ann, murmured in the

negative, embarrassed to be addressed by an elderly and oddly wigged woman while they watched their free porno film.

'Good,' she said. 'Lucky for you.' To Sue Ann she said, 'You mind?' as she reached for the VCR.

Sue Ann shook her head with relief.

'I had a child once who swallowed a penny,' Rita said, lifting the VCR. 'Tried everything we could to get it out. Finally, I grabbed him by his ankles, turned him upside down and gave him a shake. Penny popped right out.' She lifted the VCR high in the air, its rear wires going tight, and gave it a healthy shake. It whirred wildly, clicked several times and coughed out June's tape on to the linoleum floor. One of the men reached down and picked it up. Rita set the VCR down and held out her hand.

He hesitated before handing the tape over, his averted eyes looking somewhere past her. 'Say, uh, I mean, I don't suppose I could offer . . .'

Rita snatched it from him. 'Not for sale.' She gave her wig a straightening yank, waved bye-bye to Sue Ann, and hurried off to Refrigerators and Henry. He was not there. When she reached the parking lot, Henry's blue Taurus was a speeding speck disappearing down MacDade Boulevard. Rita hurried to her own car.

Henry took a deep cleansing breath. He took another. He had finally gotten the message of this day. He believed it was Zen in nature, although he was not really sure what Zen was. The unceasing ordeals of the day were meant to strip him of the human tendency to resist and to fear. I am no longer human, I am Zen. I will no longer fight. I will continue until I do not continue. I float tetherless, Zen Man, without wife or home, soon to be without a father. My release from my wife is complete, Zen, Zen, I will complete my release from Daddy, Zen, Zen. I have shifted to a place where teeth are not needed, for in Zen we do not gnash or gnaw. I am the toothless dentist, at peace with myself, at one with the world. Zen, Zen.

Zen speedily transported him back to his office. For in Zen there are no such things as red lights or speedometers. And fortunately, no police cars, either. Henry felt himself hurrying and going slow at the same time. He was no longer hungry, for in Zen the hunger for French fries is but a transient desire, easily quelled. He did not sweat, for in passionless Zen one does not work up a sweat. He liked this Zen thing: it was Novocaine of the mind. He stepped out of his Taurus. He stood before his office door. There was another note taped to the door. Juney June giving him an update on her sexual exploits? Poor June. She does not understand that in Zen there is no sex. He read the note. 'Dear Dr Miles,' it said in handwriting that was not June's. 'Sorry about this short notice, but Charlie Carnes and I are zooming off to the Poconos for our honeymoon. Love has found me, Dr Miles. I hope you find another dental assistant real soon. Yours, Mrs Charlie Carnes (the former Jennifer Olmstead).'

Henry held the note and stared at himself in the reflection of the office door. In Zen, marriages end and marriages begin. Jennifer gone. He studied the reflected bump on his forehead. Is it un-Zen-like to wonder if she took her box of panty liners with her? The bump on his forehead pulsed. He took a cleansing breath and continued to stare at himself in the cracked glass of the door. An image began to take shape before his eyes, but it was as unclear to him as the first few seconds of June's blurry ass on the videotape. He saw himself in the glass and something else, too. Shapes, letters. He backed away from the door so more letters would come into view. Ds and Os and Ts and Us danced before him. A message from Zen. He swung around. His eyes latched on to the building and the huge letters plastered against its side. DREAMI DONUTS.

Sweat popped out on Henry's forehead. A great hunger gripped him, a hunger for revenge.

'Screw Zen!' he shouted at Dreami Donuts and Marty Marks. I'll get that little sugar-sucking wife-fucking sonofabitch. He spun around and unlocked his office. He had returned to himself. He was agitated, hyper, impulsive. He was Henry. He sniffed the sweet medicinal aroma of his office and he was Dentist Man. He was going to end this day with two things scratched off The

List: he'd strike a blow against the forces of dental disease and he'd do Daddy in. Every day for the rest of my life, I do hereby swear, unless they throw me in prison, I will scratch something off The List. Wait a second, being thrown in prison, that was one of the things *on* The List. Don't think about it, Henry. Act, don't think. Resolve, isn't that right, Tommy Tooly? Resolve Daddy. Resolve Dreami Donuts.

He rifled through cabinets in room 2 until he found the red metal lock box, the emergency kit. Which wasn't locked, thank God. He popped it open. A fat bead of sweat rolled off the tip of his nose and splatted on to one of the glistening vials of injectable Daddy Death. Look at all this stuff. He couldn't. He slammed the lid. The sound seemed to echo around the rooms of the empty office. OK, OK. Next. He hurried down the hall to the employee rest area, which Jennifer alone had used for cigarette breaks. Rita never left her desk and he did not use it since he was the boss. The room smelled of stale cigarettes and sweet Jennifer. And now Charlie Novocaine Carnes would be handling her sweets. A day of unbecoming men handling the women in my life, thought Henry. He snatched a book of matches out of an ashtray and sprinted back down the hallway.

He took a last look around him. He'd had a lot of good times in this office and saved a lot of teeth. I wouldn't mind that as my epitaph: 'He saved a lot of teeth. R.I.P.' He suddenly felt very weary. Yes, he was in need of peaceful rest. It would come. The day would have to end some time.

He locked the office door and junped back into his Taurus. He wanted the car with him, the engine running. My trusty Taurus, saddled and ready. Then he did something he'd never done in the fifteen years his office had stood beside Dreami Donuts: he shifted into drive and headed right for it. He didn't bother to cut left down their shared driveway and right into the Dreami Donuts lot. He just kept going straight, from his lot, across the driveway, up over the curb, and through Marty Marks's careful row of foot-high azaleas. I hate azaleas, thought Henry.

The lights were out inside Dreami Donuts. Henry saw a lone

figure wearing a crumpled paper cap, hunched over the long counter: My Nemesis, he thought, smirking. I come crashing through his azaleas and he can barely turn around to watch. Numbed by adulterous sex and glazed donuts. He swung the Taurus around back, into the shadows between the big green dumpster and the building. He left the engine running and got out. The dumpster was tall, but if he went up on his toes he could just reach in. He grabbed a fistful of trash and withdrew his hand. The horror, the horror. His hand had slid inside a used Tiny Tasties box. He hurled the box and wrappers and styrofoam coffee cups against the wall of the building. His arm was coated up to the elbow in granulated sugar and multicolored jimmies. Rah-Rah Raspberry filling dripped from his fingers. He could feel the stuff burning into his skin. He wiped the hand on his shirt, but the red of the raspberry stuck to his fingers. What did Lady Macbeth do? But there was no time for proper hygiene if he was to flee this place and get to his father.

He kneeled over the little pile of trash. Goodbye, Dreami Donuts, purveyor of all that is wicked in my world. He opened the cover to Jennifer's matches.

Rita, who had not had the forces of Zen manipulating stoplights for her, at last reached the office. But his car was not there. Oh, dear. She did a U-turn in the office lot and spied, in the early evening shadows behind Dreami Donuts, Dr Miles's Taurus.

Three matches left. He struck the first. It sputtered and died. He struck the second, which ignited but then stuck to his raspberry fingers. He panicked and blew it out. He held the last match with the unsticky part of his fingers and lit it. Ah. He lowered the flame of revenge and resolution to the clutter. No wrappers blowing over into my yews again, Marty. Doesn't pay to cross Dentist Man, does it? A wrapper caught fire. The edge of the Tiny Tasties box began to crinkle and turn brown. Henry stepped back. He realized he hadn't exactly placed the trash against a flammable part of the building. He could only hope this righteous heat would ignite cinderblock. Smoke began to rise from the Tiny Tasties box. It burst into flame. A surge of triumph and panic knotted his stomach. He jumped back in his car and zoomed around the far side of the building, twice circling Dreami Donuts. He honked his horn and waved to Marty Marks, whose frightened face was now pressed against the plate-glass window. Marty lifted his hand uncertainly and gave a little return wave as Henry's Taurus sped out of the lot and on to MacDade Boulevard.

Marty ran outside when a second car came speeding out of Dr Miles's lot, through his azaleas, and screeched to a stop behind his building. What was happening back there?

Rita had asked herself the same question. Her eyes were not what they had once been, and Dr Miles's Taurus had obscured her view, but when she saw the smoke, she understood. She was even rooting for him, in a way. She'd seen the tape, after all. But burning down Dreami Donuts was not in his best long-term interest.

She got out of the car and began to stamp on the pile of burning trash. It was not much of a fire. She believed it came under the presently popular psychological category called 'A Cry for Help'. Her wig jostled this way and that as she stamped and hopped on the sputtering wrappers and styrofoam cups. There, that's almost got it. She lifted her leg and prepared to come down hard on a final clump of flaming trash. But it was not her foot that smothered the fire. When her leg shot up, her wig slid down over her face and, before she could grab it, on to the last of Dr Miles's inferno. The flames died instantly.

'Rita Hoops?' came Marty's voice behind her.

She turned her bald turtle-like head and stared at him. Marty did not look well. He seemed to be suffering from the same affliction as Dr Miles. She was glad that she was not a middle-aged man.

'Dr Miles tried to burn down my Dreami Donuts?' he asked.

Rita continued to stare at him. She ran a wrinkled hand over her hairless skull. She'd been wanting another wig, but could not bring herself to waste the money on a new one when the old one seemed to have so much vitality. She looked down at the smoking tangle of synthetic hair. Well, there was certainly no life in it now. She believed she'd buy something with a hint of blue this time and a few curls. She looked up when Marty addressed her again.

'So he lit the fire,' he said, his eyes fixed on her wig, 'and you put it out. With your hair.' He lifted his eyes to hers. 'I'm so very, very grateful.'

He approached her shyly. When he stood directly in front of her, he lifted the Dreami Donuts paper cap off his head, hesitated a moment, then gently lowered it on to hers. It rested on her ears, covering her baldness completely.

Rita nodded. 'Thank you, Marty,' she said, opening her car door.

When she glanced in the rearview mirror as she was driving away, she saw him standing in the ashes of Dr Miles's fire and she was quite sure he leaned forward and pressed his lips to the side of the building.

Chapter 10

June and the twins finished their supper in silence. Ed and Fred kept exchanging furtive looks. June knew she had not satisfactorily answered their questions. Especially the big question: Where's Dad? She was also acting strangely and the last thing children liked to see was one or both of their parents acting strangely.

'More meatloaf, Ed?' she tried to say in reassuring tones.

There was a long pause. 'I'm Fred, Mom. Jesus.'

'Fred, yes, Freddy, of course,' she said, reaching out to touch his arm. He pulled it away.

'You never get us wrong. What's going on?' he asked.

'Nothing's going on. I slip with your name and something's going on? What kind of sense does that make?'

Ed said, while Fred nodded in agreement, 'Number one, Dad's not here, and Dad's never missed a supper with us in his life. Number two, the living room smells like alcohol and the end table by the sofa has a big scratch on it. Number three, you look weird and you don't even call us by our right names.'

Number four, she didn't say, I duct taped a sexually explicit videotape to your father's office door and I wonder if he's gotten it yet. She looked from one twin to the other. Creepy, how they never miss a thing. What am I going to tell them?

'When did he die?' blurted Fred.

'Die?' She reached for both their arms. 'Daddy's not dead. Oh, Fred. Oh, Ed.'

'Not Daddy,' said Ed. 'Grandpa Stu.'

'Grandpa Stu.'

'That's what we figured,' said Fred. 'You know, because when Dad came by school at lunchtime, he said he was on his way to Fox Glen. So we figured . . .' Fred looked at Ed.

'He came by school?' June shut her eyes and tried to think.

'Yeah, so we figured, since he was acting weird, like you are now, and he was going to Fox Glen, it must be because . . .'

'He said he was going to Fox Glen?' No, no. He was spending the afternoon screwing hundreds of women in his Ford Taurus. 'He went by school?'

'So he's dead?' the boys said in unison. 'Grandpa Stu?'

June opened her mouth to say no, was already shaking her head, when the doorbell rang. She gripped the boys' arms and stood up. 'Grandpa Stu is not dead, OK? Wait here, don't move.' She did not want them coming with her to the door. Good news was not ringing her doorbell, of that she was sure.

One of the twins called from the kitchen as she moved down the hallway, 'So then where's Dad? Think that's the police?'

Maybe, thought June. Yes, of course, the police. Why not? Why shouldn't this day end with a major tragedy? The way has certainly been paved. The weight of whatever was out there pressed against the door, she could feel it. Henry found the videotape and drove his car into a telephone pole. If I don't open the door, I'll never have to know. If I seal this door, if I board it up for ever, the police will never have a chance to make me a widow. The doorbell rang again and June could not stop her hand from turning the doorknob and yanking it open.

'June Miles?' Lotty Daniels, holding a big cookie tin straight out in front of her, smiled toothily. 'Lotty Daniels from over on Cornell Avenue. Our boys play soccer together?'

The hand that opened the door, why couldn't she make it slam the door in Lotty's big face?

'Am I interrupting your supper? I was trying to time it close, because, here,' Lotty said, opening the cookie tin, 'I brought you dessert. A thank you dessert. Pecan Crispies.'

June nodded in amazement.

'For what your lovely husband did for me this morning. It was amazing, simply amazing how good I felt afterward.' Lotty closed her eyes in dreamy remembrance.

'You've come to my house,' June said in a monotone. Would

women start coming, bearing thank you gifts for what my husband did to them? Did to them after Fox Glen? Where does Fox Glen fit in, and Grandpa Stu?'

'Yes, I simply had to thank him. That new technique he used on me.'

June smiled, incredulous. Lotty was the most repellent and fascinating creature she had ever met. Was there anything she would not say or do?

Lotty asked timidly, 'Is he here? Is the doctor in?'

June continued to smile, her eyes deadly. 'Oh, he's not with you?'

Lotty cocked her head, unsure. 'I'm sorry?'

'Well, he was with you this morning, but I guess just because he was with you this morning doesn't necessarily mean he'd spend the day with you. Right?'

'In fact,' said Lotty, reaching into the cookie tin absently and pulling out a Pecan Crispy for herself, 'I did think I might have to see him again this afternoon. He even suggested it, but what he did this morning really finished the job.'

'I'll bet.'

'Yes. That new technique.'

'Wow.'

'He's done it to you?' asked Lotty, nibbling her cookie. 'You needed it, too?'

'Not like you needed it, apparently,' said June.

'I really, really needed it.' Lotty lifted a hand to her mouth in embarrassment. 'Oops, look at me. I ate one of your cookies. They're just so good. Here, take them quick, before I eat them all.' She thrust the cookie tin at June. 'This morning before I met up with Dr Miles, I swear I thought I'd never put another thing in my mouth.'

June nodded. 'But I guess Dr Miles fixed your mouth good.'

'He sure did. God bless him.'

'Lotty,' June said after a long moment when the two women stared into each other's eyes. 'Lotty, my two sons are in the kitchen probably listening to every word we've been saying. How do you think this conversation makes them feel?'

'I should hope it makes them feel very proud of their father. He's a wonderful man and an extraordinary dentist.'

The telephone rang. June heard one of the twins answer it. This woman was incapable of remorse. Shut the door now, June, before she further contaminates the house. Drop the cookies and shut the door. She started to do just that when Lotty spoke again.

'Periodontic acupressure, he called it. He's an extraordinary dentist.'

'Mom!' Ed yelled from the kitchen. 'Phone for you.'

'Periodontic acupressure,' June repeated.

'To fix my tooth. The technique I was talking about. He was so sweet to examine me right there in the car. I can't believe I actually flagged him down. But he stopped and was so pleasant and he fixed me right up.'

June dropped the cookies and clutched the door jamb. Pecan Crispies rolled everywhere.

'Are you . . .?' Lotty's eyes were wide.

'Acupressure,' June interrupted her with a hoarse whisper. 'Lotty, how did he do the acupressure?'

'Mom,' Ed yelled again louder. 'It's Margo Zimmerman. She says it's important.'

'The acupressure?' said Lotty. 'With his finger, of course. It hurt at first. I have to admit, I was squirming all over the place. But then the pain just evaporated. And it still hasn't come back.'

It was a *finger*, Margo. The rhythmic jiggling in the car was *pain*, Margo. And now there's a videotape, Margo, a videotape I made because of you. June called over her shoulder, 'Ed, tell her I'll be right there.' I've got to get that videotape off his door.

'Bless you, Lotty.' June embraced the surprised woman. 'I'm so happy about your tooth. Thank you for the cookies. I'm sorry I dropped them, but we'll eat every one of them. I have to go, I have to go, bless you and goodbye.' June shut the door in Lotty's bewildered face and ran to the kitchen, crushing half a dozen Pecan Crispies on the way.

She grabbed the phone from Ed and held her hand over the mouthpiece. 'You two get in the car right now. Get my keys and my wallet and go out to the car and I'll be right there.' The twins shot nervous excited looks at each other, then did precisely as they were instructed. June called after them, 'And nobody's dead, OK?'

Fred yelled back to her, 'I'll bet it's something even better!'

June looked at the phone she held in her hand and wondered if she'd be able to speak. She was trembling and feverish. She worked her mouth to get it ready and a drop of spit, like snake venom, fell from her lip on to the mouthpiece.

'Margo,' she whispered. Then louder, 'Dear Margo, what news do you have for me?'

'June!' Margo's voice leapt into June's ear. 'I waited and waited to call you with this. I mean, what with the Lotty thing this morning which upset you, I'm sure, and then to have to call you again. But this has to be done. I mean, I know if you have to hear bad news from somebody, you want it to be from me.'

June dripped more venom on to the phone. 'Oh, you bet, Margo. If it's bad, I want it from you. You know why?'

There was the slightest pause. 'Why?'

'Because I trust you. When I get it from you, I know I'm getting the straight facts. From your eyes to my ears.'

'OK. Right. So sit down. Like on the floor or something, because you're going to wind up there anyway when you hear this. You sitting?'

'Actually, Margo, I'm sort of in a big rush. So maybe you could give me an abridged version and I'll just stand here and clutch something.' Like your throat, Margo. That might steady me.

'I said it this morning and I'll say it again now: You are so strong, June. Even though you did kind of hang up on me. But that's OK. All right, here we go.'

June could hear her panting happily. 'So go.'

'He did it again this afternoon,' Margo began in a rush.

'He, as in, my husband.'

'Of course, right.'

'You saw him with Lotty Daniels again. In the Taurus.'

'No and yes. Yes, in the Taurus, but no, not with Lotty.'

'Of couse not with Lotty. Let me guess. The mayor's wife? Or no, how about those hairdressers at the Co-Ed Beauty Salon, Cindy and Terri. Both at the same time, Henry hopping to and from the back seat to the front.'

'It was a meter reader, June. In a parking lot in Morton. She looked like a Russian weightlifter.'

'A meter reader, is that right? Or maybe it wasn't the mayor's wife, or Cindy and Terri, or even a meter reader in Morton. Maybe it was you? Is that a possibility, Margo?'

'Easy now, June . . .'

'Oh, this will be very easy, Margo,' said June, breathing flames into the phone. 'It's all sex for you, isn't it? Everywhere you look, somebody's humping somebody else. Today it's my husband? What, are you following him or something? Are you stalking him? Are you one of those sex stalkers?'

'But I saw . . .'

June pressed her mouth into the receiver, her teeth bared. 'I'll tell you what you'll be seeing next. Lawyers. Do you know what slander is, Margo? I'm going to stick a slander suit so far up your ass you're going to need ten lawyers and a backhoe to get it out!' She slammed down the phone, then picked it up and slammed it twice more for good measure.

The twins were sitting rigid with anticipation in the back seat of the car when June jumped in behind the steering wheel. She turned to face them. 'How's everybody doing?' she said.

'Great, Mom,' said Ed.

'Yeah, fine, really,' said Fred.

'Would it be OK to say that all this has to do with parent stuff and that even though it doesn't look like it, things are pretty much under control?'

'Sure, great,' they said in unison.

June sighed. 'This is all just a big mix up, OK? A miscommunication between your father and me. But he's fine, I'm fine, Grandpa Stu as far as I honestly know is fine and what I'm doing now is straightening everything out. Am I making sense?'

'Sort of,' said Fred after a moment.

'Mom,' said Ed. 'You're about to drive this car real fast, aren't you?'

'Yes, I think I am.'

The twins grinned. 'We promise not to tell Dad,' said Ed.

'Yeah,' said Fred. 'Even if you run a few red lights.'

June started the car and began to back out. 'You guys are troopers. First stop, Dad's office.'

'Go faster,' they urged.

And she did, scaring herself and sending the twins into a giggling danger-high. They punched each other in the arm and shouted encouragements to her. She imagined she was in a Ben Hur chariot race with Henry, that he was driving his Taurus on a distant but parallel road and the prize they were both competing for was taped to his office door. The early evening shadows deepened as the sun dipped behind the blur of stores now turning on their lights along MacDade Boulevard.

'There it is,' shouted the twins, leaning forward in their seats.

There it was, Henry's beloved sign, shining like a beacon above his beloved office. That light would guide her to safety, put an end to this stormy day. The tape would be there, she would beat Henry to it, the light would guide her, the light that shines on all good marriages. But as she approached, she thought she saw the light flicker and dim for a moment, and when she at last pulled into the office lot with a screech of tires and a spray of gravel, the lit sign blinked out altogether, the words HENRY MILES, DDS – GENERAL DENTISTRY fading into the evening sky. June got out of the car and ran to the door, knowing even as she moved toward it that the tape was not there. She rested her head against the cracked glass of the door and moaned softly. Behind her in the car, the twins sat quietly. After a long moment, she began to make her unsteady way back to the car. She stopped suddenly and smiled at the sky. Sure, he's got the tape, but that doesn't mean he's played it yet! She lifted her nose and inhaled, as if Henry's scent could be detected in the warm evening air. He was somewhere near, she knew. She had just missed him. She was back in the car in an instant, hurtling on to MacDade. 'What do you say, guys,' she called back to the twins. 'Next stop, Fox Glen?'

If Henry had been capable of an out of body experience, if he could have lifted his spirit upward so that he hovered high above his Taurus, high above the neighborhood through which he now drove, he would have seen that he was at the absolute center of a convergence. But Henry was firmly inside his body. He had never felt so connected with himself, so in control of his destiny. He had actually lit the fire. He felt dazed with the power of his accomplishment. He had struck a decisive blow against an enemy. He had acted. He was about to act again. He turned his head slightly and gazed at the emergency kit, on top of which rested his father's dentures.

He was off MacDade, on Hillborn now, going past the high school, retracing his lunchtime route. The school yard was empty, the twins long gone. The twins, June. How had Marty coerced June into making such a tape? Had he drugged her, tied her hands behind her back and fed eclairs into her? For a coerced person, though, she looked like she was having the time of her life. How could he ever forgive her?

But he did forgive her and the realization of it made him swerve momentarily into the oncoming lane. I forgive her, I forgive her. She is my Juney June, she is what I have, the mother of my sons, and if she needed to do it with the donut maker, then who am I to deny her? She succumbed to a craving for sweets, that's all, and how many of my patients have done that? Every one of them. And have I abandoned them? Never. Dentist Man forgives them all, just as he forgives you, June. Oh June, your Henry is alive with the power of sweetness and forgiveness and resolution. You would not recognize me. He did not recognize himself.

But he did recognize the blue Buick sedan speeding toward him from the direction of Fox Glen. He honked the horn and yelled, 'Ronnie!' as the car shot past him. Halfway down the block, the Buick put on its brakes. Henry did a quick U-turn, pulled up alongside the car and got out.

Ronnie smiled up at him from the driver's window. 'Howdy, Dr Miles. I believe you're double parked, aren't you?'

'You stiffed me. You stole twenty bucks from me.'

'Another emergency acquisition, Dr Miles. Like the car. Didn't I say I'd pay you back, though?' Ronnie winked.

'How can you pay me back if you had to steal to get the money you didn't have in the first place?'

'Who's talking about money?' said Ronnie, chuckling.

Something stirred in the back seat. A figure slowly emerged from the shadows, raised itself into a sitting position and grinned toothlessly at Henry.

'Daddy.' Henry gripped the roof of the Buick.

'Hello, son,' he said, rolling down the window. 'I've been liberated.'

'It was a beautiful operation,' piped up Ronnie. 'I was in and out before they knew what hit them.'

'How?' said Henry.

'I got ways,' said Ronnie. 'Don't you believe in me yet?'

'But Daddy, I was coming for you.'

'You were, weren't you, Henry? You were up to the job, weren't you?'

'I was. I really think I was.'

Ronnie said, 'We kind of stirred them up back there, Henry. We're going to have to put this Buick in the forward mode.'

'I'm taking off into the sunset with Ronnie,' said Daddy. 'Two old guys heading out for a last gasp. Doesn't that sound like the way to do it? I wanted out. Not living with you and June. And this is better than the out you and I were planning, wouldn't you say? Stu and Ronnie and the sunset. Ronnie knew what we really wished for.' He squeezed Henry's hand, then let it go.

Henry was giddy with relief. He turned to Ronnie, who had begun to rev the engine softly. 'How is that, Ronnie?' he said. 'How is it you knew what we wished for?'

Ronnie shrugged and crooked his finger. Henry leaned close, and Ronnie whispered in his ear. 'You're a dentist, aren't you? Then I guess you believe in the Tooth Fairy, right?'

Henry, his mouth open, stepped back as Ronnie began to pull slowly away. 'Are you?' he called to Ronnie. 'Are you really?'

Ronnie poked his head out the window. 'I've told you the truth about everything else today, haven't I, Dr Miles?'

Henry watched the car begin to pick up speed. 'Hey!' he suddenly yelled, waving his arms for the Buick to stop. 'Wait a second.' He opened the door to his Taurus, reached inside, then ran down the street to the Buick.

'What about these?' he said, holding out his hand to his father.

'My dentures! Holy cow, Henry, thank you, son.' He slipped them into place, made a few sucking sounds, then looked up at Henry with a huge white smile. 'How do I look?'

Henry stepped away from the car. 'Like a million bucks, Daddy. They're beautiful.'

'So long. Bye-bye now.'

'Daddy,' he called out as the Buick disappeared into the sunset, 'put an extra tablet in when you soak them tonight. They've had a hard day!'

Henry's eyes were still misty when he started up his Taurus to head for home. He gave the padded rectangle in the center of his steering column a little pat as he shifted into gear and began to pick up speed. Perhaps it was his misty eyes, or the fatigue from his interminable day, or that he was still thinking about his father and Ronnie. Something distracted him and when he looked up he saw a car heading straight at him and behind the wheel of that car, June. Henry cut hard to the right, too hard. As he jumped the curb and headed for the tree, he looked for an instant into his rearview mirror and he was certain that he saw June begin to brake her car safely.

He never felt the tree. As his seatbelt grabbed him he heard a sound, the sound it seemed he'd been waiting all of his life to hear. The airbag opened with a loud pop, like a champagne cork, a celebration. He would survive. His face sank into the cushioning softness as the airbag continued to grow and inflate around him, to embrace him as June would embrace him, to keep him safe as she would keep him safe from everything that was crashing in upon him. It was a lovely moment and he wanted it to last forever.